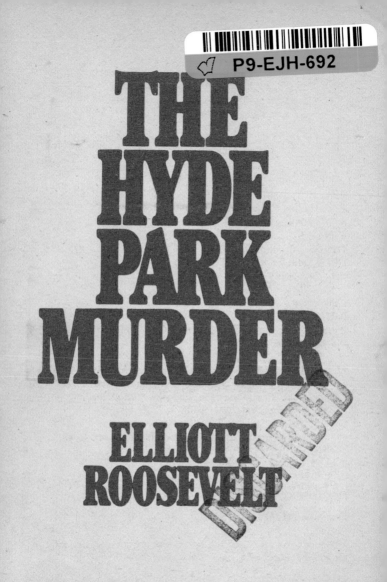

THE HYDE PARK MURDER

ELLIOTT ROOSEVELT

AVON
PUBLISHERS OF BARD, CAMELOT, DISCUS AND FLARE BOOKS

AVON BOOKS
A division of
The Hearst Corporation
1790 Broadway
New York, New York 10019

The St. Martin's Press edition contains the following Library of Congress
Cataloging in Publication Data:

Roosevelt, Elliott, 1910–
   The Hyde Park murder.
   1. Roosevelt, Eleanor, 1884-1962—Fiction.   I. Title.
PS3535.O549H9   1985   813'.54   85-1752

First Avon Printing: August 1986

AVON TRADEMARK REG. U.S. PAT. OFF. AND IN OTHER COUNTRIES, MARCA
REGISTRADA, HECHO EN U.S.A.

Printed in the U.S.A.

K-R 10 9 8 7 6 5 4 3 2 1

As always and forever,
to Patty

THE HYDE PARK MURDER

1

Mrs. Roosevelt sat in one of the weathered wooden arm-chairs on the lawn above the orchard at Hyde Park, chatting with Louis Howe, knitting, enjoying the sunshine and the long view of the Hudson. It was a Saturday afternoon, late in May 1935. She was casually dressed in a simple yellow blouse and a long brown skirt, and she wore a band of yellow silk tied over the back of her head to hold her hair in place.

Maybe it was not in her nature, or maybe it was what life had dealt her, but only very rarely could Eleanor Roosevelt draw a deep breath, look at herself and the world around her, and savor a sense of peace, contentment, ease, and well-being. Her mind was too active for that, and the situation of her life too demanding. She was conscious that the warm optimism she felt was not only rare but surprising. Idly, she began to analyze it.

It was not of Hyde Park. To the contrary, she found little comfort in visiting there. The mansion was not her home but the home and domain of her redoubtable mother-in-law, Sara Delano Roosevelt, who would find plenty of occasions this spring weekend to remind her daughter-in-law of the shortcomings she found in her, First Lady though she might be.

It was not of the developing national political situation. There was no comfort in that. Aside from the blows the Supreme Court had just dealt to some of the most important aspects of the President's program for national recovery, a strong anti-Roosevelt coalition was forming in the country, and it seemed likely that Franklin faced a bitter campaign for re-election in 1936.

It was not from her own achievments, which seemed only to engender more and greater demands and win her the vitriolic scorn of at least a quarter of the nation besides. Neither was it of her personal life, which had as many tensions as ever. It was probably, therefore, irrational, without any reason at all; and she resolved to enjoy it for the moment it would last. She abandoned the analysis.

"It was to be expected," said Louis. "I would have been astounded if anything else had developed."

In her moment of introspection, Mrs. Roosevelt had almost lost the thread of the casual conversation in which she had been engaged with Louis. "You think so?" she asked. "I find some relief in your having expected it."

"Yes," he said. "If it had not surfaced, then we would have had something to worry about. It's the undercurrents of politics that are difficult, sometimes impossible, to cope with. When your opposition surfaces and you can see it, then you can respond to it. I'm pleased."

If Louis thought so, likely her husband would think so. Louis McHenry Howe was the Roosevelts' political mentor, the man who, more than any other, maybe even more than Franklin himself, had made Franklin D. Roosevelt Governor of New York and then President of the United States. Everything *she* knew about politics, she had learned from Louis. She had never known anyone as shrewd, or as devoted. His judgments had proved well-nigh infallible. He was the most valuable friend Franklin had.

Sara Roosevelt didn't like him. He was a wizened,

gnomelike, gray little man, a wheezing chain-smoker suffering from asthma and maybe even from emphysema. The shoulders of his worn, ill-tailored suit were sprinkled with fallen dandruff from his sparse hair. His vest and trousers were gray with cigarette ash. She, Eleanor, had disliked him too, at first. Rather, she had been jealous of his devotion to her husband and his constant presence, and she had resented Franklin's deference to Louis's analyses and opinions. But she acknowledged now that Louis had skillfully created first a candidate and then a candidate's wife, first a President and then a First Lady. She could not but be grateful. And she could not but respond, too, to the friendship he extended to her in measure second only to that which he gave Franklin.

"He's not discouraged," she said. "Another man would be."

"By the Court, you mean," said Louis. He shook his head. "It may have done us a favor. Since the justices killed the NRA, we don't have to worry about its failing. If it had lived, it might have become a terrible albatross around the President's neck. By the Schechter decision, the Court cut the albatross loose and threw it in the water."

She smiled broadly. "You're an optimist, Louis."

Louis shrugged as he drew deeply on the last of the cigarette in his mouth and extracted another from the pack in his vest pocket. "Why not?" he grunted as he touched the fresh cigarette to the burning butt just under his nose.

Mrs. Roosevelt poured lemonade into Louis's glass and her own. The pitcher of iced lemonade had been sent—not brought—out by Sara Roosevelt: a concession.

"Well," said Louis. "He returns."

The President's car—an open-topped Ford equipped with handbrake and hand throttle—came slowly along the drive and stopped. The President enjoyed the occasions when he could drive around the estate and the near neighborhood, and as he stopped he tooted the horn and showed a great, toothy grin. The Secret Service car stopped at a discreet distance, and the Secret Service men dispersed around the lawn, checking the vicinity as unobtrusively as possible.

"We've had a marvelous drive," said the President as he opened the door and Gus Gennerich, his burly ex-policeman bodyguard, came around to help him from the car. "Almost ran down some ducks, but otherwise a marvelous drive."

As Gus held his arm, the President locked his leg braces to support him erect and swung his way, with Gus's help, across the lawn. Jim Farley, who had been in the front seat with him, followed; and Missy LeHand, who had been in the back with Gus, hurried around the car to walk half a step behind the President and offer more help if he needed it.

"Those *were* ducks, weren't they, Jim?" the President asked playfully. "You know, they did look and sound like Republican senators, for all the world."

Gus helped the President settle himself into one of the wooden armchairs on the lawn.

"Senators, Mr. President. That's what they were," said Jim Farley, the Postmaster General.

"I'm sorry I put on the brakes, then." The President laughed.

He reached for the glass of lemonade that Mrs. Roosevelt handed him, nodded his thanks, and took a sip. He was comfortable. She had long marveled at his ability to be comfortable. Wearing a panama hat and a rumpled summer-weight suit, he was *visibly* comfortable, in a way that she could envy. Farley, who was a stocky man, was perspiring in the heat of the sun, but the President looked as if he welcomed the heat and enjoyed it.

Mrs. Roosevelt poured lemonade for Farley, then a glass

for Missy. "Do you mind sitting on the grass, Missy?" she asked. "I'm afraid we're one chair short."

"I'll just stand," said Missy. "I can't stay. I have to make a few calls for the President."

Mrs. Roosevelt could marvel at Missy, too: at the way she managed invariably to look crisply attractive, always the unwearied dutiful secretary, ready to accept another assignment and scurry off to perform it. This afternoon she was characteristically fresh and springy, wearing an inexpensive pink-flowered dress and no hat, her hair blown loose by the ride in the open car. Though she brushed self-consciously at her hair with her hand, she still looked stylish and pretty.

The President adjusted his pince-nez and glanced casually over a newspaper clipping Farley had handed him. He chuckled. "So Bill Hearst's calling me 'Stalin Delano Roosevelt,' is he? Poor old fellow. 'Benito Randolph Hearst.' Next month he'll be calling me Saint Franklin the Good. I wish he could make up his mind."

"A disordered mind is unlikely ever to be made up," said Louis Howe acidly.

"Not disordered," said the President. "Just second-rate. That's all. Just second-rate."

"Have you seen this morning's *Times?*" asked Howe.

"Glanced through it," said the President. "What should I have noticed?"

"The indictment of Alfred Hannah," said Howe. "No political significance to it, I suppose, but it's distressing."

"Oh, yes!" exclaimed Mrs. Roosevelt. "Practically a *neighbor.*"

"More than 'practically,'" said the President. "The Hannahs are members of Saint James's Church. Al's a member of our Masonic Lodge, too. I did see the story, Louis. Distressing is the right word. I don't suppose there's a thing we can do?"

Howe shook his head. "No, you wouldn't dare touch it."

"Millions," said the President, shaking his head. "Tens of millions. It's difficult to believe that a man like Alfred Hannah could be involved in a scheme like that."

"Nothing has been proved, let's don't forget," said Mrs. Roosevelt. "He's only been indicted."

"And dismissed from his firm," added Farley. "His partners threw him out as soon as they got the word."

"Disgraced . . ." sighed Mrs. Roosevelt.

"Yes, even if he's not convicted," said Missy. "The charge will stick to him for the rest of his life, even if the indictment is thrown out. I've met him, I think. I feel sorry for the man. What does he face if he's convicted?"

"A prison term," said Howe grimly. He sucked hard on his cigarette, drawing it down to a short butt. "Think of that—Al Hannah in the penitentiary."

"Think of his poor family," said Mrs. Roosevelt. "We don't know them well enough to call, do we? I mean, it would be—"

"No, we don't," said the President. "It wouldn't be appropriate, even if we weren't in our present odd circumstances."

Missy laughed suddenly. She was embarrassed, but Mrs. Roosevelt understood and smiled warmly at her. She, too, was amused that Franklin referred to the presidency as their 'odd circumstances.' Missy's little laugh broke the mood, and the conversation turned from Alfred Hannah to the latest doings of the Kingfish—Senator Huey Long.

Late in the afternoon, Louis Howe, James Farley, and Missy LeHand left to catch the train for New York, and the President and Mrs. Roosevelt went inside to the big living room at the south end of the house. Only then did Sara Delano Roosevelt join them. She had spent the afternoon closeted in the private sitting room she called her snuggery, probably to avoid the men she called "Franklin's *political* friends," both of whom she considered too lacking in good breeding for her attention.

"You will, I trust, *dress* for dinner, Eleanor," said Sara, raising an eyebrow slightly as she eyed the skirt and blouse her daughter-in-law had worn on the lawn that afternoon.

"Of course," said the First Lady quietly.

The two women drank tea. The President, as was his custom, sat in one of the tall black leather chairs that had been given him as Governor of New York and mixed his two before-dinner martinis. He would have preferred to drink with company, but his wife rarely drank anything alcoholic, and his mother, though she would enjoy wine with dinner, strongly disapproved of what she called "cocktails." The conversation was of politics, covering many of the topics that had been covered earlier on the lawn—in order that the President's mother might have a brief review of the situation developing for 1936.

"I am pleased anyway," said Sara Roosevelt, "that I am no longer compelled to tolerate association with that unsavory Tammany ward-heeler, Alfred Smith."

The President shook his head, and his smile was forced and brief. "Al," he said sadly, "has grown old and bitter."

"It is not surprising," said Sara Roosevelt. "He was always a *hollow* man."

"I—" the First Lady began to say, when she was interrupted by the entrance of the butler, whose face shone pink with annoyance, perhaps even with alarm.

"Forgive me," he said. "Miss van der Meer insists she must see Mrs. Roosevelt immediately."

"Miss *who?* Tell her to go away. I am not receiving."

"I beg your pardon, ma'am. It is Mrs. Franklin Roosevelt that the young lady wishes to see."

"Adriana van der Meer," said Mrs. Roosevelt. She rose. "I'll see what she wants."

"It is extraordinary that she should appear at this hour," said Sara Roosevelt indignantly. "Dinner—"

"I will be dressed and ready for dinner. For the moment, I will see why Adriana is here."

Adriana van der Meer was waiting in the main hall. "Oh, Aunt Eleanor!" she cried as soon as she saw Mrs. Roosevelt, and she rushed into her arms and shook with sobs.

"Whatever is wrong, Adriana? Tell me, child. What is it?"

"Oh, Aunt Eleanor, I wish I were *dead!*" the girl cried.

"No . . ." said Mrs. Roosevelt, as soothingly as she could. "No, nothing is ever that bad. Come. Let's step out on the porch where no one can hear, and you tell me what's wrong."

On the porch the girl dabbed at her flushed face with a white handkerchief and brought her trembling lips under control. She was a tall nineteen-year-old, well proportioned and exceptionally pretty, with the pale blue eyes and flaxen hair of her Dutch ancestry. She was dressed in riding clothes: khaki jodhpurs, white blouse, boots, a floppy soft cap; and her chestnut gelding was hitched to the cast-iron post at the edge of the drive. She heaved with breath as she struggled to take complete control of herself.

"Would you like a glass of lemonade?" asked Mrs. Roosevelt.

Adriana shook her head.

"Then tell me what's wrong."

"The world is *cruel,* Aunt Eleanor." Adriana sobbed, shaking her head.

"Agreed," said Mrs. Roosevelt. "But what cruelty is it doing to you to bring you here in such a state?"

Adriana sighed. "Did you see this morning's newspaper—I mean, *The New York Times?* Did you see the story about Mr. Hannah?"

Mrs. Roosevelt nodded gravely.

"Well . . . Bob and I—that is, Bob Hannah and I—want to be *married!* I mean, we are engaged. Unofficially. I mean, we haven't told our families yet. And now . . . now my father and mother have forbidden me ever to see Bob again!"

"Because of Mr. Hannah's indictment?"

Adriana sobbed. "Yes! And I *love* him. I'd rather *die* than not see him again!"

Mrs. Roosevelt drew a deep breath. "Well . . ." she said, and she patted the girl's hand. "It has been a shock, you know, to everyone who knows the Hannahs. I should imagine your father and mother will reconsider, when they've had a chance to think more clearly about it."

"No," whispered Adriana tearfully. "My father says no van der Meer will associate in any way with an indicted felon. Never. He didn't even know Bob and I planned to be married, and he has forbidden me to see him, even to tell him I'm forbidden to see him. I telephoned anyway. I—"

"Then you've spoken to him. And what did Bob say?"

"Oh, he could hardly speak. He needs me now, Aunt Eleanor. He needs someone sympathetic, someone who loves him."

"Let us sit down," said Mrs. Roosevelt, and she led the distraught girl to a chair on the terrace on the north side of the porch. "I'm uncertain as to what I can do for you, Adriana."

"Mr. Hannah is *not guilty*," said Adriana fiercely. Her eyes hardened, and her face colored with a new, angry flush. "Bob told me a month ago that something like this might happen. He says his father is the victim of a conspiracy."

"By the government?"

"No. By the really guilty men, who want him to be convicted and imprisoned so they can get off free. Bob explained it to me. But my father says that makes no difference."

"Why does it make no difference?"

"It is a horrible scandal, no matter how it comes out; and he will not have our name in any way associated with it.

Besides, the Hannah's are going to lose everything they have, and—"

"I understand," said Mrs. Roosevelt grimly.

Adriana dissolved. "Oh, I wish I were dead!" she wailed.

"Bob wouldn't want that, would he?"

"Oh, no. He's so *wonderful* . . . He is everything a girl could wish in a husband, Aunt Eleanor. And I love him. We had such plans!"

"What can I do for you, Adriana?" asked Mrs. Roosevelt. She was compelled to think of the time. It was not unlikely that her mother-in-law would issue from the house shortly. "Is there anything I can do to help you?"

"One thing maybe," said Adriana, sniffing. "If I were visiting you and if Bob happened to come to visit you, too . . . You see?"

"Then you could talk to him," said Mrs. Roosevelt.

Adriana nodded. "I *must,* somehow."

"Alone, you mean?"

"Yes. I'd be so grateful to you! I didn't know who else would understand and . . . and would have the special position that might make it possible."

Mrs. Roosevelt glanced toward the front door. "Since you ride, dear, why don't you just have the young man meet you somewhere in the woods, where you can talk?"

"My father is having me watched. One of his stableboys is down the road now, waiting for me to start back."

"He followed you?"

"At a discreet distance."

Mrs. Roosevelt frowned. "Despicable," she said. "He wouldn't try to follow *me,* I dare say."

"No, I'm sure he wouldn't."

"If he did, he might find a Secret Service man blocking his way."

"Yes," said Adriana.

"Well, then," said Mrs. Roosevelt. "I'm not certain I'm doing the right thing, to help you defy your parents; but suppose tomorrow morning I should be out for a little canter and should happen to ride by your home ... You should be ready about ten. We will ride together. In fact, I shall ask you to lunch."

"You are very kind. I thought I could turn to you."

"Your young man, though. How will he know what to do?"

"He will telephone you this evening."

Mrs. Roosevelt smiled. "You anticipated a bit too much, Adriana," she said. Her smile broadened. "Or perhaps you didn't."

"I was confident of your generosity," said Adriana quietly. Then she smiled, too. "Also of your sense of romance," she added.

2

When she woke the next morning, Mrs. Roosevelt could hear rain beating on the roof; and she was afraid she would not be able to go out riding, to keep her appointment with Adriana van der Meer. By eight, when she was having breakfast, the rain had stopped; and by nine-thirty, when she mounted a trim black mare, the sun shone brightly on wet grass and trees, and the hills smelled green.

She did not find time to ride often anymore, but she had the clothes for it: khaki coat and breeches, boots, white shirt with narrow maroon necktie. Her hair was held in place by a band of silk knotted behind—a style she much favored. She settled confidently into the soft English saddle and took the double reins in her right hand. The horse did not know her and at first tested her, pawing and side-stepping; but when it felt a firm hand on the reins it submitted to her control. She walked it at first, on a testing circuit of the rose garden. Then, on the graveled path toward the woods and the bridle path, she urged it into a canter.

She glanced back. Williams of the Secret Service was following, bouncing awkwardly on a bay stallion. He would keep a discreet distance: never out of sight but never so close as to intrude.

Her mother-in-law had suggested that riding, on such a morning, when water might be shaken from the trees and fall on her, and when besides she *should* accompany her husband to church, was not a very good idea. The President, though, had contradicted his mother. It would be good for Babs, he said, to get some exercise, to take the sun. He had asked where she might go on her ride, and she had told him she might ride to Val-Kill Cottage, the little stone house they had built a couple of miles from the mansion, on the brook called by the Dutch name Val-Kill. That was in fact one of the places where she meant to go.

But first she meant to ride north a mile or so, to the van der Meer estate. She could ride a part of the distance on the bridle path but then would have to turn onto the Albany Post Road for the last half-mile before turning into the gate behind the sign that read:

RIVER HAVEN
C. VAN DER MEER
PRIVATE!

Her mother-in-law had been right about the water that would fall from the trees. She brushed low-hanging branches heavy with rain, and by the time she turned in at the van der Meer gate her riding clothes were spotted with water. It was her appearance, partly, and partly a sense of uncertainty about the game she had promised to play against Adriana's parents, that were the source of her intense self-consciousness as she nudged her mare into a canter again on the curving gravel drive from the road to the house.

The house was hidden from the Post Road by a stand of ancient spruces. It was a rambling century-old farmhouse, built of native fieldstone, much of which was now shaggy with ivy. A long porch crossed the entire front, following the angles of the additions that had been made to the main house over the years. Great old oaks and elms shaded the house from all sides, giving it—as Mrs. Roosevelt thought—a somewhat dark and gloomy aspect.

As she rounded the stand of spruce and came in sight of the house, she was surprised to see Adriana already mounted on her chestnut, sitting before the house. At first, she thought Adriana was just waiting for her; but, on closer inspection, she could see that the girl was engaged in earnest conversation with her father, who stood on the porch in the posture of a man whose patience was being tested.

"Ah, good morning, Cornelius. Good morning, Adriana! Aren't we fortunate that the rain stopped?"

Cornelius van der Meer stepped out of the shadow of the porch and onto the steps, where he greeted Mrs. Roosevelt with a curt formal bow, which perhaps he supposed her status as First Lady required of him. "We are honored," he said. He was a formidable man—formidable in his height, his big solid head and big solid face, his firm wide mouth, and his great, round, cold eyes. His yellow hair was plastered tight to the sides of his head with oil, and the dome of his bald head was white and splotched with liver spots as if he had just been splattered with mud. From where he stood on the porch step, he looked up at Mrs. Roosevelt astride her horse, and the upward turn of his eyes gave him an air of suspicion so vivid that she wondered if he did not know she was taking Adriana to a meeting with Bob Hannah. "We've not had the honor for a long time."

"If it is indeed an honor, you owe it to Adriana, who invited me," said Mrs. Roosevelt with a warm smile. "Actually, it's a pleasure for me. We don't see each other nearly often enough anymore."

"We—" he started to say, but was interrupted by his wife, who emerged suddenly from the house.

"*Eleanor!*" cried Christina van der Meer. "How very nice!"

"Christina! It is a pleasure to see you. Could we, by any chance, encourage you to come riding with us?"

Mrs. Roosevelt returned Adriana's appalled glance with an innocent smile. It was perfectly apparent that the plump little Mrs. van der Meer, dressed in a flowered spring frock, was not coming horseback riding. Obviously, she and her husband were about to leave for church.

"Actually, I haven't ridden horseback for years," said Mrs. van der Meer.

"It is good exercise, you know," said Mrs. Roosevelt. "I am so pleased to see that Adriana rides."

"Well, we are pleased that you've asked her to ride with you."

"And we'll have lunch, I believe," said Mrs. Roosevelt. "So I'll send her home about . . . oh, about two."

"If you'll telephone, I'll send a stableboy to ride home with her," said van der Meer. "I worry about her riding far from home alone. A young girl, you know . . ."

"If I don't accompany her home myself, I'll send one of the Secret Service men with her," said Mrs. Roosevelt. "There is one lurking somewhere nearby, you understand."

"Ah . . ." said van der Meer uncertainly. "Well, if it's not too much trouble."

"It won't be," said Mrs. Roosevelt.

"Well, then," said Adriana, turning her horse. "Good-bye until this afternoon."

"Don't forget any part of your instructions," her father called after her.

"I shan't," Adriana muttered through her teeth as soon as her back was to her parents. "I shan't *forget* them."

They rode to Val-Kill. Mrs. Roosevelt had telephoned last evening to be certain that no one would be there that Sunday morning, and when they rode their horses up to her house, it was as deserted as she had expected—even a little more deserted, since Bob Hannah had not yet arrived. Adriana telephoned the Hannahs to find out if Bob had left and learned that he had.

"I am grateful to you," she said quietly to Mrs. Roosevelt.

"I don't know what solution you are going to find to your problem, child," said Mrs. Roosevelt, "but I wish you the very best. You've suffered a cruel blow, but I am confident things will work out somehow."

"I love him," said Adriana firmly. "I thought about it all night. I won't let them separate us."

Mrs. Roosevelt drew a deep breath. "Well . . . be circumspect," she said.

Adriana nodded. "You needn't wait."

Mrs. Roosevelt smiled. "You want to be alone with him," she said. "Very well, Adriana. Please be sure the house is locked up when you leave." She paused. "Needless to say, I . . . uh, have every confidence that you and your young man will conduct yourselves, uh, *not improperly* while you are alone here."

"Of course, Aunt Eleanor," said Adriana soberly. "And thank you once again."

As she rode back toward the Albany Post Road, Mrs. Roosevelt saw Bob Hannah driving fast in the opposite direction, toward Val-Kill, in a black Model A Ford coupe. If he saw her, he gave her no greeting. The glimpse she had of him was only enough to recognize him and to note that he was grim-faced and purposeful.

She knew him far less well than she knew Adriana, who had been a neighbor's child and a visitor at the mansion since she was a toddler. She tried to remember what she knew about Robert Hannah, to put together a coherent impression. He was older than Adriana, probably about twenty-five. His family spent more time in New York than at Hyde Park, and she recalled that he had gone to school in the city. He was a Harvard man, as was his father. She did not recall having heard what he was doing since his graduation, except that she had a vague recollection that he was taking some postgraduate degree. Maybe he was studying law. He was, anyway, a handsome, well-spoken young man. It was easy to understand why Adriana was in love with him.

She could only wish them well. To do much more was beyond her power.

The telephone rang at four. Cornelius van der Meer was on the line. "I am sorry to disturb your afternoon, Eleanor, but Adriana has not returned. Is she still with you?"

In one distressing flash, Mrs. Roosevelt knew what had happened and what responsibility she bore for it. The purposeful young man in the Model A Ford coupe had swept up his rebellious and determined girl, and God knew where they were by now. The couple had used her friendship and trust to effect their evasion of the wrathful Cornelius van der Meer and their escape . . . again, God knew where—perhaps to Canada. What could she say? The impulse to confess was strong. An impulse to defer confession until she could obtain a few more facts was also strong—and for the moment stronger.

"Why . . . no. I, uh, rode back with her as far as your gate. That was at two."

"She did not come home," said van der Meer. "She rode off somewhere else. I think I know where."

"Oh, dear," said Mrs. Roosevelt. She hated the lie, but she was siezed with the idea that she could perhaps do something curative if she only had a little time. "I am sorry, Cornelius. I—"

"It's not your fault, of course," he interrupted. "It's a family matter. The girl has become infatuated with an entirely unsuitable young man, and I suspect she has gone to see him, contrary to my specific, emphatic instructions. I am sorry to have troubled you, Eleanor. I shall take care of the matter."

When she put down the telephone, the President looked up from a volume of his stamp collection, which he was studying at his small desk in the east end of the living room. "You look stricken," he said. "Sounded stricken. What's happened?"

"Adriana van der Meer went riding with me this morning. She did not return home. Her father thinks she has gone to see Bob Hannah. I think it's more than that. I think they've eloped."

"Uh-oh," said the President with a smile that quickly spread into a grin. "I bet you were playing Cupid. You gave her the opportunity. 'Fess up, Babs."

"I took her to Val-Kill," admitted Mrs. Roosevelt. "He met her there. Oh, Franklin, I've got to go up there immediately. They might still be there. Or—"

"Or she left her horse there," suggested the President. "Take the car, Babs. Call me from there."

She drove his car, the latest of his cars equipped with hand controls, and sped up the road to Val-Kill, having gotten away without a Secret Service man to accompany or follow her. In a few minutes, she reached the house, where, sure enough, Adriana's chestnut gelding remained tethered, impatiently pawing the earth and snorting.

She had no choice but to telephone Cornelius van der

Meer. "Adriana rode with me to Val-Kill cottage this morning," she told him, "and apparently she returned here." (A lie again, and she hated it, but it would be difficult to explain the truth to him now.) "Her horse is here."

"Ah," he said. "It's all becoming very clear now."

Mrs. Roosevelt wondered how much he meant was clear. "Uh . . . you haven't found her?" she asked, knowing full well he hadn't.

"No, but I know why I haven't," he said. Anger darkened his voice. "I am sorry this has touched you, Eleanor. I am afraid it's a police matter, but I will see to it that your name is in no way associated with any part of it. I'll send a boy for the horse, and we won't say where she abandoned it. Please don't worry about it."

"Oh, but I *will*," Mrs. Roosevelt protested. "After all, Adriana is like my own daughter. I—"

"I told you there is a young man in the picture," van der Meer interrupted. "Alfred Hannah's son. I think he's taken her. She is infatuated with him and no doubt went willingly. I am notifying the sheriff and the state police."

"But—"

"I'll have them brought back. I know his car and the license number. I'll find them. They can't have gone far in two hours."

"Cornelius would be well advised," said the President, "to abandon this posture of moral outrage and face the fact that his daughter is of the age when she can marry as she chooses, with or without his blessing and certainly without his consent. It's been a long time since I practiced any law, but I remember enough to know that."

They were seated at the round dining table—the President, Mrs. Roosevelt, and Sara Delano Roosevelt—the President in one of the spartan wooden armchairs, his mother in the other, his wife in one of the straight chairs without arms. Their Sunday evening dinner was before them, a simple meal of soup, bread, and fruit, with coffee, since the cook had Sunday off and the meal had been prepared by the maid. A few yellow tulips stood in a glass holder in the footed blue bowl in the center of the table. The President's mother wore a floor-length silk dress, his wife a simpler, shorter dress, and the President himself a wrinkled light brown suit.

"The girl's family are, of course, *correct*," said Sara Delano Roosevelt with a quick nod of her gray head. "It would be quite unsuitable for their daughter to marry the son of a man who has been engaged in a criminal conspiracy and now faces a term of imprisonment."

"He has not been convicted yet," said Mrs. Roosevelt. "It is by no means certain that he will be."

"Nevertheless, the matter smacks of the unsavory," said her mother-in-law.

"The question is," said the President, "if he will manage to get her to their Gretna Green, wherever that may be, and marry her before Cornelius catches up with them. My money is on the boy. If I recall, he's a quick, tough lad. They'll have to get up early to track him down."

"Mr. van der Meer will cut them off without a cent," said the President's mother. "And of course the Hannahs will be in no position now to establish them. They will have cause to regret their impetuosity."

"I am much tempted to phone," said Mrs. Roosevelt.

"Phone whom?" asked her mother-in-law.

"The van der Meers. The Hannahs," said Mrs. Roosevelt. "To find out—"

"Indeed, you must not, Eleanor," said her mother-in-law indignantly. "The matter is none of our affair."

The President grinned. "I wish I could be completely confident of that," he chuckled.

His mother seemed to ignore his comment. "Hannah," she said. "Don't I recall that he was a partner in Deutsch, Lindemann and Company?"

"Yes," said the President. "Brokers. Specialists in public utility stocks and bonds. Survived the Crash quite nicely. They've put a lot of money into efforts to frustrate some of our new programs."

"They cling to the quaint old idea that investment is a private matter, I suppose," said his mother with keen irony.

"They cling to their own version of caveat emptor," said Mrs. Roosevelt. "Let the investor discover for himself that there are no assets behind the securities he buys."

"If I sell you a horse," said her mother-in-law, "is it not only fair that you should open its mouth and see for yourself if it has teeth?"

"Yes, Mother," said the President. "But suppose the purchaser is a small businessman in, say, Rhinebeck, New York—and what he is buying is shares of an electric utility company. How does he look at the teeth of that?"

"He relies on the honesty and good judgment of the management of the company, also that of his broker," she answered.

"Precisely," said the President. "And if they are dishonest, then he is stuck, and they become rich by stealing from him. That's why we passed the securities acts—to force them to give him an honest, accurate statement of what's behind the stocks and bonds he buys."

"He shall then depend, in other words, on your young men in government, rather than—"

"That's right," said the President.

He and his mother were interrupted by the sound of the telephone ringing in the kitchen. Conversation stopped as all three waited for the maid to come in and tell them who was calling.

"It's for you, ma'am," the maid said apologetically to Mrs. Roosevelt.

Eleanor took the call in the living room.

"Mrs. Roosevelt?" said a tense voice on the line. "This is

Alfred Hannah calling. I am sorry if I'm disturbing you, but my son insisted you would want to know that he has been arrested in Plattsburgh, New York. Miss van der Meer is with him. She said you would understand why they wanted me to call you. She, uh, is asking for your help."

The traffic light had been switched off for the night, but from habit Robert Hannah stopped at the main intersection in Rhinebeck, New York, and hesitated before shifting into low gear and driving on—long enough that the state trooper sitting beside him glanced at him warily. Bob Hannah cast a sidewise glance at the dimly lighted, tucked-in-for-the-night Beekman Hotel and wondered if anyone still lingered in the bar. For an instant he swelled with the resentment that people in trouble instinctively feel toward the untroubled. Quickly he subdued that feeling and tried to focus rationally on the situation.

Somewhere on this same highway, half a mile or a mile ahead, Adriana rode south in a police car driven by a state trooper. She sat in the back seat, beside the trooper's wife, who had come along from Plattsburgh to guard against her jumping out of the car and running away.

Adriana had almost won her argument against coming home in the police car. She had insisted that he, Bob, drive her home, so they would not come back to Hyde Park like criminals being returned by the police. It was only when the sergeant of troopers had told her that that was just how Bob would return to Hyde Park—under arrest and in handcuffs—if she did not cooperate, that she resentfully agreed to the arrangement they were following.

She had been a great deal more forceful in speaking with her parents. He had heard only one side of the conversation: "I will *not*. I don't care anymore how you feel about it. . . . I want Aunt Eleanor there when I arrive. . . . Because I want a friend there. . . . No, you are not my friends. Not anymore. . . . Well . . . I will not speak a word with either of you unless she *is* there. . . . That is your problem. You seem to be quite resourceful, so solve it."

Mrs. Roosevelt, Adriana had told him before they left Plattsburgh, would be at the van der Meer house when they arrived. He was skeptical, but Adriana insisted it would be so.

It had been Adriana's idea that they run away together. He had been reluctant to impose any further cause for worry on his harried father and mother; but he had discussed it with them, and both of them had told him wearily that he should use his own judgment; they were for now unable to give much thought to his problem. Besides his car and a few clothes, he had brought a little more than three hundred dollars in cash with him—all he had. Adriana had brought no clothes—was in fact still wearing her riding habit—but she had somehow managed to get away with fifteen hundred dollars. She had been, unfortunately, a little vague about where she got it.

Their plan had been to drive to Canada and there marry, return in a few days to confront the van der Meers with a fait accompli, and face the realities after that. Her fifteen hundred had made the realities a good deal less bleak. What she had wanted him to do was return to Harvard and finish law school. They could live on that much money, she said, until he was admitted to the bar and was placed in a first-class Wall Street firm.

He had not, in the space of the few hours they were together before the state police stopped them outside Plattsburgh, been able to tell her that Robert B. Hannah, son of Alfred Hannah, might not be entirely welcome on Wall Street in 1935 or 1936. The consequences of the corporate collapse that was going to follow his father's indictment would be painfully felt for years to come, and the resentments would burn for decades. No matter that his father was, as he believed, a victim. It was his name, the name Hannah, that would be attached to the developing disaster. He had tried to tell her what she was accepting by marrying him. The scandal, the shame, might be the least of it. She might experience social ostracism. They might face near-impoverishment.

Bob doubted that Adriana had any real appreciation of the depth and scope of all this—as much as he had tried to explain it to her. She was an intelligent girl, but she had a young woman's capacity for putting out of mind any complication that stood in the way of what she had decided to do. To his earnest attempt to explain it all to her, Adriana replied only that she loved him. Well . . . he loved her, too, of course. My God, how could he not love her?

The state police car was parked before the house when he drove around the stand of spruce and came in sight of the brightly lighted van der Meer house. And there too— he could hardly believe it—was the familiar old Model A with hand controls, the President's Hyde Park car.

"I'll see you and your father both behind bars," growled Cornelius van der Meer as soon as he opened the door. The man's face was high pink, and the veins on the sides of his head throbbed. He shook his fist. "In the state penitentiary, by damn!"

Adriana brushed by her father and threw her arms around Bob. "Daddy," she hissed over her shoulder. "Do try to be a human being, just for five minutes." She clung tightly, fearfully to Bob as they crossed the front hall and entered the living room.

Bob glanced apprehensively around the big living room—at Mrs. van der Meer in a conspicuous state of collapse on a couch, her face half covered with a small white handkerchief; two beefy state troopers in uniform, standing uneasily in the middle of the room, hats in their hands; Mrs. Roosevelt, sitting in a wing chair by the cold fireplace, her head cocked to one side, regarding him with open curiosity; and, before the fireplace, in his wood-and-steel wheelchair, Mr. Roosevelt, too!

Bob gasped. *"Mr. President!"*

The President smiled weakly and nodded, but he looked weary. His cigarette holder drooped, and the cigarette had gone out.

"Mr. President. Mrs. Roosevelt. I'm sorry you've been dragged out in the middle of the night. Even so, it's . . . very good to see you. I'm grateful."

"Adriana has always been like another daughter to us," said Mrs. Roosevelt brightly, her warmth not in the least diminished by the hour or the circumstances.

"And I could hardly let Ma Perkins here go running off to play neighborhood peacemaker in the middle of the night and not come with her," said the President. "I will appreciate it, though, if we can reach some sort of armistice in a few minutes and get to bed. I have to take a train to Washington in the morning."

"It can be settled very expeditiously," said Cornelius van der Meer aggressively, "if the officers will simply take this hoodlum off to jail, lock him up, and throw away the key."

"Really, Cornelius," protested Mrs. Roosevelt. "You are being tiresome."

"Anyway, old man," said the President, "what would the charge be?"

"He kidnapped my daughter!" yelled van der Meer.

"Adriana," said the President. "Were you kidnapped?"

"Yes," she snapped. "By them"—pointing at the two troopers—"bringing me back here by force. Or by him"—she pointed at her father—"using his influence to make them do it."

"And how old are you?" asked the President.

"I'm nineteen."

The President glanced up at the two state troopers and shrugged. "The girl is of age," he said. "She went voluntarily . . ."

"I don't believe the officers are needed any longer," said Mrs. Roosevelt decisively. "Christina," she said to Mrs. van der Meer. "Haven't you coffee and sandwiches available?"

Mrs. van der Meer nodded. "I suppose so," she whispered.

"I believe the maid is still in the kitchen with Gus," said Mrs. Roosevelt. "She will be happy to prepare a nice snack for you two gentlemen, and you may remember Gus Gennerich, who was Mr. Roosevelt's bodyguard when he was Governor of the State of New York."

"Corporal Dugby's wife is waiting in the car outside," said Adriana.

"Bring her in, Corporal," said Mrs. Roosevelt.

"Just a minute here," said van der Meer, shaking a finger. "There was money stolen from this house today. What about that?"

"Do you want to send *me* to jail?" Adriana asked him defiantly. She remained locked to Bob, with her arms tightly around him, her head on his shoulder. "I confess. Right now. I took all the money I could find in the house."

"Adriana . . ." murmured Bob, shaking his head.

"*I'll* go to jail," shrilled Adriana. "Right now. I'll go with the officers right now, if that's what you want."

"Do you want your daughter placed under arrest, Mr. van der Meer?" asked Corporal Dugby firmly.

"No, I don't want my daughter placed under arrest, for the love of Pete."

"Then we'll be going, sir. Good night."

"Uh . . . the sandwiches?" sniffed Mrs. van der Meer.

"Thank you, ma'am, but we'll be going," said the corporal. "Good night. Good night, Mr. President, Mrs. Roosevelt."

For a long moment, as the state troopers left the house, the living room was silent. Adriana released Bob from her arms but gripped his hand tightly and did not move half a pace away from him. Van der Meer stood staring at them, his temples still visibly throbbing. The President lighted a cigarette.

Finally, Adriana tossed her little handbag on the floor at her father's feet. "You'll find your money in there," she said. "We would have used it to finish Bob's education, but we'll manage somehow without it." She looked up into Bob's eyes. "Let's go, honey," she said quietly.

"*Adriana,*" said van der Meer grimly but with control. "I will disinherit you. You won't have a dime. How do you like that, Hannah?"

Bob shook his head. "I'm sorry for Adriana's sake," he said. "And I'm sorry for you, Mr. van der Meer."

Adriana's face was red, but it was hard, and her eyes were dry. "May I take some clothes?" she asked.

Her mother sobbed. Her father shrugged.

"Oh, dear," murmured Mrs. Roosevelt, shaking her head. "Does it all have to be so . . . so *bitter?* Can't you see your way clear, Cornelius, to—"

"To what?" interrupted van der Meer. "To consent to my daughter's marriage to the son of an embezzler?"

"My father has not even been *charged* with embezzlement!"

"Stock manipulation, then," sneered van der Meer. "Larceny."

"He has only been charged, Cornelius, not convicted," said Mrs. Roosevelt.

"He will be proved innocent," said Bob. "When the evidence is in, it—"

"Oh, sure," said van der Meer scornfully. "What I hear, and from reliable sources in the city, is that the evidence will bring out worse things than have already been charged. Far worse. And my daughter will be married to this puppy. Living in"—he swelled with breath, and his face reddened—"in squalor."

"Mr. van der Meer," said Bob, "if you can adopt a decent attitude, I will be more than happy to postpone our marriage until my father is proved innocent. Adriana can live at home until—"

"Oh, no!" protested Adriana vehemently. "I'm not staying here, a virtual prisoner in this house. Oh, no. I've made the break, Bob. I made it today, for you. We're going to be married now."

"What are you going to live on, Adriana?" her mother asked tearfully. "I can't insist that your father give you an allowance, when you are so . . . undutiful."

"We will manage," said Adriana. She squeezed Bob's hand. "Others do."

"I would like," said Bob gravely, "to have a good relationship with Adriana's family. I am willing to be reasonable."

"You would like," sneered van der Meer, "a share of the family money—particularly since whatever the Hannahs have is likely to disappear in the general catastrophe your father has precipitated."

"Others precipitated," Bob insisted. "You will see, Mr. van der Meer. When the evidence is in, you will see. You will be embarrassed for what you've said."

"All may be quiet on the Western Front," said the President impatiently, frowning and drawing distractedly on his unlighted cigarette, "but it's anything but quiet on the Hyde Park front. Why can't you all retire and sleep on this problem? Adriana, you can't get married tonight. Cornelius, old man, you can't make a wise judgment in the middle of the night, at the end of a trying day, with your emotions tight as a drum. There has to be a reasonable compromise somewhere. Why don't you take some time and look for it?"

"I will not sleep another night in this house," said Adriana.

Bob sighed heavily. "I can't ask her to. I can't leave her here."

"Then get out," said van der Meer coldly. "Both of you. See how you fare."

"No!" shrieked Mrs. van der Meer, rising to her feet. "You cannot throw our daughter out of the house in the middle of the night and . . . No!"

"*Christinaaaa*," van der Meer protested through clenched teeth.

"Adriana, you can't go with him!" Mrs. van der Meer cried, pointing dramatically at Bob. "Where would you go? Where will you sleep? Not—"

"No," said Adriana.

"What future will you have?" cried Mrs. van der Meer.

"Really, Christina," blurted Mrs. Roosevelt irritably. "They might have more attractive prospects if all of you would act more calmly. This conversation is going 'round in circles."

"Been around three times now, at least," said the President. "Gus!" he called over his shoulder.

Mrs. Roosevelt stood. "I can make . . . this offer," she said quietly. "Adriana can go to Val-Kill cottage and stay there until some resolution of this dispute is reached. Nancy returned this afternoon, so Adriana will not be alone there. In a few days, much may change."

"I doubt that," said van der Meer.

Gus Gennerich came in from the kitchen and stood behind the President's wheelchair, ready to push him toward the door. The President lifted a hand to indicate he would stay another minute.

"Let me ask you something, Cornelius," the President

said. "If Alfred Hannah were acquitted, would you withdraw your objection to this young couple marrying?"

"If he were *cleared*," said van der Meer. "Cleared. Acquittal is not enough. I do not want Adriana married into a family that—"

"I know," the President interrupted. "But—"

"It will be months before the case is tried," said van der Meer.

"He may be cleared before that, if the evidence is brought out," said Bob.

"But you would not object, Cornelius, if Bob's father's reputation were restored to what it was before the indictment?"

Van der Meer glowered at Bob. "Besides, he's a fresh young fellow."

"That objection is overruled," said the President. "Would you consent to the marriage if Alfred Hannah's name is cleared?"

"It won't happen," said van der Meer.

"But if it does?"

Van der Meer's forehead creased in a dark frown. "I don't think she's using any kind of good judgment."

"But *if* . . ." insisted the President.

"She loves him, Cornelius," whispered Mrs. van der Meer.

Van der Meer shrugged. "She loves horses, too," he muttered.

"All right, all right," said the President. "Here is my suggestion. We've always thought of Adriana almost as another daughter of our own. We do wish her well. Suppose Adriana comes down to Washington with us and lives as our guest in the White House for a while. She'll find enough in Washington to claim some of her attention. Bob can come and see her from time to time. If Alfred Hannah's name is cleared, there can be a fine big wedding sometime next year. If it's not . . . well, then, at least ev-

eryone will have had time to think calmly about it. How
about that, old man? How about that for an idea?"

"It's very good of you, Frank," conceded van der Meer.

"Adriana?" asked the President.

She glanced up into Bob's eyes, and he nodded. She nodded.

"Christina?"

"Oh, yes!"

The President settled an eye on Mrs. Roosevelt. "I'm
sure Mary Margaret McBride will agree," he said, nodding
and allowing a smile to spread. "She doesn't have nearly
enough to think about these days and is at terrible risk of
sinking into boredom." He lifted a hand to Gus Gennerich.
"Push, pal," he said. "Let's go home."

4

In railroad jargon, the presidential train was called
POTUS—President of the United States. From the siding
at Hyde Park, a big, panting steam locomotive would pull
the presidential cars out onto the New York Central
tracks for the run down the spectacular Hudson Valley to
New York City. In a yard in the Bronx, the train would be
switched to the Pennsylvania tracks for the run to Phila-
delphia, where usually it was switched to the Baltimore &
Ohio for the remainder of the journey. The presidential
car, a special armored Pullman, was accompanied by a second car for aides, Secret Service men, and communications
equipment; and often an additional couple of cars were

added for newspaper and radio reporters. Nervous though the Secret Service men could sometimes be, the presidential cars were often attached to ordinary trains, which became POTUS for the day; and that was how it was on this May morning in 1935.

Officially, the presidential car, painted kelly green, the color of the Southern Railway, was an anomaly, a Pullman car without a name; so usually it was called by the name it had had before it was armored and refurbished: the Ferdinand Magellan. The interior of the car had been torn out and reconfigured, and the rear compartment was a spacious lounge furnished with sofas, a desk, and wingback chairs. The President, who never tired of studying the scenery through the thick glass of the bulletproof windows, found riding the train most restful. Often he traveled at night and slept comfortably aboard the car. Day or night, POTUS never traveled more than thirty miles an hour. The swaying of the car, if it traveled faster, was painful to the President's lower back.

Adriana van der Meer, who of course had never been aboard the presidential train before, amused the President and won a new measure of warm sympathy from Mrs. Roosevelt by her open-eyed wonder. She had packed her things and come to the siding to board the train at seven o'clock, so she had had no sleep at all; yet she was bright and alert and pretty in a blue and yellow spring dress. The President, casual in his shirtsleeves and wearing a jaunty bow tie, sat behind his little desk and studied the morning newspapers that had been brought up on an early morning train to be delivered aboard POTUS. Mrs. Roosevelt sat on one of the couches, with her knitting on her lap and spread out around her. They had coffee and Danish. The scene was, as she reflected with amusement, almost domestic.

"Something here you'll want to read, Adriana," the President said, tapping a finger on a page of *The New York Times*. "An analysis of the Northern United debacle."

"Mr. Hannah's problem?" asked Adriana.

The President nodded. "Concise summary of the story here. If you don't know exactly what problem your future father-in-law has, you can get a good grasp on it by reading this."

"Northern United was a shell," said Mrs. Roosevelt. "Isn't that right? Its securities were worthless."

"Well, not one hundred percent worthless," said the President. "There was enough behind it to sustain the fraud."

"Bob has tried to explain it to me," said Adriana. "I'm afraid I haven't really understood. He finds it hard to be objective, you know."

"Explain it, Franklin," said Mrs. Roosevelt. "Adriana should know."

The President ran his eyes quickly down the rest of the newspaper story. "Well, most of it's here," he said. "Don't you know what the indictment charges?"

"*I* don't, exactly," said Mrs. Roosevelt.

"Uhhm," he muttered, lifting his chin high and regarding the First Lady with a skeptical frown. He understood that she did know and that he was being prompted to explain to Adriana, rather than to leave her to learn the facts from the newspaper. "Well . . . Northern United is a utility holding company. That is to say, it doesn't own any power plants or electric lines or water-power dams or gas works, or much of anything else, tangible. What it owns is the stock of companies that do. Or that's the theory, anyway. Understand?"

Adriana nodded. "I understand about utility holding companies. But one of the companies owned by Northern United was Northeastern United . . . right? And the problem with that was . . . ?"

"Well, that's just one of the elements of it," said the President. "Northern United owns twenty-eight percent of the stock of Northeastern United, which it lists on its books as being worth a great many millions of dollars. The problem is, one of the chief assets of Northeastern United is twelve percent of the stock of Northern United, which Northeastern in turn lists on *its* books as being worth a great many millions of dollars. And beyond that, Northeastern United is itself only a holding company which owns no physical assets but only the stock in still other companies. The relationships among some twenty-nine holding companies and utility companies are so tangled that it requires a huge wall chart with lines that look like the webs of a regiment of inebriated spiders to trace them."

"And the point," said Mrs. Roosevelt, "is to construct a gigantic fraud and reap immense profits from it."

"At the expense of thousands of innocent people," added the President. "Thousands, maybe tens of thousands, of people invested their savings in these companies, supposing they were sound when in fact they were only a tangle of paper."

"Bob told me the stock went down terribly," said Adriana. "Ninety percent."

The President nodded. "Worse than that. When the market opened for trading on January second, Northern United was selling at one thirty-eight and seven-eighths. When trading was suspended last Monday, it was selling at seven and three-quarters."

Adriana's face was solemn and pale. "What did Bob's father do?" she asked.

"Let's ask what he is charged with doing," Mrs. Roosevelt suggested quietly.

The President folded the newspaper and pushed it away from him. "He is accused of distributing false information about the assets of these companies," he said. "He is accused of concealing the true state of affairs from prospective investors. He is accused, in essence, of having cheated many thousands of people out of many millions of dollars."

"For his own profit," added Mrs. Roosevelt.

"Yes," said the President.

At Ossining the tracks passed close to the walls of Sing Sing, the big old New York State penitentiary, where generations of big-city criminals were confined when they were sent "up the river." There for a moment the train made its third momentary stop since leaving Hyde Park.

"I wish I could be in New York next Monday," Adriana said conversationally as the train picked up speed pulling out of the Ossining station. "That great new French liner will be docking, and I think it would be wonderful to see it."

"The *Normandie*," said the President, nodding. "I'd like to see it myself. Its maiden voyage. They say its the finest ship afloat."

"Oh, it would be—" Adriana started to say. She stopped because there was a sharp rap on the door.

"I'm sorry, Mr. President," said Whitcomb of the Secret Service, "but a young man came on the train at Ossining and says you would be willing to see him if you knew he's here."

"What's his name?" asked the President.

"Hannah. Robert Hannah. He insisted I bring his name in."

The President chuckled. "Let him in," he said. "I may have him thrown off at Yonkers, but let him in for now."

"Oh, I didn't—" said Adriana, her face gleaming red.

"I'm sure you didn't," said the President.

Adriana stood, Mrs. Roosevelt knitted calmly, thoughtfully, and the President poured himself another cup of coffee as Whitcomb brought Bob Hannah to the door and held him there until the President nodded that it would be all right to let him enter the compartment.

"Bob!" cried Adriana. "You shouldn't have come."

"I know," said Bob Hannah soberly. "It's another imposition, Mr. President, Mrs. Roosevelt. Please let me explain."

"I believe that would be appropriate," said Mrs. Roosevelt dryly, not looking up from her knitting.

"I've thought through what I'm doing," said Bob. "I haven't acted impulsively."

"Would you like a cup of coffee?" the President asked.

"Uhh . . . yes. Please."

The offer of coffee had effectively stopped the speech the young man had been about to launch—exactly as the President had intended—and he stood nervously, faintly blushing, as he watched the President pour from a china pot into a cup. He was dressed in a light tan double-breasted suit, a wide maroon silk necktie, and tan and white shoes. He carried a worn leather briefcase.

"You have been very kind," Bob ventured. "I'm not sure your kindness is based—"

"Cream and sugar?" asked the President.

"No thank you."

"Well then, sit down. To what do we owe the visit?"

Bob sat down on the couch opposite Mrs. Roosevelt, who now had stuffed her knitting into her bag and sat looking at him curiously. He sat erect and stiff. He cast an appealing look up into the face of Adriana, who touched her fingers lightly to her lips, kissed them, and gestured to toss the kiss to him.

He drew a deep breath. "Last night you heard me insist my father is innocent of the charges brought against him. I can't imagine you believed I was right. You had no reason to believe me. I . . . have some evidence. I would like to show it to you. I can't ask you to accept that it proves my father's innocence, but I do hope you will see that I wasn't just talking wildly last night. I have reason beyond . . . beyond emotional commitment, filial duty, to believe my father is the victim of a conspiracy. If you will let me show you what I have—"

"Of course we'll look at what you have," said Mrs. Roosevelt.

"I came aboard the train because I thought it might be the only chance I would have to impose again on the time and patience of the President of the United States and the First Lady."

"You aren't asking me to intervene in your father's case, are you?" the President asked.

"No, sir. I just want you to see that you didn't make a mistake in helping Adriana and me."

"Well, let's see what you have, then," said the President.

Bob unbuckled the straps on his briefcase. "Start with these," he said. He stood and put before the President, on the desk, half a dozen slips of pink paper. "Do you see what those are?"

The President nodded. "Show them around," he said grimly.

The slips of paper were carbon copies of stockbrokers' buy-sell orders. These were buy orders, initialled A. H., ordering purchases of shares of stock in Northern United Utilities. "He was buying for his own account," said Bob. "I have the confirmations here to support the slips. On January sixteenth my father bought a hundred shares of Northern United at one twenty-five and a half. On February fourth he bought fifty at eighty-seven and five-eighths. On February twenty-sixth he bought . . . Well, you can read the buy orders. He kept on buying until the middle of April, when the stock had fallen to thirty-five. He put more than fifty thousand dollars in Northern United, this year. Why would he do that if he understood the corporation was a shell and that he would lose his money? He lost money in the collapse of Northern United, the same as everybody else. More than those slips show. He had been investing regularly for the past two years. He had almost a quarter of a million dollars' worth of the stock, and he bought it with his own money."

"You are aware, I suppose," said the President, "that a number of interpretations could be placed on his actions in that respect."

"I suppose so," said Bob.

"You have records of his recent purchases," said the President. "Do you have records that show how much Northern United he *sold* over the past eighteen months?"

Bob shook his head.

"What's the total picture? If he lost a quarter of a million in 1935, how much did he *make* over the past five years?"

"I don't know, Mr. President," said Bob. "I can't help but wonder, though, why he would keep buying, when the stock was going down wildly, if he knew something was wrong with the company."

"That's a good point," said the President. "It deserves an answer."

"I have more evidence," said Bob, lifting his chin, drawing a long breath through his nose.

"Bring it out," said the President.

Bob reached into the well-worn leather briefcase and pulled out a manila file folder. "This is more significant," he said, "but it takes some effort to read it. I've typed a copy . . ."

He handed the folder to the President, who opened it, pressed the bridge of his pince-nez with one finger, and peered at the odd contents of the folder. What it contained was a second folder, this one of onionskin paper, in which a once-crumpled sheet of carbon paper was pressed flat— plus a typed sheet.

"From someone's wastebasket, I suppose," said the President, touching the onionskin folder with one finger.

Bob nodded. "The sheet of carbon paper a secretary used when she typed a letter. I rescued it from the wastebasket, carried it home, straightened it, and held it up to a light to read it. The sheet I typed is an exact copy."

The President read the typed sheet and handed it to Mrs. Roosevelt. It read:

New York
March 5, 1935

Martin—

Over the weekend we examined all the documents in that certain file, as per agreement. On re-
ceipt of your assurance that you have done your
part, we will have our little bonfire. Your part of
course includes disposing of your copy of this note,
as our part includes disposing of so much that you
have written. It would be difficult to exaggerate the
importance of our preparing a "clean" file for the
attention of the gumshoes who will arrive soon. All
depends on our mutual faithfulness and discretion.
You are assured of ours. We place our confidence in
yours.

"Who," asked Mrs. Roosevelt, "do you suppose signed
this missive?"

"It could have been one of two or three men," said Bob.
"The 'Martin' to whom it was addressed is clearly Martin
Fiske."

"Why 'clearly'?" asked the President.

"Martin Fiske," said Bob, "is the president of Northeastern and a director of Northern. He was one of the architects of the holding-company structure that failed and
cost so many people so much money."

"How do you come to have this piece of carbon paper in
your possession?" asked Mrs. Roosevelt as she handed the
typed copy to Adriana for her to read.

Bob Hannah drew a deep breath. He glanced from the
President to Mrs. Roosevelt to Adriana. "I, uh, have made
it a point to gather evidence of what was going on at
Deutsch, Lindemann and Company with respect to Northern United and the other companies. I've been doing it for
some time."

The President lifted his chin and nodded at Bob with his
famous presidential grin. "Been going through their
wastebaskets?"

"More than that, Mr. President," said Bob solemnly.

"Specifically, Bob," said Mrs. Roosevelt. "Would you tell us how you came into possession of this piece of carbon paper?"

Bob glanced at Adriana. "I've cultivated the friendship of some of the secretaries in the office," he said. "It's a small matter to be around at closing time and *just accidentally* happen to pull things out of the wastebaskets."

"You've done more than that, I imagine," said the President.

"To be quite frank with you, Mr. President, I have," said Bob humorlessly. "My father can be naïve about his associates. I've suspected them for a long time. A lot of what I know can't be documented, but some of it can."

"What have you done, Bob?" Adriana asked in a thin, troubled voice.

"Aside from rooting through their trash?" he asked. "Quite a lot. Some people, I am sure, would consider what I've done entirely unethical. I've *eavesdropped.* I've done worse than that. Don't ask me to tell you more. If the government investigators had done what I've done, my father would not be under indictment. Others would be. I don't have the evidence in a form that any court could accept, but I know my father is a victim of the manipulations of a vicious gang of felons. I *know* it, Mr. President, Mrs. Roosevelt. I am not just guessing. I know it."

Mrs. Roosevelt looked at the President. "Who should see his evidence?" she asked. "Who should hear him?"

"Babs . . ." said the President on in-drawn breath. "You *must not—*"

"Talk to Joe Kennedy," she interrupted.

The President nodded emphatically. "Talk to Joe Kennedy," he agreed.

"The chairman of the Securities and Exchange Commission . . ." said Bob.

"The chairman of the Securities and Exchange Commission," said the President grimly.

"He made a fortune—"

"Doing the same kinds of things your father is accused of doing," the President broke in. "But he's reformed."

"Not reformed enough to trust him," Mrs. Roosevelt suggested with a sly smile.

"Babs . . ."

"'Never trust an Irishman.' How many times have you said it?"

"Babs!"

Bob Hannah grinned. "Good advice, Mr. President. But they even let them into Harvard now, you know. They don't keep their pigs in the parlor anymore."

"Lace-curtain Irish," muttered the President. "I'll say something for him, though. He was ready to bet on the country when a lot of rich men weren't. It's hard to fault him for profits he made by investing in recovery."

"At least," said Mrs. Roosevelt, "the chairman will have information about the overall matter."

"And you will be circumspect," said the President.

Mrs. Roosevelt nodded, smiling primly. "I always am," she said. "After all, I've been around in political circles almost as long as you."

Absent the odd horn-rimmed glasses, he would have been the archetypal Boston Irishman. With his sandy hair and pink complexion, his broad, ready smile, and his lively blue eyes, he *looked* Irish. He spoke with a Boston twang, softened a little by a trace of Irish accent.

"I am grateful to you, Mr. Kennedy," she said. "I know there are heavy demands on your time."

"None ever so heavy that I do not have time for *you*, Mrs. Roosevelt," he said with a toothy smile.

"You are kind," she said.

She had invited Joseph Kennedy, the first Chairman of the Securities and Exchange Commission, to meet with her late in the afternoon, for tea, and she had set the meeting in the Green Room, one of the more intimate and less formal of the public rooms of the White House.

"Your family is all well, I hope," she said.

"Quite well," he said. "And yours?"

"Quite well."

He nodded. "Good. Mine are a bit far-flung at present. Jack"—to her ear he pronounced it "Jeck"—"is in London, doing some work at the London School of Economics. He'll be over there about a yee-ah."

"I have always been glad," she said, "that I was able to receive a part of my education at an English school. It was a very useful experience, most broadening."

Kennedy nodded over his teacup.

Mrs. Roosevelt smiled and clasped her hands before her. "I asked you to stop by because I want to talk with you— quite confidentially, please understand—about a matter that distresses me. Also please understand that I mean to keep the discussion on an entirely proper plane. I am interested in exchanging information to the extent that we can, ethically; but most emphatically I am not attempting to influence the course of an investigation being carried out by the staff of the Commission. You may have guessed what matter I have in mind."

"The Alfred Hannah indictment," said Kennedy immediately.

"Yes."

A professorial frown crossed his forehead. "A very distressing matter, that," he said. "I've of course known Alfred Hannah for years. And his partners. He has been

indicted by the state of New York, you understand. Not by
the federal government, not for violation of one of our new
securities laws."

"Yes, I understand."

"Unofficially," said Kennedy, "I can tell you that there
would have been a federal indictment if there had not been
a state one. In fact, there may be a federal indictment yet.
The facts justify one."

"And the federal crime might be. . . ?"

"Under the new federal securities laws," Kennedy said
somberly, "it is a crime to distribute false and misleading
information about a stock issue, to encourage people to invest in companies that are not sound, companies in which
they would not invest if they had accurate information.
The laws require the filing with our commission of regis-
tration statements, called by a variety of names. What it
all amounts to, stripped to its essence, is that people who
issue and sell securities must make accurate disclosures of
the facts about the companies behind those securities."

"Blue-sky laws," she said.

"That's what the states call them. All the states have
their own securities laws."

"But, as I understand it, Alfred Hannah has not been
indicted under the New York blue-sky law."

"No. He's been indicted for larceny, larceny by trick. It's
not that he *withheld* information about Northeastern
United and the other companies; he's accused of distributing *false* information. It was outright, old-fashioned
fraud."

"Isn't it odd," she asked, "that a man of his standing and
experience could be so stupid? I mean . . . wasn't it actually stupid to do what he's accused of doing?"

"Immensely stupid," said Kennedy. "I was amazed to
hear about it. I mean, let's do understand, Mrs. Roosevelt,
that Alfred D. Hannah is no saint. He's been involved in
some shady promotions in his time, ones that skirted a

very fine line between legitimate and illegitimate; but this one involved outright theft. It was cleverly hidden, and he might have gotten away with it, but he was stupid and careless toward the end."

Mrs. Roosevelt held the palms of her hands pressed together, and now she touched her pursed lips with her index fingers. Her frown deepened. "Do you know why I am interested?" she asked.

"Well . . . the Hannahs are neighbors of yours, I believe. At Hyde Park."

"And so are the van der Meers. Do you know Cornelius van der Meer?"

"Yes. We are acquainted."

"Their younger daughter, Adriana, is in love with Alfred Hannah's son, Robert. The indictment is a real tragedy to the young couple. The President and I have always admired young Adriana, so we have listened to young Robert's protestations of his father's innocence."

"Do you believe he is innocent?" Kennedy asked bluntly.

"We neither believe nor disbelieve," she said. "Could I, however, show you in confidence some evidence that might shed some light on the matter?"

Kennedy frowned. "I . . . am not sure I can properly look at any evidence *in confidence*," he said. "If I am shown relevant evidence, I can't keep it secret from the SEC investigators."

"I quite agree," she said. "On the other hand, I do not want to exercise an improper influence; and if your investigators knew a piece of evidence had come to your hands from *me*, they might feel pressed to give it more weight than it deserves."

"Allow me to worry about that, Mrs. Roosevelt," said Kennedy. "We have some pretty bright young fellows on the Commission staff."

"Yes," she said. She smiled. "I have heard that."

"In what form is this evidence, and where did it come from?"

Bob Hannah had left in her care the worn leather briefcase he had carried aboard the presidential train at Ossining, and she had brought down to this meeting the stock purchase orders and the sheet of carbon paper Bob had shown to the President. She handed the purchase orders to Kennedy.

He nodded over them. "He was still buying Northern United, almost to the end. We know that."

"Isn't that inconsistent with his knowing the company was a shell?" she asked.

"Maybe," said Kennedy. "Our figures indicate that Alfred Hannah lost about two hundred and thirty-six thousand dollars in the collapse of Northern United stock. On the other hand, he may have profited ten times that much from the overall utility-holding-company scheme. He—"

"Even so," Mrs. Roosevelt interrupted, "why would he keep on buying? Even if he were only spending ill-gotten gains, why would he spend them on a stock he knew was worthless?"

"I can think of three reasons," said Kennedy. "First, he didn't know the company was hollow. Second, he was trying to shore up the market in Northern United stock, to delay or prevent the collapse. Third, he was trying to throw our investigators off the track."

"I find it hard to believe the third possibility is very likely."

Kennedy shrugged. "I'd really like to know why he was buying the stock."

"Well, let me show you the second piece of evidence," she said.

She handed him the sheet of carbon paper in its folder, as well as the typed copy of the letter taken from the carbon paper. Joseph Kennedy studied the typed copy intently and glanced at the sheet of used carbon paper.

"'Martin,'" said Kennedy. "Martin Fiske, hmm?"

"The sheet of carbon paper," said Mrs. Roosevelt, "was retrieved from a wastebasket in the offices of Deutsch, Lindemann and Company."

"From whose wastebasket?"

Mrs. Roosevelt shook her head. "I don't know."

"It would be well to know," said Kennedy.

"I did not cross-examine the . . . the person who brought that sheet of carbon paper to us."

Kennedy re-read the typed copy of the note and for a moment held the carbon paper up to look at the letters impressed on its greasy surface. "Can you tell me who brought this to you?" he asked.

"You can guess, can you not?"

"Robert Hannah."

Mrs. Roosevelt nodded. "Yes. The young son of Alfred Hannah. It is quite obvious, I am sure, why he was prowling through the trash in the offices of Deutsch, Lindemann and Company."

"Would he talk to one of my investigators?"

"I can't speak for him. I'll ask him. Is there any impropriety in your sending an investigator to talk to him?"

"None."

"Good. Then. . . ?"

"It will be arranged," said Kennedy.

The man sent by Joseph Kennedy arranged to meet with Mrs. Roosevelt, Bob Hannah, and Adriana van der Meer at the White House in mid-morning two days later. His name was Lionel Pickering, and he was a new graduate of Yale Law School—a sobersided young man with the severe air of a Calvinist divine. He wore steel-rimmed spectacles, and his Adam's apple bounced up and down under the rim of his stiff collar. Although he had undoubtedly shaved no more than three hours before, the black stubble of his whiskers darkened the pale skin of his chin and jawline.

His lips were unnaturally red. Mrs. Roosevelt wondered if he bit them.

"We, uh, need not dwell on the, uh, proprieties," he said nervously. "Mr. Kennedy has instructed me most emphatically about them."

"You will not be improperly influenced by the fact that this meeting is in the White House and that I acknowledge to you my own and the President's interest in the matter to be discussed," said Mrs. Roosevelt. "We have every confidence in the integrity of Mr. Kennedy. I would like to transfer that confidence to you."

"I am flattered," said Pickering.

"You have examined the evidence I showed to Mr. Kennedy?"

"I have."

Pickering's glance returned repeatedly to Adriana, who sat with her legs crossed, her pale blue eyes fixed on him with apparent calm. He was unable to conceal his reaction to her, which obviously was that she was a vision of feminine grace. When, on the other hand, his eyes passed over Bob Hannah, they darkened with another judgment that he could not conceal: that here was a sly and threatening character, the son of a cornered lion, ready to slash in any direction.

"So what do you think of the evidence I brought to the President and Mrs. Roosevelt?" asked Bob Hannah.

"It is suggestive," said Pickering.

"'Suggestive,'" Bob repeated. "What does that mean?"

Pickering's chin rose in carefully measured defiance. "The Commission staff," he said, "is in possession of reams of evidence in the Northern United matter. No individual item proves much, but the aggregate proves a great deal. This evidence"—he glanced at the purchase slips and the sheet of carbon paper that lay on a table before them— "suggests exactly what you would hope it suggests. But by itself it proves nothing."

"You need more," said Bob.

Pickering nodded. "Precisely."

"Why hasn't your investigation discovered evidence like this?" Adriana asked of Pickering.

"These . . . documents," said Pickering, again glancing at the slips and the sheet of carbon paper, "were found in the trash at the offices of Deutsch, Lindemann. We can hardly subpoena the office trash from a brokerage house. Practical considerations aside, the Constitution of the United States limits our subpoena power. What is more, we cannot conduct what is called a fishing expedition. We have to go in looking for specific evidence, of specific violations. In a word, you have done, Mr. Hannah, something the Commission's investigators could not do. You are a student of the law. I'm correct, am I not?"

"You are correct," Bob Hannah conceded.

"Then . . . then to what does all this lead?" asked Adriana in a voice made shrill by frustration. "If these papers prove nothing and you can't get more—"

"I have another question," Bob interjected. "What would the SEC have done if the state indictment had not been handed down?"

"I'm afraid I don't follow," said Pickering.

"Well, let me put it this way—has the state indictment impeded your investigation?"

"I really don't feel at liberty to comment," said Pickering.

"What are you suggesting?" asked Mrs. Roosevelt.

Bob Hannah sighed loudly and rose from his chair. "Mr. Pickering is not at liberty to say this," he said, "but I think the state indictment effectively foreclosed the SEC investigation. The publicity, the fact that the State of New York was acting . . . I can't help but wonder if the state authorities did not indict my father *as a means of heading off the federal investigation.*"

"That's a serious charge," said Mrs. Roosevelt.

"Mr. Pickering!" shrilled Adriana. "Surely you can say whether or not you think the state indictment has impeded the federal investigation."

Pickering stiffened, not with indignation as it appeared, but with discomfort. "I . . . The line between propriety and impropriety is very fine here," he protested. "I . . . I will say this much—that, quite unofficially, speaking personally and not for the Commission, the thought *has* occurred to me."

"In a federal indictment, my father would have been only one of the men charged," said Bob aggressively.

"I can't say that," Pickering objected immediately.

"But it is true."

Pickering licked his red lips. "I can't say it," he insisted. "Don't ask me to comment further."

Mrs. Roosevelt smiled warmly. "You need not comment further, Mr. Pickering," she said. "Although we could not quote you, you have communicated your meaning quite effectively."

As was not her custom, Mrs. Roosevelt joined the President, Louis Howe, Harry Hopkins, and Missy Lehand at their late-afternoon cocktail hour. As the three men shared the martinis the President loved to mix as a stimulant to conversation, and as Missy drank Scotch, Mrs. Roosevelt sipped from a glass of dry sherry—the Tio Pepe she had learned in England to regard as the *only* sherry a host or hostess of taste would offer to guests.

"Is it possible?" she asked Louis. "That's all I'm asking. Does it make sense?"

Louis McHenry Howe slapped cigarette ash off his vest. Only very rarely, during all the years she had known him, had he let his ashes fall on his clothes. He was an untidy man: a careless genius, but he had always had dexterous control over the cigarettes he chain-smoked. It troubled her to see his hands shake, to hear him wheeze and cough.

She wondered how she and her husband would face the campaign of 1936 if Louis were too ill to be active.

"If you are prepared to assume," said Louis, "that the Manhattan District Attorney, or someone in his office, is corruptible, then you can believe perhaps that the Hannah indictment was obtained as a means of derailing the SEC investigation. That's two unlikely things you have to believe. It's a little too conspiratorial for me."

"Bob Hannah is a persuasive young man," said the President. "His evidence is suggestive but much less persuasive."

"Is Joe Kennedy corruptible?" asked Mrs. Roosevelt.

"I'd say no," Louis answered.

"His staff?" she persisted.

Louis shrugged. "Who knows? A collection of idealistic young men . . ."

"The D.A.'s office in New York?"

"I see what you're driving at," said Louis. "A collection of Tammany politicians."

Mrs. Roosevelt smiled sweetly at Louis Howe. "Exactly," she said. "Although there may be nothing wrong, if there is, that's where it would be."

"There's enough money involved," said Harry Hopkins, "to corrupt better men than your typical courthouse hack."

"This is all speculation," said the President. "Those purchase slips and that sheet of carbon paper that Bob Hannah showed us prove nothing. We really should not be sitting here wondering if there is corruption at the SEC or in the Manhattan District Attorney's office on the basis of no better evidence than that."

Louis Howe blew a thick white stream of smoke toward the ceiling and coughed painfully. He did not allow himself to be distracted. "I don't need any evidence whatever," he remarked, "to tell me there is corruption in New York courthouse politics. It's there, by definition. But I do need evidence to tell me specifically who has been corrupted in this specific instance. And obviously we have no evidence along that line."

"I need to repeat a warning, Babs," said the President to Mrs. Roosevelt. "Be careful. We cannot afford, from any standpoint, to become identified with an effort to interfere in the Hannah prosecution. Ethically, politically . . . We cannot. We must not."

Yesterday morning, thank God his last morning in the squalid little Washington hotel where he had stayed to save funds, he had not shaved; and by the time he had reached New York, in mid-afternoon, he had borne a visible stubble on his chin and cheeks. His mother, with whom he had spoken briefly in their New York apartment before she caught the train for Hyde Park, had remarked on his untidy condition and had suggested that even the family's distressing situation at the moment did not require or justify his going about looking like a bum. But it did, as she could not possibly understand, and this evening, as he left their East-Seventies apartment and walked to the subway station, he wore a two-day growth of beard. With that on his face, and with the clothes he was wearing, he was not sure Adriana would know him if she saw him casually on the street.

His oversized pants, bought this morning for ten cents in a second-hand clothing store on Second Avenue, were too big and were pinched in at the waist by the worn leather belt the man had thrown in for two cents more. His collarless shirt, the same: outsized and shabby. He had washed and dried it before he could bear to wear it. The stained tan corduroy jacket he wore against the chill that would develop in the spring night had cost him seven cents. Shoes, twenty-five cents—sturdy, high-topped, the laces spliced with big round knots. On his head he wore a brown and white tweed wool cap. The gold-framed round spectacles—his father's spare pair—remained in his pocket until they would be needed; the world swam before his eyes when he squinted through them.

In the nickel-plated lunch box he carried—five cents at another stall on Second Avenue—he carried a Leica III, a German camera worth more than a hundred dollars, and a new device, a Weston Photronic exposure meter, which for twenty dollars was supposed to tell him how to expose the thirty-five-millimeter film loaded in the Leica. Besides the lunch box he carried a tool kit, a leather pouch filled with mostly second-hand tools he had picked up during his afternoon's shopping for a total of a dollar and a half.

When he emerged into the blue-gray darkness of the spring evening, Bob Hannah affected the persona he had practiced a bit during the afternoon: the weary workman trudging to yet another job, burdened to be working at this time of day when his brood sat down around their supper without him. He had drunk two heavy shots of brandy before he left the apartment, to fortify himself for the work ahead; and it was not difficult to play the role he had created.

Wall Street. It was almost deserted at this time of day, at a quarter past eight. Offices blazed with light in the buildings around, but they were the lights switched on by the cleaning women; except for a few late-struggling young lawyers, the denizens of Wall Street had fled for the night to their apartments and flats, some to homes in

Westchester or Connecticut. Few men who counted for much remained in Wall Street at eight in the evening.

So few people were on the street that he felt no compulsion to fix the little gold-rimmed spectacles astride his nose. He walked without them. So successful was his disguise that twice he was approached by furtive men who grunted "Socialist Labor Party meeting, comrade. Eight-thirty. Don't forget."

He stopped at a small red-lighted tavern and drank a nickel beer. It was tasty, and it had occurred to him that the smell of beer on his breath would be better than the odor of brandy.

At eight-thirty he stood before the twenty-four-story building where Deutsch, Lindemann & Company had kept offices for as long as he could remember. From the time when he was eight years old, he had frequented this building and that office—but never like this, never sneaking in, never before anything but welcome. He sighed, squared his shoulders, and walked up the three steps to the revolving doors to the lobby.

Thank God, nothing had changed. The doors were not yet locked, and he entered the cavernous, marble-floored lobby, dim-lighted now and filled with the sharp odor of the disinfectant soap that had been splashed over the floor and whipped around with great, swishing mops. No one was about. He glanced up at the arrows that indicated the positions of the elevators. All were in the cellar but one: the elevator used by the cleaning crew working its way up through the building. That one elevator was at the fourteenth floor.

Once it had been an adventure to come here at night, with his father, stopping by to pick up some forgotten document or simply to bring his son in to use the bathroom. Now he remembered that he was no longer welcome, and he took his father's spectacles from his shirt pocket and fixed them on his nose to complete his incognito. He tried the door to the left of the bank of elevators. It was not locked either, and he passed through it into the stairwell and descended to the cellar of the office building.

He found what he wanted: a short stepladder stenciled with the name of the building. He carried it to the elevators and began pressing the button, setting up a persistent ringing on the fourteenth floor.

He watched the arrow turn. The elevator reached the basement, and the old woman inside threw the lever that opened the heavy doors. "Who you?" she demanded. Her face was fluid in his father's lenses.

"'Lectrician," said Bob. "Got a bad fixture on the eighth floor. Gotta be fixed at night. Can't come in and upset the big wigs in their office hours."

The old woman looked at him with an expression of hostility. "Who you work for?" she asked.

"Like I said, 'lectrician," said Bob. "Webster. Boss says I gotta fix the sumbitch right now, tonight. Eighth floor," he said, jerking his thumb upward. "You got the key?"

The old woman, fat and ruddy in her gray cleaning-woman dress, shrugged and pulled the doors shut. "What's the matter?" she asked.

"I dunno," he said. "Light wouldn't come on. Put in a new bulb, it still wouldn't come on. Switch maybe. Hope its a switch. I can put in a new switch in five minutes. Here, uh . . ."

He handed her a bit of crumpled paper on which he had penciled the name Deutsch, Lindemann—spelling it "Dutch Lindman."

She nodded. "Eighth floor," she said.

"Who they, so damn important they couldn't have their light fixed this afternoon?" he asked.

"Brokers," she said. "Capitalists." She spat on the elevator floor. "*The* worst."

"Parasites, huh?"

"Parasites," she agreed.

"We gotta miss the meeting."

"Hell with the meeting," she said.

She found the right key on her big keyring and let him into the offices of Deutsch, Lindemann & Company. He carried in his stepladder and told her he hoped he wouldn't be more than fifteen minutes. Well, maybe twenty—she shouldn't wait. He would ring when he wanted the elevator again.

When she had gone, he jerked the spectacles off his watering eyes and put on white cotton gloves. He walked through the offices, to be sure no one was working late. The office was deserted, silent, and smelled of the same disinfectant with which the lobby floors had been mopped. He switched on the lights in several offices and set up the ladder inside one. Then he returned to the reception room, opened the door to be sure no one was in the corridor outside, and set to work on the lock.

The locks in the building were not flush locks with bolts shooting through plates in the door frames, but rim locks, mounted on the insides of the solid oaken doors, with bolts that shot into steel cases screwed to the oak frames. They could be opened by turning brass knobs inside or by inserting complex notched keys from the outside. They were dead-bolt locks, without springs. He had been intrigued, as a child, with the way his father had opened and closed this heavy, polished-brass lock. It was as familiar to him as a childhood toy.

He knew precisely how to overcome it. He had planned this visit and was prepared. With a screwdriver from his leather bag he removed the six big screws that held the steel case on the oak frame of the door. They did not come easily. For a moment he thought one of them would defy him, and he felt his face redden as he applied all his force to twist the screwdriver. The screw did yield at last, as did the five others, and in a few minutes he was able to pry the case from the frame. The bolt and the cylinder lock were meaningless without the case on the doorframe. The door swung in, the thick steel bolt protruding uselessly.

From his bag he extracted an assortment of screws he had brought with him. Being unsure of the exact size of the screws he was now going to replace, he had brought several sets. It was easy to match his screws to the ones he had removed. He made the match and threw all the extra ones back into his bag—together with the six screws he had removed. He replaced them with big thick screws that nearly matched. The difference was that he had used a hacksaw and vise and had cut the new screws short, leaving only a few threads to go into the wood of the doorframe. He put the six cut-off screws in the six holes. The case was now back in place—but only tenuously. It would hold only so long as no one gave the door a firm push.

When the old woman came back down, he was waiting at the elevator, with the ladder.

"Sumbitch was a busted switch," he said. "Somebuddy must have give her a whack, busted her inside. I put in a new one."

As he had thought she might, the old woman went to the door and unlocked it. As he stood in the corridor and waited, she walked through the offices for which she felt responsible—as though her quick inspection could have discovered any theft he had performed in the treasury of documents he meant to explore later tonight. When she returned, satisfied, she locked the door. To his relief, the case did not fall off the frame inside the door.

She returned him to the cellar, where he could replace the ladder in the building supply room. "Still gonna make the meeting," he muttered as he left the elevator.

"Hell with it, I say," she rejoined as she closed the elevator doors.

*   *   *

Expecting the cleaning crew to return to the cellar before they left the building, he climbed the stairs to the second floor, used the bathroom there, and sat on a wide marble window sill at the end of the hall, waiting for the time when he could safely return to the eighth floor. He watched the street below. A few cars passed, one carrying a load of noisy drunks. A policeman patrolled on foot. Shortly a steady rain began to fall.

He waited until after eleven before he climbed the stairs to the eighth floor. The arrows above the elevators indicated they were all in the cellar now. That meant the cleaning people had left the building. Except for a single low-wattage bulb burning at each end of the long corridor, the eighth floor was dark. He paused for a long moment before the door of the Deutsch, Lindemann offices. He put his ear to the door and listened, knowing it was irrational to suppose he could hear anyone stirring inside.

He put on the white cotton gloves that would prevent his leaving fingerprints and turned the doorknob. He pushed. The door did not give. He put his shoulder to it and pushed hard. It swung back. He stepped inside and closed it. The lock case had fallen noiselessly onto the carpet, and his six sawed-off screws were scattered.

His first job was to replace the case with its strong, full-length screws. The faint light from the window was enough for this work. He gathered up his sawed-off screws and dropped them into his tool kit, then used the screwdriver to screw the case back to the door frame. He took a flashlight from his lunchbox and examined the lock carefully. He had made no scratches.

He had the whole night now to explore the offices of Deutsch, Lindemann & Company, to see what evidence, if any, could be found in the desks and files of his father's former partners.

He began in the office of Arthur Lindemann. Uncle

Arthur. As he sat in Lindemann's chair and used the screwdriver to jimmy the simple little lock on his rolltop desk, he remembered Uncle Arthur's expansive promise, never redeemed, to see to it that a pony was delivered to the Hannah place at Hyde Park. ("Fine boy like Bob ought to have a pony, Al. By golly, I'll send one.") Uncle Arthur was as rich as Pierpont Morgan, everybody said; anyway he was as potbellied and florid.

The lock surrendered easily enough, and Bob rolled up the cover and exposed the desk and its cubbyholes—in one of which a pint bottle of Scotch lay on its side. For ten minutes he read, by the light of his flashlight, the accumulation of papers stuck in the cubbyholes. Some of the letters and memoranda dated as far back as 1928 and had turned yellow. They were disappointing. There was nothing that seemed significant. He went through the drawers then. Again, the collection of documents in folders made it apparent only that Arthur Lindemann was a sloppy, forgetful collector of paper. He was careless in another way—the key to his filing cabinet, which was secured by a more difficult lock that might have had to be broken, lay in the little drawer in the middle of the cubbyholes.

It was well that Bob had all night. The yellow-oak filing cabinet had four big drawers, all jammed tight with paper, all jumbled together in no perceivable order. There was no alternative to riffling through everything.

He thought he had been at it an hour—though actually, when he checked his watch he saw he had been at it only half that—when at last he came on something possibly significant: a file marked with the name James F. Cote. He read quickly through the papers in that file. So . . . Cote.

James F. Cote was a judge. Until 1933 he had been district attorney. He was a political power in New York City. He was also, it seemed, a client of Deutsch, Lindemann, a

buyer of substantial numbers of shares of common stock—
which, oddly, were transferred not to his own name but to
a variety of accounts in the names of others. It was particularly interesting that he had bought a thousand shares of
the stock of A. G. DeLoach & Company. Now, was there a
file for DeLoach, too? There was. Bob's hands trembled as
he examined the papers in the DeLoach file.

He opened his lunch box and took out the Leica. On the
surface of Lindemann's desk he set up a copying station.
He had no tripod, but he set the camera on a couple of
books to get it at the right height. With the tape he had
brought for the purpose, he measured the distance from
the lens to the file folder he propped up against an end of
the rolltop. He directed Lindemann's gooseneck lamp toward the folder and switched it on. He measured the light
with the Weston meter and adjusted the camera to expose
the film in that light. Then, one by one, he attached sheets
of paper to the file folder with paper clips, making an
exposure each time, methodically copying documents
from the Cote and DeLoach files. When he was finished
and was ready to put the file back, he had made fifteen ex-
posures.

Before he left Lindemann's office, he looked around intently. He was satisfied he had left no sign he had been
there. He moved on, into the office of Griffin Bailey.

Griff Bailey. Never Uncle Griff. Mr. Bailey. Mr. Bailey
to everyone, small boys and big men, all of whom were
awed by his cold and lofty dignity. He was tall, spare, pallid of face, and his characteristic posture was one with
chin lifted, looking down his thin nose at whomever or
whatever happened to be before him. ("Al, there is a button open on the boy's shirt.")

His desk was like his personality: grimly tidy, with
nothing allowed to clutter its polished surface or relieve its
formidable austerity.

His files were the same: neatly arranged, purged of

every unnecessary scrap of paper. Going through them was a matter of minutes. Bob found nothing of significance to his father's case.

He sat down in Bailey's chair, a little discouraged. Slowly he pulled out the drawers of Bailey's desk. In the center drawer he found a leather-covered ring binder. It was Bailey's desk calendar. Bob flipped through it, expecting nothing, but as he flipped pages he began to grin.

In Bailey's very tidiness, in his obsession with neat organization, was his weakness! He logged his every visitor, his every telephone conversation. For each day, from the beginning of 1935 to this very date, the calendar represented a record of everyone Griffin Bailey had talked to, each name written in a pinched hand, each one followed by a note of what was said. The notes were written in abbreviations and symbols that looked at first as if they were a code; but, looked at more closely, were just a simple, highly individual shorthand that would probably yield to easy deciphering by anyone who studied it.

Bob did not have the film to copy a hundred pages. He had brought extra rolls, but this was more than he had expected. If he tried to select pages to photograph, it was as likely as not that he would miss something important. If he took the book with him when he left, the firm would know the offices had been entered and the files rifled. He decided he would copy twenty pages or so. If absolutely necessary, he could return another night.

As he set to work to set up another copying arrangement on Bailey's desk, Bailey's telephone began to ring. At midnight! It rang eight times before it stopped. Then somewhere in the office another telephone rang. It, too, rang eight times. There had to be a reason. Something was wrong. Could he have set off an alarm system he didn't know about? Quickly he dismantled his copying arrangement, packed the camera in the lunch box, and closed Bailey's desk.

He returned to the reception room. He went to the window, and holding himself cautiously to one side so as not to be visible to anyone staring at that window, he peered down at the street. Irrationally, he looked for police cars. He saw none. He saw no one. After a few minutes his breath came more easily, and he decided to return to Bailey's office and to what he had been doing.

Just as he passed through Bailey's door he heard the harsh scratch of a key being pushed into the lock on the door from the corridor. He was inside Bailey's office when he heard a voice. It was Griffin Bailey!

He had only seconds to hide himself and his equipment. In panic he did the only thing he could do; he crawled into the kneehole under Bailey's desk. It was the only hiding place in the office, and it would be no hiding place at all once Bailey sat down and thrust in his feet. He held his breath.

"Siddown, honey," said Bailey.

Bob could not see anything, but apparently Bailey was accompanied by a young woman—someone, anyway, that he called "honey."

"Oh, Mr. Bailey, I . . . I don't feel right about this," she breathed in a high, girlish voice.

"You felt well enough about it over dinner and through the show," said Bailey.

"It's not that I don't . . . respect you and all," she went on in the same voice.

"Tell me straight, Mary," said Bailey. "Am I hearing the conventional little protest girls think they have to make to save their respectability, or are you really trying to back out on me?"

"I wouldn't back out on a promise, Mr. Bailey," the girl said solemnly. "I just want you to know I've never done anything like this before."

"Okay, fine," said Bailey curtly. "You've never done anything like this before."

"I don't want you to think I'm a bad girl. I mean, I don't want to jeopardize my job or anything."

Bob heard Bailey laugh. He had never heard the man laugh before, had even wondered if he were capable of it.

"I mean . . . you said it wouldn't."

"Mary," said Bailey, still laughing, "I don't know if you're stupidly naïve or endearingly clever. C'mon now. It's after midnight."

Though Bob pressed his cheek to the carpet and tried to see through the inch-wide crack between the carpet and the front panel of the desk, he could see nothing. He did not need to see to know what they were doing. The sounds impressed the scene as firmly on his mind as a full, well-lighted view would have—maybe even better.

"Tell you what," Bob heard Bailey say when the sounds of their activity had ceased. "You slip down the hall to the ladies room and do whatever you want to do, and I'll make one quick phone call."

Phone call! If he sat down at the desk . . . Bob scrunched himself as far into one corner of the kneehole as he possibly could, knowing he could not compress himself enough to avoid the feet that Bailey would shove under the desk as soon as he sat down to make his telephone call.

Then he heard him dialing. He was sitting on the edge of the desk apparently.

"Hans? Griff. Any word? I don't give a damn what time

it is. You call me if . . . Okay. Okay. Be sure you do. I'll be
home in half an hour. You can call me there."

Bob heard the scratch of a match, and in a moment he
smelled the pungent odor of cigar smoke.

"Ready, kiddo? I'll take you home. You're a good girl,
Mary. You keep up the good work."

Bob heard the outer door slam. He crawled out and
straightened his painfully aching joints. As he set up his
camera again and set to work photographing the leaves of
Griffin Bailey's calendar book, he wondered about the midnight telephone call. What word was Bailey expecting in
the midnight of the night? It seemed unlikely to relate to his
legitimate business in this brokerage office. At any event,
he had formed an amended opinion of the austere Griffin
Bailey.

It was one o'clock before he moved on to the office of the
third of his father's former partners, Austin Brinker.

Austin. The best of them. The best-looking: a tall, spare
man with jet black hair invariably smooth and shining,
with black pencil mustache always neatly trimmed, his
pin-striped, double-breasted suits always impeccably
tailored and fitted. Austin was personable, capable of
drawing the line between friendship and familiarity. He
was respected on Wall Street. Bob's father had placed
more confidence in him than he had in either of the others.

Nevertheless, Bob began an examination of Austin
Brinker's desk. He would search the man's desk and files
as thoroughly as he had the others'.

The desk drawers contained nothing but papers relating
to current stock deals—also a bottle of brilliantine, half a
dozen combs, a mirror, nail files . . . A folder lying open on
the desktop contained the documents relating to a corporate takeover: Ferguson Laboratories was buying stock
in General Chemical. That could be useful information
for someone with money to invest. He took the key to

Brinker's filing cabinet from the center drawer of the desk.

The files contained nothing. He pulled out the folders for Northern United, Northeastern United, and several of the other companies involved in the fraud of which his father stood accused. They were thin. They contained only innocuous papers. Comparing them to the files for a hundred other companies, it was apparent that Brinker's files had been purged, just as Bailey's had. Other files contained assorted scraps of paper: telephone notes, memoranda, correspondence, even cryptic notes scribbled on matchbook covers; but these thin files contained only tidy records of purchases and sales in the stocks of these utility companies. It was only negative evidence, and Bob knew how little it would count for in proving any kind of a case; yet it proved to him that Austin Brinker, too, was at least a consenting participant in whatever the partners had done to his father.

He visited one more office: his father's. Although a few of his father's pictures and mementos remained on the walls and on his desk, the office was neat and bare, obviously unused. Files lay loose or flat in the drawers—so many had been removed under subpoena that those remaining no longer packed the drawers tightly enough to support each other. The odor of cigar smoke, which had always characterized this room for Bob, had dissipated, leaving nothing on the antiseptic air but a faint smell of furniture polish.

Despondent, he sat down in his father's chair. The film he had exposed tonight would have some impact in Washington perhaps, but it would not change anything much. He had hoped—with far too much optimism, he well knew—that the risk he was taking by breaking into these offices tonight would produce something dramatic, something that would at a stroke prove his father's innocence.

What he had found was suggestive. That was all it was: suggestive.

He was tired, and in the near-darkness of the office his mind filled with images of another time, of happy times as he remembered them, when he had sat here and had seen his father as a giant of corporate finance, confidently trading in the great bull market. In those days, businessmen were American heroes, and he had seen them come to this office, to see his father and the other partners in Deutsch, Lindemann. He had met Andrew Mellon, Charles G. Dawes, Owen Young, W. C. Durant, John J. Raskob, Albert Wiggin, and Thomas W. Lamont. One memorable day he had even met J. P. Morgan. In another context, he had met Al Smith and Jimmy Walker. They had all come here. The offices had always been busy, always noisy, with the ticker chattering away in the outer room, often surrounded by half a dozen excited men. He had been here, too, five years ago, when the Crash was in progress. He had not been alone in admiring his father's calm strength in those days. His father had been a different man then.

Bob remembered October 24, 1929. He had left school at noon and come downtown because he had heard what was happening. His father was conferring in his office with a group of frightened men and had given him only a curt nod of greeting. He had pushed his way into the center of the little knot of clerks around the ticker. The numbers were coming through:

R   WX
6. 5½. 5. 4.   9. 8⅞. ¾ ½ ¼. 8. 7½. 7

In minutes, both Radio Corporation of America and Westinghouse had slipped two points. Then one of the boys had told him the ticker was running ninety minutes or more late. They were not sure, therefore, if Radio had dropped from 66 to 64 or from 56 to 54, or if Westinghouse had dropped from 189 to 187 or from 179 to 177. Anyway, a disaster was developing.

Drawing a deep breath now in the gloom of his father's office, Bob remembered too how. . .Yes! He remembered . . .

He pulled himself up from his father's chair and hurried back into Arthur Lindemann's office. That afternoon, October 24, 1929, Uncle Arthur had let him see something he probably had not meant to let him see. His father had pressed him into service as a messenger, running down to the Exchange, returning, carrying notes from one partner to another, returning to the exchange. (It was only by going to the floor and hearing the clerks reading off prices that one could learn if Radio was at 64 or 54.) Late in the afternoon he entered Uncle Arthur's office without knocking, carrying a list of prices he had obtained from a floor clerk. Uncle Arthur had waved him into a seat and finished what he was doing before he turned and accepted the list.

And what Uncle Arthur had been doing was opening a secret compartment in his rolltop desk. He had pulled out one of the wooden dividers between two cubbyholes, exposing a thin brass trigger in the slot at the rear. Hooking a finger in that trigger, he had pulled it, releasing a latch that clicked somewhere inside the desk. He had then tugged on the walls of the bank of cubbyholes, and they had swung out, revealing a voluminous secret compartment. He had taken out a package, closed the desk, and handed the package to Bob. "Heft that, son," he had said. "That's how much a million dollars weighs. It goes to the Morgan bank."

Bob sat down again in Arthur Lindemann's chair. Once again he jimmied the simple lock on the rolltop. Nervously he tugged on the dividers between cubbyholes. The third

one he tried pulled out. The trigger was there. He pulled
it. The latch clicked. Bob opened the secret compartment.
It contained just what it had contained before: a package
of money, probably not as much as the million dollars he
had seen there before but a fortune anyway.

He was not tempted to take it, not really. Though it
might have solved many problems, it would have created
others, probably more difficult. He blew a loud sigh. He
had hoped to find something more. He slammed the secret
compartment shut.

Then it occurred to him that the desk was symmetrical.
If there was a secret compartment on the right side, might
there not be another on the left? He pulled, one after another, at the dividers between cubbyholes to the left, and
again one came out and exposed a brass trigger. But this
compartment was empty. Almost empty. In the near-
darkness he all but overlooked the key that lay in the
shadow of a corner. A key. Forgotten? Or carefully hidden
in one of the compartments Arthur Lindemann trusted to
the extent of a million dollars? Bob picked it up.

It was a long, thin, flat key, like one for a safe-deposit
box—though it had no number on it and so seemed unlikely to be the key to a safe-deposit box. No name was
stamped in the steel, either. For a minute or so he sat
there staring at it. It would be useless to photograph it, he
supposed. He had no way to take an impression. He wondered how often Arthur Lindemann used it. He wondered,
if he took it, how long it would be before Uncle Arthur
would discover it was missing.

He shone his light on it and tried to make a Sherlock
Holmes kind of guess about how much it had been used. It
was not worn in any way—but then, how much would a
key wear if it were used once a month, or once a week?

Unless it were simply something discarded, left in the
secret compartment by oversight, it was important. If it
had nothing to do with his father's situation, then maybe

it was important for some other reason. Deciding impulsively, Bob dropped it into his pocket.

It was after two o'clock now. He explored the offices one more time, looking through secretaries' and clerks' desks. He made another circuit through the partners' offices, assuring himself that he had left no telltale sign of his visit.

For a moment he pondered his decision not to take the money from the secret compartment in Arthur Lindemann's rolltop desk. It was unlikely Uncle Arthur would call for a police investigation if it disappeared. Almost certainly it was money he would not want the state and federal tax authorities to know he had. And what slight chance was there that he would remember the afternoon of October 24, 1929, when he had let Al Hannah's son see the secret compartment? Bob struck his palm with a fist. He would not take the money. He might take something else, though, from these men who had conspired to destroy his father. What he had seen in the folder carelessly left open on Austin Brinker's desk might be worth more than that hidden money if he could find a way to use the information—and they would never know, could never even suspect.

He left the offices of Deutsch, Lindemann & Company, relieved himself in the men's room at the end of the hall outside, and entered the stairwell. He began to descend the stairs, tiptoeing as quietly as he could. He supposed there was a watchman in the building, who would be alert to any sound anywhere, now that the cleaning crew were gone. The windowless stairwell was pitch-dark, and he was compelled to use his flashlight. He covered the lens with his fingers, so that only a tiny part of the beam escaped, making a dim light that he shone at his feet.

He expected that the lobby door through which he had entered the building would be locked now. His plan was to exit through a rear door or window, maybe onto the loading dock. If he could not get out, he planned to hide among the trash bins until morning.

He reached the landing at the seventh floor and stopped there to listen. The building was silent. He worked his way down to the sixth. By the time he reached that landing he knew he had begun to hear an alarming sound. The elevator was coming up!

Why, for heaven's sake? Why, in the middle of the night? And in an instant he knew. He had used the urinal on the eighth floor and had habitually, instinctively, pulled the flush lever. A watchman or night janitor in the cellar had heard the rush of water in the pipes.

He entered the sixth-floor corridor and watched the needle turning on the elevator indicator. The elevator went to the tenth floor and stopped.

Why the tenth? It could be, possibly, that someone had returned to his office at half past two. Far more likely, the night man had been able to tell, from the pipes or meters, that a toilet or urinal had been flushed between certain floors, between the tenth and fifth maybe. Very likely someone was beginning a search of floors from ten down. Likely it was more than one man. Maybe, too, the police had been summoned.

Bob returned to the stairwell. He had four floors' head start, and he hurried down, unsure of where he was going, for it was certain the doors downstairs would be locked and probably guarded. There were few places to hide in the building, big as it was, and if he were compelled to remain inside until morning it was almost certain he would be caught. Caught, he was a burglar. Nothing more. His reasons for entering the Deutsch, Lindemann offices were meaningless before the law—he well knew—and he would go to prison. His heart pounded as he ran down the stairs.

When he reached the second floor, he ventured out into

the corridor again. He checked the elevator indicators. The elevator that had gone up remained where it had stopped, on the tenth floor. He tried the doors of some of the offices. All were locked. He went to the windows at the end of the corridor and looked out at the street. He saw what he most feared: two police cars. Flushing the eighth-floor urinal had been the same as tripping a burglar alarm. The night watchman had known someone was in the building without authorization, and he had called in help.

Bob entered the second-floor men's room. It contained three toilet stalls and two urinals—no place to hide. He pushed up the frosted-glass window and peered down at the street. The window was only ten or twelve feet above the pavement. If the police cars had not been there he could have climbed out and risked the drop. It seemed almost certain, though, that one or more policemen remained on the street.

He left the men's room and trotted down the hall to the ladies' room at the far end. In there—where he had never been before—there were four toilet stalls and a small sofa. He unlatched and pushed up the window. This window opened on the alley behind the building.

He learned out and stared searchingly into the gloom. He saw no one, heard no one. The drop was the same. He pushed the window all the way up and climbed out onto the sill. He sat and let his legs hang outside. He dropped his bag of tools. They landed with a small thud, and he waited, staring, listening. Then he gathered his courage, clutched his lunch pail with the camera inside to his chest and pushed himself out.

He fell to his knees, and the lunch pail escaped him and clattered on the alley pavement. He crawled forward and recovered it. He stood up and looked around. Then he began to edge along the wall of the building, keeping in the darkest of the shadows as much as he could. If he could . . .

"Okay, feller, game's over. Get your hands up and turn around."

He saw the light first, then the revolver leveled at his belly. He raised his hands, lunch pail in one, tool bag in the other. He looked into the ruddy, bespectacled face of a watchman.

"Well," the man said. "You're lucky you didn't bust an ankle." The man was peering open-mouthed at his face. "Young feller, ain't you?"

Bob nodded. He felt weary to the point of collapse more than he felt afraid. He lowered his arms slowly, as if they were too heavy to hold up.

"Knock off yer cap," the watchman said. "Slow like. Don't try nothin' dumb."

Bob reached up with one hand and shoved the cap off his head.

The watchman frowned. *"What's yer name?"* he demanded, scowling.

They would find out sooner or later. "Hannah," Bob sighed.

"What I thought. Young Hannah. Thought I knowed ya. Been up to the eighth floor?"

Bob nodded.

"So. Sure. Find anything?"

"I didn't steal anything," Bob said. "Just took some pictures."

"Yeah." The man nodded. "Figgers." He glanced around, up and down the alley. "Evidence, huh?"

Bob nodded. "That was the idea."

"Yer dad know what you're doin'?"

"No."

"No . . . Figgers." The watchman shook his head and blew a noisy breath through his nose. "Yer dad's a different sort of feller. Done *me* a good turn once't. Lent me 'nough to cover my rent when I'd lost my week's wages on the ponies. Others'd turned me down. Yer dad . . . Well, I owe him one. So bust ass out o' here, young Hannah. Bust ass, and don't let me see you again."

Bob had no voice. "Thanks . . ." he whispered hoarsely. "What's your name?"

"Never mind that. Get goin'."

Bob turned and started once more along the wall.

"Not that way, you damn fool! T'other way. Go! Go on, now—and don't you never come back like this. You hear me, son? Don't you never do a damn-fool stunt like this again."

Stumbling as he trotted along the alley, Bob resolved he never would.

Mrs. Roosevelt was five minutes late. It was five past eleven when she entered the President's oval study on the second floor of the White House; and she was solemn and distracted as she greeted Bob Hannah, Adriana van der Meer, and Lionel Pickering, who had been waiting for her. One of the most difficult aspects of being First Lady was the necessity of effecting a complete shift of mind and attention as she passed from one appointment to another, and as she sat down in the leather armchair before the fireplace her mind had not yet entirely made the shift from her ten-thirty appointment to this one.

"Good morning," she said simply.

She was wearing a dark blue linen jacket and skirt, and a loose white silk blouse with a floppy collar that fell over her shoulders. She carried a small leather briefcase into which she had shoved the documents from her ten-thirty meeting, and she put the briefcase aside on the floor.

Bob, Adriana, and Pickering were probably not aware that she was a little late. They sat together on the leather couch facing her, absorbed in the President's naval prints that hung on the walls of the room and in the model of a World War I naval vessel that filled most of the space on the mantel. They were fully aware, too, that this room was a part of the private quarters, a room not often seen by visitors.

For a moment Mrs. Roosevelt was too alert, her eyes hard and glistening, as she made the effort to focus on this meeting and these people. That moment did not last. "Well," she said. "We meet again. I understand there are things to tell."

"Important things," said Adriana. She was wearing a summer frock of flowered pink and white silk, the loose folds gathered at her breast by a gold-and-diamond brooch. "Wait till you see."

"I wish it were more," said Bob grimly. Once again he was carrying his battered old briefcase, and he unbuckled it now and began to pull out eight-by-ten prints of the photographs he had shot in the offices of Deutsch, Lindemann & Company last week. "I hope you will understand the significance of some of this."

"I don't want to know where you got this material, do I?" said Lionel Pickering.

"Unless you ask, I won't tell you," said Bob.

"*I* may ask later," said Mrs. Roosevelt.

Bob selected a dozen photographs. "These are copies of papers from a file folder marked with the name James F. Cote," he said.

"Jim *Cote?*" exclaimed Mrs. Roosevelt. "In New York?"

"Judge Cote," said Bob. "Former District Attorney Cote. Former Ward Leader Cote. Jimmy Walker's friend—"

"My husband's friend . . ." warned Mrs. Roosevelt.

"Al Smith's friend," said Adriana loftily. "I am not sure he is any good friend of the President."

"Anyway, a political power in New York," said Bob.

"These papers are . . . ?" asked Pickering.

"Records of stock purchases and sales," said Bob. "It's the record of a confidential account Deutsch, Lindemann and Company maintains for Judge Cote."

Pickering had taken some of the sheets from Bob's hands and was perusing them with interest. "Oh, I'm sorry," he said suddenly and offered them to Mrs. Roosevelt.

"You go right ahead, Mr. Pickering," said she. "I will examine them at my leisure, later."

Pickering returned to his intent study. "I'm not sure what this has to do with your father's case, but—"

"Cote could arrange any indictment he wanted," said Bob.

"Well, I don't know about that, but—" He looked up from his papers and spoke to Mrs. Roosevelt. "Judge Cote, it seems, has bought and sold more than two hundred thousand dollars' worth of corporate stocks during the past eighteen months or so."

"And what does that suggest?" asked Mrs. Roosevelt.

"It might suggest nothing at all," said Pickering, "except for the fact that he has taken the stock in the names of others and except for the further fact that some of the companies are ones that do substantial business with the city of New York."

"Besides that," said Adriana, "where does a man who has served the past ten years as a district attorney and judge get his hands on two hundred thousand dollars?"

Mrs. Roosevelt reached for the photographs Pickering held. She frowned over them. "Extraordinary . . ." she murmured.

She recognized some of the company names. Others she did not. Some of the companies were clearly ones that supplied goods and services to the city government. Although

Arthur Lindemann's notes said flatly that the stocks had been bought for the account of James F. Cote, the certificates had been taken in a number of other names—Patrick McCarnahan, Anthony Fiorenza, Donald Murphy, others.

"Check the honorable judge's docket, you'll find something interesting," said Bob. "He is the judge assigned to the suit brought by Mayor La Guardia against A. G. DeLoach and Company. Notice that the honorable judge bought a thousand shares of DeLoach stock in December—putting it in the name of Fiorenza."

"Still . . ." said Pickering. "Assuming that anyone is going to be surprised to learn that Judge Cote is corrupt, how does that affect the case against your father?"

"The *firm* is corrupt," said Bob. "Deutsch, Lindemann and Company has been used as a vehicle for political payoffs."

"That doesn't follow," said Pickering. "I'm sympathetic, but unethical stock dealings by a judge don't prove that the broker was acting as a vehicle for political payoffs."

"Well, look at this, then," said Bob, handing over another photograph.

Pickering's face colored as he frowned over this document. He handed it to Mrs. Roosevelt and waited for her to examine it.

"You see," said Bob. His lips were pinched tight as he nodded. "That proves it, huh?"

"These two documents show," said Mrs. Roosevelt thoughtfully, "that A. G. DeLoach sold a thousand shares of his company's stock to Deutsch, Lindemann and Company, to the account of Anthony Fiorenza, in return for a promissory note signed by Fiorenza. Tell me what that proves, gentlemen."

"It proves, for one thing, that DeLoach received no money for his stock," said Pickering. "Only a note."

"But then," said Bob, "Deutsch, Lindemann and Company sold the DeLoach stock in February—for cash."

"At a loss," said Pickering thoughtfully.

"*But for cash*," said Bob, tapping his palm with one finger. "Credited to the account of Anthony Fiorenza."

"So you think Fiorenza holds—"

"No," said Bob. "There is no Anthony Fiorenza. I made inquiries. A man with enough credit to buy a thousand shares of DeLoach simply by signing a note is not a street bum. He has to be somebody. I checked banks—"

"Murphy? Carnahan?" asked Pickering.

"No," said Bob. "There is no Murphy and no Carnahan either. If I'd had time to check through enough files, I'd have found transactions in their names, too—I have no doubt."

Pickering pursed his lips and blew a stream of breath against his fist. "It is difficult to believe that a firm under investigation, as Deutsch, Lindemann and Company has been, would keep documents like this in its files."

"There has been no investigation involving Judge Cote's dealings," said Adriana.

"Exactly," said Bob. "Even if the SEC had gone into the office with a subpoena for the utility holding-company files, that would not have entitled you to look at the Cote file."

Pickering glanced at Mrs. Roosevelt, then at Adriana. "Officially I don't know you have been in the Deutsch, Lindemann offices. Officially I have no idea how you gained access to these documents to photocopy them. Officially I can't ask you, but I would be curious to know what you found in their files on the utility holding companies."

"Nothing," said Bob. "Their files were purged—except, of course, for my father's, which were taken by the New York district attorney. Arthur Lindemann—dear, direct old Uncle Arthur—seems to have purged his most effectively, simply by ridding himself of the lot, folders and all. The others purged theirs with great care, leaving nothing in them but tidy documents of no significance."

"That is quite significant in itself, I should think," said Mrs. Roosevelt.

"But it's not evidence," said Bob.

Lionel Pickering gathered up all the photographs he had looked at and began to glance through them with the air of a man who could not believe what he saw. "All of this," he said, "tends to prove gross misconduct on the part of the firm. But your father—"

"My father is no angel," said Bob. "I'm not sure I want to know how much of this he knows about. I'm convinced, though, that he is the victim of a conspiracy, within the firm and outside. Deutsch, Lindemann has been involved in illegal stock manipulation, embezzlement, political corruption . . . and God knows what more. They've decided to make my father a scapegoat. They're throwing him to the wolves, to save themselves."

"Not proved," said Pickering.

"The Scots verdict," said Mrs. Roosevelt. "The evidence you have suggests something of the kind but fails as yet to prove it."

"Indeed, I am not sure what you intend to prove," said Pickering.

"I told you last week," said Bob firmly. "They deflected the SEC investigation, which might have turned up a lot of this, by securing a state indictment against my father. The SEC has stood aside—you can't deny it has—to allow New York to make its case against Alfred Hannah. By the time the SEC returns to the investigation, they will have destroyed every last shred of evidence you might have found."

"They haven't destroyed it yet, apparently," said Pickering dryly.

"It was only by luck that I found what I did," said Bob, "and I would bet my hide that very shortly the documents I took pictures of will themselves be destroyed. The others won't let Arthur Lindemann continue to be careless of his files. He's an old man. In some ways he hasn't learned yet to live in this century. But the others will clean his files for him. They may have done it already."

Pickering drew a deep breath. "I will report to Mr. Kennedy," he said. "It may be that we should reopen the SEC investigation immediately."

At eight the President entered the State Dining Room—Mrs. Roosevelt on his right, his son Elliott on his left, to lend the support he needed to walk with his braces. The string quartet in one corner of the room interrupted a bit of Mozart and swung into a soft but spirited version of "Hail to the Chief." The President nodded to the musicians and chuckled. He was wearing white tie, and Mrs. Roosevelt wore a sleek floor-length gown of gold and white silk. Their guests applauded quietly as the Roosevelts crossed the room to the head table and the President was helped to his chair under the portrait of the brooding Lincoln that hung above the fireplace.

To the President's right sat the retiring Chief of Staff of the United States Army, General Douglas MacArthur, resplendent in his dress blues and wearing for decorations only his Medal of Honor and the Distinguished Service Medal he had just been awarded. Beside Mrs. Roosevelt, who sat to the left of the President, was the Secretary of War, George Dern. To General MacArthur's right sat Major General Malin Craig, his replacement as Chief of Staff. Also at the head table were Colonel George C. Marshall and Major Dwight D. Eisenhower who, it had already been announced, would soon accompany General MacArthur to the Philippines, where General MacArthur would be military adviser to President Manuel Quezon. Mrs. Eisenhower was among the wives who were also seated around the table. Mrs. Roosevelt had arranged for Adriana van der Meer to be present at this dinner, and Adriana sat at one of the smaller round tables to the side, beside Thomas Corcoran—Tommy the Cork.

"I could only wish, Douglas," said the President as soon as they were seated, "for two more guests who would make this occasion even more pleasent—General Pershing and your mother."

"Mother would be honored, Mr. President," said the General gravely. "I am afraid, though, that neither she nor General Pershing will venture out of the hospital many more times. She is eighty-four, you know."

The General himself was fifty-nine, and his dark hair was retreating. His dark, sharp eyes were youthful, though, and his uniform had been expertly tailored to his tall, hard figure. He was conscious of the dramatic effect of his appearance and played on it without embarrassment.

"I want you to keep a bag packed in Manila, Douglas," said the President. "If anybody in Europe even gives us an evil frown, I'll be calling you home to take command of an army."

"Assuming we have one, Mr. President," said the General smoothly.

The President laughed. "We'll have one, Douglas. We won't forget your preachments. You won't be far enough away for that."

The General nodded and favored the President with a knowing smile.

"Do you think, General," asked Mrs. Roosevelt, leaning forward to speak past the President, "the Philippines will be able to defend itself in the event of a major war?"

"I have no doubt of it," said General MacArthur. "The gallantry, the courage, of the Philippine people is unparalleled."

"Against a determined attack by Japan?" she asked.

"In ten years," said General MacArthur positively, "the Philippines will be strong enough to repel the most determined attack that any nation could launch."

"Is that your judgment, too, Major?" the President asked Eisenhower, who was listening intently from across the table.

"Uh, uh . . . yes, sir," said Major Eisenhower. "The General and I have given, uh, considerable study to the, uh, British amphibious operation at Gallipoli in 1915. Uh, putting ashore an army against, uh, any sort of competent defenders is, uh, *difficult*."

"Correct," said General MacArthur. "That abortive operation demonstrated once and for all that brave defenders can turn back five times their number coming ashore from the sea. The point will be to make the Philippines so expensive to invade that no sensible commander will want to undertake it."

"Well, let's hope, Douglas," said the President with a smile, "that you don't have to prove your point."

When, a little later, the President was helped to his feet to offer a toast to General MacArthur, Adriana watched and listened dewy-eyed. Her father had served with the General in France in 1918, and she had heard his name all her life. The President spoke of the General's service and commended him as "an officer who has demonstrated his devotion, not only to his service, not only to his country, but to honor as well."

Then General MacArthur stood to respond. She would not remember all he said, but she would try later to reconstruct the brief poem with which he concluded. He had spoken of military preparedness, and at the end he said:

> "They talk of peace eternal
> And may that peace succeed.
> But what of a foe that lurks to spring?
> And what of a nation's need?
> The letters blaze on history's page,
> And ever the writing runs,
> God, and honor, and native land,
> And horse, and foot, and guns."

The General had just resumed his seat when Adriana saw Missy LeHand hurry into the dining room, conspicuous in her informal clothes, and quickly hand a note to the President. The President's face darkened as he read it, and then he handed it to Mrs. Roosevelt. The First Lady started and glanced at *her*—that is, at Adriana. She drew Missy down and spoke to her urgently. Then Missy came to the round table and asked Adriana to accompany her out of the dining room.

Missy led her quickly into the Red Room and closed the door, so they could be alone.

"Adriana," she said. "I'm sorry to have to be the one to tell you this, but Bob Hannah called from New York a few minutes ago. His father is dead. He jumped out the window of his office."

Heavy, wet clouds hung so low around the church that it seemed St. James's might presently disappear, might be swept away to a netherworld where the unreality of the hour might be reality. Bob found his own wooden courage ugly, but he maintained it, solemnly greeting everyone who came to the funeral, receiving their polite words, directing them on to his tearful mother. He stood in the door until the last moment.

Even Mrs. Roosevelt had come. It was good of her. She and Adriana sat together in a pew, talking quietly, looking up to speak to people the Secret Service agents allowed to approach them. Together in another pew, Arthur Lindemann, Griffin Bailey, and Austin Brinker sat in stiff silence, staring at the casket.

They had stopped to shake his hand, to say the correct words. It had been difficult to speak to them. What couldn't be said, by him or them, had dominated the moment. They had stopped to speak with his mother. Their progress, then, to their pew had been a retreat.

Always there had been tension. Always. He remembered another rainy spring day, ten years ago, when the three of them had come to Dutchess County for a Saturday afternoon they had expected to spend on the lawn. He remembered vividly what he had heard his mother say after they had left—"There is no way, Al. There is no way they will ever be our friends. So quit trying."

Arthur Lindemann, dapper in a vanilla-ice-cream-colored linen suit, with boater on his head and cane in hand, had brought a mysterious dark-eyed girl with him. Griffin Bailey had been accompanied by Mrs. Bailey, a woman who reminded people of Mrs. Warren G. Harding: unnaturally severe and pitiably ugly. Austin Brinker—handsome in a white suit—had come alone. Perhaps his wife had refused, or perhaps he had not wanted to subject her to the company.

Bob's father had bought champagne—real champagne, hauled down from Canada by his bootlegger, who had charged, as the phrase was, an arm and a leg for it. Uncle Arthur had drunk the champagne happily, as did his girl friend until she was tipsy. Mrs. Bailey sipped grimly from one glass and did not finish it. Austin Brinker, Bob remembered, had tried to ease the tension by telling amusing stories. But somehow it had not been possible. It had been apparent, even to a teenaged boy—and it would have been apparent even if he had not heard his mother's comment—that these people did not like each other.

Al Hannah, Bob reflected, had never been a handsome

man. He had been shrewd. There had been in him a pur-
posefulness that probably made some people uncomfortable. And for some reason, he had seemed anxious to
please. His wife, Bob's mother, had always been soft and
beautiful. All of them admired her—even Mrs. Bailey, resentfully. Bob remembered how protective his father had
been of her, especially, it seemed, from his partners.

He had formed judgments of his father's partners, even
then; and in the years since he had not amended them. His
father was the source of the tension. Something had always been wrong between his father and the rest of the
partners. Brinker was the most graceful of them, trying
apparently to make the best of whatever the situation was.
Lindemann, the senior partner, obviously disliked anything that interfered with his enjoyment of life, and somehow Al Hannah did. Uncle Arthur's gruff heartiness had
been unsubtly forced that day. And Griffin Bailey . . .
Well, Bailey had always been severe, judgmental, and
sometimes it seemed even hostile. His father had always
been ready to make peace, as it seemed to Bob, but he
never could.

Now they sat together and stared at his casket. And
whatever had caused the tension was still there.

Except for Arthur Lindemann, none of them went to the
cemetery. But the old man did, driven by a chauffeur; and,
carrying a cane, he made his way across the wet earth to
the grave. Bob watched him approach his mother and say
something to her that seemed for a brief moment to
lighten her face. He was a smooth liar.

At the end he walked over to Bob. "My very deepest
sympathy, Bob," he said. "If there's anything I—"

Bob turned his back on him and walked away.

"It was inappropriate, in my judgment," said Sara Delano Roosevelt, the President's mother. "It is difficult for
me to believe that Franklin wished it."

"He did wish it," said Mrs. Roosevelt, the First Lady. "But frankly, I would have come whether he wished it or not."

"Yes," said the President's mother. "I suppose you would have." She put her teacup aside. "In any event, this closes the whole matter. We shall hear no more of it."

They were seated in the small original parlor of the mansion at Hyde Park—the room Sara Roosevelt liked to call the Dresden room because her husband, the President's father, had brought back and installed a Dresden chandelier in that room, many years ago. Mrs. Roosevelt was dressed in black. She had returned only a short time ago from the funeral for Alfred Hannah at Saint James's Episcopal Church.

"I may tell you," said Mrs. Roosevelt, "that Franklin would have come for the funeral himself if he could have made the trip more easily. He is by no means convinced that Alfred Hannah was guilty of any wrongdoing, and he considered it his duty as a friend to be represented at the funeral at least."

"We differ in our opinions on that," said the President's mother primly, with an air of finality that suggested she meant to dismiss the subject.

"Indeed we do," said Mrs. Roosevelt.

"And . . . the girl?" asked the President's mother. "Adriana van der Meer?"

"She is very much in love with Mr. Hannah's son and means to marry him. She was with him throughout the funeral. She was a great comfort to him."

"I do not see how her family can allow the marriage. First, the accusation of crime, then a suicide . . . I cannot understand how the van der Meers can approve of an alliance between their family and—"

"Whether they allow or approve it or not, it's going to happen," said Mrs. Roosevelt. "Adriana is of age and will marry as she chooses. That's how it is nowadays."

"How very unfortunate," sniffed Sara Roosevelt, tossing her chin.

Mrs. Roosevelt smiled. "I would not have dared marry against my family's wishes. Neither would you have, I imagine. Girls today do dare. Adriana is very much in love. It is touching to see."

"It is widely supposed," said Sara Roosevelt, "that the suicide proves the man was guilty. I hear it said that in effect Alfred Hannah admitted his guilt. Otherwise, why would he have done away with himself?"

Mrs. Roosevelt shook her head sadly. "The opinion you are expressing is commonly held, I'm afraid."

"How very convenient it was," said Bob Hannah bitterly. He was dressed in black, and his face was puffy, his eyes red. "Now the case can be closed and everything written off. One man arranged the Northern United fraud, was caught and indicted, and he killed himself. Deutsch, Lindemann and Company regrets the way one of its brokers cheated so many people out of their money, but of course any firm can have a bad apple in the barrel."

Adriana, also wearing mourning black, clasped his hand. Her face, too, was pink and swollen from weeping. "It was very kind of the President to send such warm personal condolences to Bob's mother," she said. "She was touched."

They sat together—three of them: Mrs. Roosevelt and the two young people—in one end of a railroad car, isolated from the rest of the passengers by two Secret Service men, who had tied a cord across the aisle to mark a boundary and guarded it with grim jealousy. The train was on its way to New York City, where Mrs. Roosevelt and Adriana would spend the night before traveling on to Washington tomorrow.

"Will you think me paranoid if I say I doubt very much that my father actually jumped from that window?" Bob asked Mrs. Roosevelt. "It is so unlike him, so out of character. Besides, my mother says he was not particularly depressed that day. I can't . . . I just can't . . ."

"Of course you can't," said Mrs. Roosevelt softly.

"He received a telephone call, my mother says. About eight. They had finished dinner. He told her he had to go to the office, that someone had some information for him, something important to his case. He didn't say who it was. She asked him if it was really important enough to go back downtown at that hour. He said it was. He said he wouldn't be gone long."

"We must find out who called him," said Adriana. "And what that person said to him."

Mrs. Roosevelt frowned. "What could anyone have said to him that would cause him to—"

"To kill himself," said Bob. "To do that to my mother." He shook his head. "I can't believe—"

"*We* can't believe," interrupted Adriana. "We can't believe he jumped."

"You're suggesting he was *pushed* out?" asked Mrs. Roosevelt, leaning closer to them and speaking in a whisper.

"Thrown out," said Adriana.

They were silent for a long moment, and then Bob went on: "I don't want you to think I'm paranoid, Mrs. Roosevelt, but it is at least as logical to think that something like that happened than to think my father would have killed himself that way and at that time."

"Murder?" whispered Mrs. Roosevelt.

"As likely as suicide," said Bob. "Neither was likely, one would have thought. But he's dead."

"The police . . . ?"

Bob shrugged. "They went up. No one was there. The offices were locked and dark, except for my father's. His window was open. They telephoned his partners. Each of them professed to be hugely shocked."

"He still had a key—and the locks had not been changed?" asked Mrs. Roosevelt.

"Yes, he still had a key. And the lock on the outer door has been there for many years."

"In other words, it was not necessary for someone to let him in?"

"The police made that point. He could let himself in. It was not necessary for someone to be there to let him in. So the only evidence that anyone else was there was that he told my mother he was going to the office to meet someone. And the police are inclined to discount that."

"What no one has explained," said Adriana tearfully, "is why, if he wanted to . . . put an end to himself, would he go all the way downtown to his office?"

"He had a pistol at home," said Bob. "He could have used it on himself if that was what he wanted."

Mrs. Roosevelt shuddered. "Oh," she said, shaking her head. "It *is* inconceivable."

"But the inconceivable is what the world is accepting," said Bob.

"Bob's father was murdered," said Adriana firmly.

"We must not be too quick to leap to that conclusion," said Mrs. Roosevelt.

His mother had stayed at home in Dutchess County, and Bob was alone in the family apartment in the city. They would have to give it up, he supposed. There was talk of lawsuits that would be filed against his father's estate, with the purpose of taking from them whatever remained, little as it was likely to be. He wandered through the comfortable rooms, depressed, picking up personal things his father had cherished, putting them down, picking up something else. He was past weeping, at least for tonight. The sadness was duller now, not the sharp pain it had been for days.

Adriana had insisted she would stay in New York with

him. Mrs. Roosevelt had forbidden it, saying she had promised the van der Meers that Adriana would be in Washington, at the White House. Adriana had argued then that he should come on to Washington. She did not want to leave him alone. He had promised he would come down in two or three days. He had, he had told her, things he must do in the city.

What things? He had spoken again with the detectives, who said the matter of his father's death remained an open file; but it was apparent their minds were closed on the subject. He had answered a dozen letters of condolence that had arrived at the apartment while he and his mother were in Dutchess County for the funeral. He had returned many telephone calls. He sat down now at his father's desk and began to write a letter to Adriana. Her letter to him, which must have been written on the train between New York and Washington and posted at the station, lay in the middle of the big green blotter. He picked it up to read again:

> *My Dearest Love,*
> *Life seems determined to deal us the hardest blows that can fall on two people. It cannot diminish my feelings for you, though, and I know it cannot change yours for me. We will not change. We will never love each other any less. I—*

The telephone rang. He picked it up.

"Mr. Hannah?"

"Yes."

"Mr. *Bob* Hannah?"

"Yes."

"Don't ask who's callin'. It's a friend. I got somethin' to tell you. Need to meet you."

"You've got something to tell me about what?"

"You can guess. You interested, you gotta meet me."

"Is it about—"

"Never mind what it's about. Not on the telephone. Now listen careful. There's a bar in Chinatown called Gum Loo. Just ask the first Chink you see on the street, he'll know where it is. If he doesn't, ask the second. Come dressed like you amount to somethin'. They'll point it out to you. Nine o'clock. It'll be worth your while, I promise ya."

"I'll be there," said Bob, but he realized he was speaking on a dead line.

It was too much like the call his father had received. Although he could not imagine that his father had gone anywhere in response to that kind of talk, the coincidence troubled him.

He opened the center drawer of the desk and pulled out the pistol his father had kept there. It was a .38 Smith & Wesson revolver, with the legend REGULATION POLICE stamped on the blue steel of the barrel. It was of course loaded. His father had always kept it loaded. Bob stared at it for a moment. Then he stood and thrust the barrel into the waistband of his trousers. He was wearing a cream-white double-breasted suit, and with the jacket buttoned the pistol was entirely out of sight. A concealed weapon. It was a criminal offense to carry it, but he decided he would just the same. He put on a Panama straw hat and left the apartment at eight-fifteen.

At nine o'clock it was not quite dark on the streets of Chinatown, and yellow lights glowed from restaurants and shops onto sidewalks thronged with hurrying, purposeful Chinese and gawking tourists. Incomprehensible signs in red and black characters shouted to the night and the un-seeing Chinese, who never glanced up at them. Knots of pigtailed men talked in shrill tones on the corners, their heads bobbing, their hands remaining clasped before them.

Bob stopped a young man who seemed likely to know English. "Excuse me, can you tell me where the Gum Loo bar is?"

"Gum Loo," the young man repeated thoughtfully. "Gum Loo. Can direct you to much nicer bar."

"I'm meeting a friend there."

"Ahhh." The young man turned and pointed south. "Two block. Then"—pointing west—"one block. Gum Loo."

"Thank you. Thank you very kindly."

"Much nicer girls at New Hunan," the young man said, pointing north.

"Well . . . I'm not looking for a girl," said Bob.

"Come New Hunan afterward," said the young man. "Tell man Lee send you."

"I'll keep that in mind."

It wouldn't have been difficult, Bob decided a few minutes later, to find a much nicer bar. The Gum Loo was dark and smoky, and the cloth on his table was freshly stained. It would not have been difficult either to find much nicer girls. As soon as he was seated he was approached by three in succession, two Chinese, one a blonde, none of them attractive. A waiter in a filthy long apron rudely demanded to know what he wanted, and he ordered a beer. Although no one else in the bar seemed to have noticed him, he felt menaced in the Gum Loo, and he slipped his right hand inside his jacket and adjusted the revolver in his waistband.

He checked his watch. He had judged his time well, and it was just nine o'clock.

"Looks like you make a point of bein' on time. So do I."

Bob looked up. The man was in his sixties, gray-haired, with a stubble of gray beard on his lined face. He wore round, gold-rimmed eyeglasses and was poorly dressed in ill-fitting, much-washed trousers, a blue shirt, and a gray tweed cap.

"Don' know me, do ya?"

Bob frowned. "Yes, I think I do," he said hesitantly. "You didn't give me your name."

The man sat down. "I'm not goin' to now, neither. You'll buy me a beer, I suppose?"

"Sure."

The man snapped his fingers, and the waiter who had been rude to Bob hurried to the table. "Rheingold," the man said peremptorily.

The man was the night watchman, the one at whose feet Bob had dropped in the alley behind the office building. He glanced around the bar as though he needed assurance that no one knew him, then abruptly he relaxed. "That was a fool stunt," he said. "I mean bustin' into the Deutsch, Lindemann office. You coulda got yourself killed, you know."

"I knew that when I went there," said Bob.

"Didja? Well, you got a better idea of it now."

"Exactly what does that mean?"

"Just what you think it means."

"That my father . . . ?"

The watchman nodded. "That's my 'pinion. I didn't see it happen, you understand, but it's plain as daylight to me."

Bob regarded the watchman through narrowed eyes. "You didn't call me down here to tell me your opinion."

"Nope. I didn't."

"Then . . . ?"

The watchman slowly raised his chin and looked at Bob from beneath the reflections caught in the thick glass of his spectacles. "They's them," he said, "that would look to be paid for what I'm goin' t' tell you." He nodded again, sagely. "They's them that would. But, like I told you, your father was a different sort of man than most, and so am I. I—"

The man paused to let the waiter put a bottle of beer and a glass on the table. He watched the waiter walk back toward the bar.

"Think about the times you been in your father's office," said the watchman. "How'd he make the winda stay open in summer when he wanted some air?"

Bob rubbed the corner of his mouth with a finger. "Uh, he . . . he, uh . . . He had a pair of wedges."

"Right. That old buildin', most of the sash cords has rotted away. Different men in different offices had different ways of proppin' the windas open when they wanted air. Your father, like a lot of others, had the janitor make him a pair of wood wedges. When he wanted to prop the winda open, he pushed them wedges up in the groove where the sash had to run. Done it for years. But that ain't the way the winda was propped open the night he was supposed to have jumped out. It was propped open with a walkin' stick—Mr. Lindemann's walkin' stick, from his office. Now why, I ask you, would your father, who'd been proppin' up that winda for years with his own set of wedges, go all the way in Mr. Lindemann's office to get a walkin' stick to prop it with?"

"I can't imagine," said Bob hoarsely.

"No. He never done it. Somebuddy else done it, is my idea. Somebuddy else thrown him out that winda, and I'd bet a dollar to a doughnut he was already dead—or maybe just unconscious—when it happened."

"I believe he was murdered," said Bob quietly. "I need evidence of it."

"Well. There's some for you." The watchman poured beer into his glass and drank thirstily. "Somethin' fishy about the way it all happened."

"Did you tell the police this?"

"Not me. They had their ideas all set in their minds. They wouldn't pay no 'tention."

"Do you have any way of knowing *who* was in the office that night?" Bob asked.

"Buildin' was still open that time of night. Whoever it was coulda come in the front door. I can tell you one thing, though. Whoever it was didn't go up on the elevator. Whoever was in that office with your father walked up eight flights and ran down eight. And got away, clean."

"Knew the building," said Bob.

"Huh?"

"Knew the building. To get in and out without being seen, he had to know the building: where the doors are, where the stairs are; and what's more, he had to know the schedule: when the doors are locked, how the cleaning people work—"

"Like *you* knew," said the watchman over the rim of his beer glass as he took another great swallow.

Bob managed a little smile. "If I'd just known enough not to flush the toilet."

The watchman nodded humorlessly.

"Plus, of course, he had to have a key to the Deutsch, Lindemann offices."

"You're thinkin', bub," said the watchman. "You keep thinkin' like that, you're goin' to figure it out."

"*Jim Cote!*" The short, swarthy man sitting in Mrs. Roosevelt's White House office with Louis Howe and Adriana tapped his knee with his forefinger and raised his famous high-pitched, animated voice. "Ironclad evidence," he said. "Where's the evidence? It would take ironclad evidence to make a case against Jim Cote, and even with that he'd probably beat the rap."

Louis Howe, struggling for breath but pressing two fingers close to his mouth to hold the stub of a cigarette in place as he drew the smoke deep into his diseased lungs, forced a little smile. "We are grateful that you took the time to see us, Mayor," he said.

"Indeed we are," said Mrs. Roosevelt. "You came on short notice, and we are grateful."

"Well . . . a visit with Mrs. Roosevelt at the White House," said Mayor La Guardia, loosening and settling back in his chair but still speaking in his characteristic staccato. "A chat with Louis McHenry Howe. And to meet so charming a young lady as Miss van der Meer. I'd have come up from Antarctica, let alone down from Capitol Hill."

Mrs. Roosevelt laughed softly.

Mayor La Guardia shrugged and lifted his brows and turned down the corners of his mouth. "I had to be in Washington anyway. This makes the trip worthwhile. And I'm glad you confided in me about this thing, even if I don't see the evidence to make it stick. What did you think I could do about it?"

"We are not entirely sure, Mr. Mayor," said Mrs. Roosevelt. "We wanted you to know about it anyway."

"I, uh, have appealed for caution . . . for restraint," said Louis Howe. "We don't speak for the President, you understand."

"Except in the appeal for caution and restraint," said Mrs. Roosevelt with a broad smile.

Mayor La Guardia's mobile, animated face twisted itself into a caricature of himself amused—one of the faces of La Guardia that was beloved by political cartoonists. "I will be cautious and restrained," he said, raising a finger.

Adriana did not smile. The Mayor noticed, and he turned and spoke directly to her. "You understand, I hope. I mean, you've told me about a walking stick used to prop open a window. That doesn't prove much, Miss van der Meer."

"Will you at least check with your police department, to see if it's true?" asked Adriana.

"Sure," said Mayor La Guardia. "I'll go that far."

"It is difficult," said Mrs. Roosevelt, "for me to involve myself in this kind of thing, even tangentially, without creating the impression of political interference. I'm sure you have a similar problem."

"The hounds bay," said Mayor La Guardia dryly.

"The element that *I* supposed would interest you," coughed Louis Howe, "is the fact that Judge Cote bought stock in A. G. DeLoach and Company—when he is the judge assigned to try your suit against DeLoach."

"It would be worth a lot to somebody to keep *that* fact concealed," said Adriana aggressively. "Wouldn't it?"

Mayor La Guardia nodded. "Yes. Someone would do something pretty evil to keep that secret."

"Like murder," said Adriana.

Mayor La Guardia settled his little reading glasses on his nose and peered at one of Bob Hannah's photocopies, which Adriana had handed him shortly after he sat down. "Murphy and Carnahan," he said. "Now, that I can believe. Two Irish Democrats. But *Fiorenza?* An Italian?" He shook his head. "When they made up names for their fake stockholders, they should have made it three Irishmen."

Mrs. Roosevelt accompanied Mayor La Guardia on his courtesy call to the Oval Office. (The Mayor of New York could not, after all, visit the White House and not spend a few minutes with the President.)

"You know what they say about me," he told the President as they shook hands. "Any man who shakes my hand had better count his fingers." He cackled. "Let's see there . . . You seem to have all ten, Mr. President."

"It's marvelous to see you, Mayor," said the President. "I imagine it's a futile hope, but I hope my wife hasn't been trying to drag you into her crusade to save the name of Alfred Hannah. She has made that something of a cause."

"His name!" chortled La Guardia. "His name is mud to me. He was just another one of those loathsome Wall Streeters who spent his life squeezing the little man out of his earnings and savings. *However*, if somebody threw him out a window—and did it to cover up some large-scale graft, which is what Mrs. Roosevelt has suggested—then

I'm gonna stick both hands into this sticky mess and see what's in it."

"I was not aware you had decided to involve yourself," said Mrs. Roosevelt innocently.

"I didn't want the little girl to hear me say it. I don't want the Hannah boy to know it either," said Mayor La Guardia. "I don't trust them yet. They're believers, enthusiasts. They may not use good judgment."

"Have you looked at *The Wall Street Journal* this morning?" asked the President.

"Are you changing the subject?" asked Mayor La Guardia.

The President grinned and shook his head. "Not in the least. United Northern went belly-up yesterday afternoon," he said. "Filed for bankruptcy. Three more utility companies are expected to file today. What's more, the First Congress Bank, up in Boston, closed. Had too much money out on loan to United Northern. The disaster is spreading."

"I'm more interested in contractors that sell to the city of New York, make payoffs, and maybe channel them through big Wall Street brokerage houses like Deutsch, Lindemann and Company," said the Mayor. "If Alfred Hannah was murdered, it was because of *that*, not because he cheated investors in utility companies."

"May I suggest a starting point for your investigation?" Mrs. Roosevelt asked Mayor La Guardia.

He inclined his head in a deferential little bow.

"Find out the name of the watchman who told Bob Hannah about the walking stick," she said. "Then get the names of all the people who would have been working in that building that night. Someone must have seen who went up to the eighth floor that night—who, besides poor Alfred Hannah? If you question all those people, you might find out who it was."

"I have set up a special investigation unit to look into

things like this for me," said Mayor La Guardia. "I'll have the name of that watchman by this time tomorrow."

"Your unit is . . . circumspect?" she asked.

Mayor La Guardia nodded. "I've got a few boys I can trust."

"Will you keep me informed?"

"You will receive a report every twenty-four hours," said he dramatically.

"I'm afraid Lionel Pickering has taken more than a casual liking to Miss van der Meer," said Joseph Kennedy. "So much so that I may have to take him off the case."

Mrs. Roosevelt smiled broadly. "Really! I'm afraid it will do him little good. She is quite deeply in love with Bob Hannah."

"Pickering knows that," said Kennedy. "But he regrets it. Even apart from being smitten with her himself, he thinks she is using poor judgment."

"Poor judgment in what regard?" asked Mrs. Roosevelt.

"This is why I may have to take him off the case. I am not sure he can be entirely objective about young Mr. Hannah. He's convinced he's a scoundrel."

"Oh, dear."

Kennedy let his round horn-rimmed glasses slip down his nose, and he peered intently at Mrs. Roosevelt through the narrow gap between their rims and his sandy eyebrows. "Pickering is a meticulous investigator," he said. "When he takes on a matter, it gets full treatment. In this instance, for example, he has extended his investigation a little beyond the scope I expected. I'm unsure of his motive, but I'm most interested in what he's found out."

"And what is that, Mr. Kennedy?" asked Mrs. Roosevelt.

Kennedy pressed his glasses back into their proper place. "We are supposed to think, as I understand it, that young Mr. Hannah is financially distressed. Are we not?"

"His father lost everything," said Mrs. Roosevelt quietly. "Such is my understanding."

"Yes. Well, from the time he was about eighteen years old, the younger Mr. Hannah had a small account of his own with Deutsch, Lindemann and Company. He traded in the market in a small way, one supposes with his father's advice and assistance, almost certainly with his father's money, at least at first. More than a year ago he closed that account and established a new one with Butcher and Loeb—I suppose because he was already disenchanted with what was happening at Lindemann. Anyway, he continued to trade in the market until early this year, when he sold most of what he had. I'd guess he liquidated to try to help his father."

"How much money are we talking about, Mr. Kennedy?"

"He never had more than twenty-five thousand, so far as we can tell. When he stopped selling, he had about two thousand left, invested in three or four stocks. Now . . ." Kennedy paused and drew a breath. "Officially I'm not supposed to know he broke into the offices of Deutsch, Lindemann and Company; but, of course, I do know, and I know he did it on the night of June fourth. The next afternoon Robert Hannah bought one thousand shares of Ferguson Laboratories, Incorporated at twenty and five-eighths."

"Twenty thousand dollars!" Mrs. Roosevelt exclaimed. "But—"

"You wonder where he got the money," Kennedy interrupted. "For my part, I'm not so much concerned about that. He bought the stock at twenty and five-eighths. Six days later he sold his thousand shares at thirty-one and seven-eighths. In six days he made himself a profit of more than eleven thousand. I'd guess he found himself a partner who put up the money and shared the profit. I'd also guess it was not difficult to find a partner willing to invest twenty thousand dollars in Ferguson—once he told that partner how he knew Ferguson was about to go up ten or twelve points."

"How *did* he know, Mr. Kennedy?"

"The night of June fourth he went through the confidential files of Deutsch, Lindemann and Company. On June sixth Ferguson Labs announced that it had bought a controlling interest in General Chemical—which meant it had acquired General's aniline patents, which General had been unable to exploit profitably for want of capital but which Ferguson can and will exploit. That announcement sent Ferguson stock up eleven points. Which—"

"Are you suggesting," Mrs. Roosevelt interrupted, "that Bob learned of that forthcoming announcement while he was . . . uh, examining the files at Deutsch, Lindemann?"

"The information was there," said Kennedy. "The acquisition of General was handled for Ferguson by Austin Brinker, one of the Deutsch, Lindemann partners. If Bob Hannah opened Brinker's files, he saw the documents. What is more, he is knowledgeable enough to understand their significance."

"And Mr. Pickering. . . ?"

"Lionel Pickering is very upset. He thinks Hannah made a tidy profit on the side from his midnight excursion into the offices of Deutsch, Lindemann—which, of course, he didn't choose to tell any of us. Pickering thinks he's been exploited to some extent. He thinks *you* are being exploited. Above all, he thinks the charming Miss van der Meer is in love with a scoundrel. He resents Hannah. That's why I'm concerned about his objectivity."

"What an unfortunate turn," said Mrs. Roosevelt.

"The matter puts you in an embarrassing position," said Kennedy. "It puts Pickering and me in a worse one. We are supposed to prosecute the misuse of insider information, but we can't do a thing about the way Hannah used insider information, because we can't admit we know how he got it. I can tell you one thing for sure, though—Pickering will never again trust young Mr. Hannah, and neither will I."

"*Unfortunate,*" murmured Mrs. Roosevelt. "Most unfortunate."

* * *

Adriana van der Meer was living on the third floor of the White House in a little suite consisting of a bedroom, sitting room, and bath. She was close to Missy there, and the two had become friends. When Mrs. Roosevelt finished the official day that had begun with the visit of Mayor La Guardia, she flipped through the notes that had accumulated on her desk during the afternoon and recalled that Adriana had left word that she would like to spend a few minutes with her when she could find the time. Adriana was upstairs, and at seven Mrs. Roosevelt went up to see her.

"Oh, I'm sorry," she said. "I can come back a little later."

"Not at all," said Adriana. "Please come in, if you don't mind if I continue."

"Not at all," said Mrs. Roosevelt. "Go right ahead."

Adriana was sitting at her dressing table, brushing her hair. She was wearing only a brassiere and a pair of panties. To Mrs. Roosevelt it seemed an intrusion to enter her room and sit down to talk while the girl was so far undressed, but apparently such a thought did not occur to Adriana, who made no move to pull on a dressing gown and only turned on her bench and faced Mrs. Roosevelt as she went on brushing.

"I've been asked to dinner by Mr. Pickering," said Adriana. "He fully understands the relationship between me and Bob, so I suppose it's all right."

"Uh . . . I suppose it is," said Mrs. Roosevelt tentatively after searching for something better to say and thinking of nothing. "Mr. Pickering seems like a fine young man."

"Yes. He's a little stiff, but he's sincere. He's taking me to the Mayflower Hotel."

"That's nice."

"I hoped you would feel it's all right. I wanted you to know all about it before I went. That and—"

"Well, there is something I wanted to ask you, Adriana," said Mrs. Roosevelt. "I'd like to know how Bob and his mother are managing. Do I not understand that they are virtually bankrupt?"

"Yes," said Adriana. "The house at Hyde Park is Mrs. Hannah's, inherited from her family. She has a bit of money to live on, from the same source. So far as Bob is concerned, he feels he cannot ask his mother for money, and he has none of his own. He is living in their New York apartment, which they will have to give up soon; and after that, he is not sure what he will do. It is really most distressing."

Mrs. Roosevelt nodded solemnly. "I am sure it is," she said thoughtfully.

Adriana tipped her head to one side as she pulled at her blonde hair with her brush. "I'm worried," she said. "That's the other thing I wanted to talk to you about. I haven't heard from Bob in two days."

"I suppose you can't expect to hear from him every day," said Mrs. Roosevelt.

"The night he broke into that office," said Adriana, frowning, "he could have been killed. He could have been arrested as a burglar."

"Yes," said Mrs. Roosevelt.

"It was a reckless thing to do," said Adriana. "But it worked, from his point of view. I mean, he got the evidence he wanted—some of it, anyway. His father was alive then, and Bob's motivation for doing something reckless was less than it is now. I'm afraid he may be doing something worse."

"What, do you suppose?"

Adriana put down her brush. "He said something about a confrontation. He said something about making 'Uncle Arthur squirm.'"

"Arthur Lindemann?"

"Yes. He thinks Lindemann is a doddering old fool. He may be right about that, but the others aren't, and—"

"If his father was in fact murdered," said Mrs. Roosevelt, "then—"

"Then Lindemann or one of his partners arranged it," said Adriana. "Which means . . ." She shook her head. "He could be in very great danger, Aunt Eleanor."

"Dot's simple enough," said the gray old man behind the scarred counter. "Dot's the key to a bank safe-deposit box."

Bob Hannah shook his head. "Did you ever see a safe-deposit-box key without a number on it? How would the bank know what box it opened?" He shook his head again, more emphatically. "They always have numbers—and usually the name of the bank."

The old locksmith turned the key over in his hand, squinting at it over the tops of his rimless octagonal eye-glasses. "Yesss," he muttered. "Dot's right. Vell, a key like dis . . . Vere'd you say you get it?"

It was of course the key from the secret compartment in Arthur Lindemann's desk, but Bob was not going to tell the locksmith that. "It was in my father's desk," he said. "After his death, I asked at the banks I knew he dealt with, and it's not the key to the box he kept at Morgan Guaranty, which was the only safe-deposit box he had. It's important to my mother to find out what it's the key to. That's why I decided to ask a locksmith."

"Ahh," murmured the old man, now peering more intently at the key. He wore a scraggly gray beard and a black vest over a collarless white shirt. "Could be I compare dis to many keys I haff in my shop," he said. "Dot vould take a lot of time. Could be you pay?"

"I expected to pay you for your trouble," Bob said.

"Two dollars?" asked the old man skeptically.

"Five dollars if it doesn't take so much time," said Bob. "I need to know right now."

"Ahh . . . five. In advance?"

"In advance," said Bob decisively. He pulled the money from his pocket and slapped it on the counter.

The old man rubbed his chin, frowned at the money—thinking perhaps that he should have asked for more—and turned to the shelf behind the counter. He took down a worn, dirty book. "Uhmm," he grunted as he began to leaf through the book, shifting his attention back and forth between the key and the pages of the book. "Uhmm. Interesting key. Not so unusual. Not common, but not so unusual."

It was a hot summer day, and Bob had loosened his necktie and wore his double-breasted suitjacket unbuttoned and pulled apart. He pushed his hat to the back of his head, cocked his hip, and watched the old man with an air of impatience. The shop, on Second Avenue, was dark and dusty—and remote and anonymous.

"I tell you what," said the locksmith. "I tink dis is a key—"

"I'm not paying five dollars for what you think," Bob interrupted.

"Five dollars ain't enough to pay me to take smart talk from a young fellow," said the locksmith. He slammed the book shut.

Bob put his hand on the five-dollar bill. "I need definite information," said Bob, modulating his voice a little less agressively. "I came to a man who is supposed to know locks better than any man on the East Side. I'm offering ten times what you might usually get for the information. What's the difference how I talk?"

The old man shrugged. "Vell . . ." he said, turning the corners of his mouth down into an exaggerated grimace.

"By me, a deal is a deal." He reopened the book. "I tell you vat," he said, peering hard at a diagram on a page. "You find a small fireproof box manufactured by Safe Cabinet Company." He nodded. "It's a little safe, really, but opens mit a key like dis, not a combination. Some of dem sliding-out drawers, like. Safe Cabinet Company, dat's who makes dis."

"You're sure."

The locksmith nodded. "No question. Some dese safes painted to look like wood, like nice furniture, you know. Find in house sometimes, where real safe look bad. But tough to open, no key. Fireproof, too. Nice equipment."

Arthur Lindemann lived on East Sixty-fifth Street, in a handsome, well-preserved and maintained three-story brownstone. Summer weekends, he went to the Jersey Shore, to an old resort hotel where he spent Saturday and Sunday playing pinochle on the long, shaded porch that overlooked the beach and the ocean. His summer routine had not varied in forty years. Even so, before Bob approached the brownstone he stopped at a candy store three blocks away and dialed the Lindemann telephone number. He let it ring six times, then hung up and dialed again. No answer.

It was Saturday afternoon. He was dressed in a brown suit, with white shirt and bow tie, and he carried one of his father's leather briefcases. He supposed Arthur Lindemann's neighbors knew his summer routine and would be suspicious, might even call the police, if they saw anyone enter the brownstone at night. On the other hand, if a well-dressed young man with a briefcase came to the house in the bright sunshine of mid-afternoon, and if he entered the house without hesitation, as if he had a key—well, then they might take no particular notice.

He knew the house. He had been there many times. Unless Uncle Arthur had installed an alarm system recently or had hired a guard—both of which possibilities were extremely doubtful—it should be easy to enter, make a search, and leave, without creating a fuss, without being caught.

His mouth was dry as he walked east on Sixty-fifth, toward the brownstone, and he unwrapped a stick of Juicy Fruit gum and began to chew. He tried to walk with a casual air, with no furtive looks around to see if anyone was watching. At the bottom of the stone steps he hesitated for a moment, to renew his resolution. Bracing himself, straightening his shoulders, he climbed the steps, miming familiarity and confidence as best he could.

He took the glass cutter from his jacket pocket as if he were taking out a key. During the week he had practiced at cutting glass, which was a special skill not immediately acquired. He had bought panes of glass the thickness of those ordinarily used in doors and had cut corners off them until he was proficient at drawing the tiny cutter wheel across the surface with just the pressure necessary to make a clean cut. Without hesitation now—because hesitation would look suspicious to anyone watching—he drew the cutter wheel down the glass. He was glad to hear the odd, ripping sound that signaled a successful cut.

The horizontal cut would be a little more difficult, because of the awkward position he would have to take. He had practiced making that cut with his left hand, and that was how he did it. Again, the cutter wheel crossed the surface of the glass with the sound of a coarse rip.

Tentatively now he tapped the lower left corner of the pane, inside the two lines his cutter had incised. The glass resisted. He tapped along the lines with the steel handle of the cutter—painfully aware of the tap-tapping noise that would alert anyone who heard it. As he tapped he could see the glass fracture along the lines. A few more taps. He rapped the corner again with his knuckle, and the square he had cut in the lower left corner of the door window swung back, broke loose from molding and putty, and fell quietly to the carpet inside. He reached through, turned the knob, and opened the door.

Only when he was inside did he take the white cotton gloves from the briefcase and pull them on to avoid leaving fingerprints. He rubbed the doorknob thoroughly. He picked up the little square of glass and carefully reinserted it in the hole, fixing it in place with his chewing gum.

The house was dead silent, and he walked into the parlor to the right of the entrance hall with a sense of intrusion that he had not felt at all when he broke into Arthur Lindemann's office. The house was completely unguarded against this unexpected entry. There in a glass ashtray lay the half-smoked cigar abandoned by Uncle Arthur when the taxi driver rang the bell. There was the half-read newspaper. The room spoke eloquently, and what it spoke of was interruption: temporary interruption, with an expectancy of return.

Bob looked into the kitchen. It was the same there. Unwashed dishes lay in the sink, waiting for the maid who would come on Monday. Uncle Arthur had eaten breakfast before he left. He had had a Scotch last night. He had left a light burning in the kitchen—his precaution, probably, against burglars.

It was upstairs, in the entirely private part of the house, that Bob expected to find something. He climbed the steps to the second floor. There he went through Arthur Lindemann's bedroom and guest bedroom, and his bathroom. Uncle Arthur had bathed and left a damp towel hanging over the side of the tub. The odor of his shaving lotion hung on the air.

Bob climbed to the third floor. There, a bathroom was rigged out as a photographic darkroom, and the room above the second-floor bedroom was set up as a studio, with a big, old, wooden view camera on a tripod, huge lights hanging from tracks on the ceiling, and assorted props—an iron bed, an immense wooden trunk, yards of draperies in assorted patterns, fake trees painted on cardboard. The back wall of the room was cluttered with tacked-up photographs, most of them of young women dressed in romantic or grotesque costumes and some hardly dressed at all.

In still another third-floor room, Arthur Lindemann kept a small home office, with a rolltop desk much like the one in his office downtown. There, beside the desk, was what Bob was looking for: the safe the old locksmith had described, the heavy steel single-drawer file, painted to look like mahogany. The brass tag stapled to the front bore the legend SAFE CABINET COMPANY, MARIETTA, OHIO.

Bob fingered the key in his pocket. He would be half surprised if it fit. Why would Arthur Lindemann keep hidden in his downtown office the key to a safe at home? It didn't seem to make any sense, but—

His attention was suddenly distracted, drawn to the rolltop desk by a pair of photographs framed together side by side in frames joined by hinges. Both pictures were of a woman, and both were autographed: one, *Best and many thanks—Jo,* the other *Thanks, Arthur—Jo.* He recognized the woman. She was the Hollywood actress Gloria Swanson (born, as he vaguely remembered, Josephine May Swenson). In one picture she stood on a lawn with her arm around a foolishly grinning Arthur Lindemann—much younger, much trimmer. In the other, although she was melodramatically posed and displaying her famous toothy smile, she was entirely, shockingly nude—a picture that certainly could not be displayed in public. It had obviously been taken in the studio in the other room. Bob stared for a moment, bemused, then turned decisively away from the desk and reached into his pocket for the key to the safe.

"Okay, buddy, just stand still and don't make any funny moves."

He turned. In the last moment, probably while he was staring at the two photographs, a man had quietly stepped into the room and faced him with a drawn revolver. As he turned, the man used his thumb to draw back the hammer.

"Police," said the man, flipping over his lapel to show the badge pinned underneath. He was a plainclothes detective. "Sergeant Joe Murphy. Yer under arrest."

Bob's knees weakened, and he stepped back and let part of his weight rest against the desk; otherwise he would have fallen. "Uh, I—"

"Shut up. Turn around," said Sergeant Murphy, gesturing with the barrel of the pistol.

Bob turned. Immediately he felt the detective's huge hand grab his right wrist and pull it behind his back. He felt the hard steel of a handcuff closing. The detective grabbed the other wrist, pulled it back, and locked the other cuff around it, fastening Bob's hands behind his back. Grabbing Bob by the shoulder then, he roughly jerked him around so they once more faced each other.

"See what y' got here," said Sergeant Murphy. He opened Bob's briefcase. "Nothin' much. Expected to carry off a lot of stuff, I s'pose."

Bob leaned weakly back against the rolltop desk, closing his useless hands into tight fists. Sergeant Murphy was a burly, hard-muscled man, dressed in a worn and wrinkled black suit. He stood facing Bob, frowning, pushing out his cheek with his tongue. He glanced around the room, as if by surveying it he could see if anything were missing. Helpless to do anything else, Bob could only watch and wait.

"Let's go, Hannah," said Sergeant Murphy, jerking his thumb over his shoulder.

Bob obeyed, though his legs were still wobbly; and, stumbling and drawing short breaths through his mouth, he stepped past the detective and through the door. They walked down the two flights of stairs to the first floor, Bob moving slowly and carefully for fear of falling with his hands pinned behind him and landing on his face. The detective stamped impatiently but said nothing until they reached the door where Bob had cut the glass.

"Nice work, that," he said then. "Very professional."

Bob stopped to wait for Sergeant Murphy to open the door. He glanced at him. "How'd you know my name?" he asked hoarsely.

"Same way I knew you'd be coming to break in here, sooner or later," said Sergeant Murphy. "I know a lot about you, Hannah."

"You were waiting for me?"

"All day. I was sitting there in Mr. Lindemann's chair, reading his newspaper, when I heard you go to work on the glass. I slipped down into the cellar while you walked around the house. Then I followed you upstairs."

Bob filled his lungs with a painfully deep breath. "Well?" he asked, nodding at the door.

"We aren't going out just yet," said Sergeant Murphy.

"We. . . ?"

"We're goin' down the cellar."

"What for?"

The detective grabbed him by the fabric of his jacket and pulled him around. "Move," he grunted. "You talk too damn much, Hannah."

Shoved forward, Bob could do nothing but stumble along the hallway toward the back of the house, to the door that opened onto the cellar steps. Sergeant Murphy reached past him and opened the door, and Bob stood facing the darkness, unable to see the steps. He turned his head to say he couldn't move until he could see—just in time to catch the detective's heavy fist on his cheek instead of on his ear, where it had been aimed.

In terror, he realized he was falling, falling into the cellar darkness, falling with his arms locked behind him, unable to do anything to catch himself or to break his fall. Instinctively he twisted to fall on his side or back, not on his face. His forehead banged a rough brick wall; then his shoulder crashed on a wooden step, his whole body turned over in a violent cartwheel, and his face was bashed hard against another step. His hip cracked against something hard. His knee brushed what was probably a rail. His back and the back of his head slammed hard onto a brick or concrete floor.

A lightbulb glowed suddenly. Though he was stunned and dizzy, he could see he was on the cellar floor, lying on his back. Sergeant Murphy was coming down the steps.

The detective stood over him, shaking his head. "Told ya to be careful of the stairs," he said. "Didn't I? *Didn't I?*"

Slowly Bob was becoming conscious of pain, different kinds of pain, in his head and back, in one knee, in an elbow, on his scraped face and forehead.

"*Didn't I,* Hannah? Didn't I warn you to be careful of the damn stairsteps?" He kicked Bob in the ribs. "Didn't I? Speak up? Didn't I tell you to be careful?"

"Yeah, yeah," Bob gasped.

"Yeah," said Sergeant Murphy. "'Watch out,' I said. 'Watch out fer the steps.' I mean, I'll take care of you, boy. I'll take good care of you. Get up."

Bob shifted his body gingerly. He winced and gasped.

Sergeant Murphy kicked him again, harder. "I said get up."

Bob rolled over painfully. Awkwardly, without the use of his arms, he managed to scramble to his knees, then to lift himself to his feet by sliding his body up the rough brick wall. He stood unsteady, facing the frowning detective. His left eye was closing, and he could taste blood.

"Now let's see here," said Sergeant Murphy. "I figger you and I understand each other a little better now, so suppose you tell me what you expected to find, breakin' into Mr. Lindemann's house and rummagin' through his rooms."

Bob shook his head. "Anything," he said. "Nothing in particular."

"Just a general fishin' expedition, huh? Like what you did in the offices downtown?"

Bob's mouth hung open. The detective's face swam in his blurred vision. He shook his head.

The detective's fist chopped hard against his nose, flattening it to his face. The blood spurted. "Speak, you son of a bitch! When I ask you a question, you answer!"

"Wha you want?" Bob mumbled.

"What'd you think you'd find?"

"I didn't know," Bob gasped.

"I jus' bet you didn't," said Sergeant Murphy scornfully. He nodded, twisting his mouth in a grimace of contempt. "What you figger—you gonna go through the others' houses the same way?"

Bob fought to settle the thoughts spinning through his head. Who was this man? What did he want? How could he placate this Sergeant Murphy enough to survive him?

"Huh?" Murphy demanded, cocking a fist. "Huh? How you figger?"

Bob spat blood on the brick floor. "You know all about it," he said. "What would *you* do? What would anybody do, whose father was murdered—"

"*Murdered?* What's this murdered? Your old man jumped out a window. The file's closed on that. Or . . ." Murphy tossed his head and grinned. "Or you put a lot of faith in that business of the walkin' stick?"

"No . . ." How did Murphy know about the walking stick? "No, I don't put any faith in that."

"But you know about it," said Murphy. "You heard about it from somewhere."

"Somewhere . . ." Bob breathed weakly.

"Forget it," growled Murphy. "Since you don't put faith in it, the best idea would be to forget it. That'd be the smart thing to do. That'd be the healthy thing to do."

Bob nodded.

"You listenin' to me? You listenin' careful?"

Again Bob nodded, but his head lolled, and he spat blood.

The detective struck out with the flat of his hand, knocking Bob off balance with a hard slap to the cheek. "That's so I got your attention, sonny," he sneered. "Now you listen. This is your last chance—one more chance than some people think you oughta have. You pull anything more, you're gonna wish you hadn't. You understand me? Huh? *Do you understand me?*"

Bob nodded. The blood from his nose ran down over his upper lip and into his mouth, and he bent forward and blew, to be rid of some of it. "I understand you," he grunted.

"Okay. Siddown."

Bob slipped down, more falling than sitting—afraid that if he didn't, and quickly, Sergeant Murphy would knock him down. The detective knelt beside him and unbuckled Bob's belt. Roughly he pulled the belt out and used it to bind Bob's ankles together.

"Gonna let you have a little time to think," said Sergeant Murphy. "Anyway, let you out on the street in broad daylight, people gonna wonder what happened to you. I'll come back after dark. Meantime, you think it over. You decide if you've lost the game and are ready to give it up. You decide, Hannah. You relax and think about it. Don't hurry. You got plenty of time."

The burly man stamped up the steps, closed the door, and left Bob lying on the brick floor in black darkness.

12

The darkness was not complete. After a little while he could see a thin white line of light coming under the door at the top of the steps. Without that bit of light on which to focus his eyes, he might have succumbed to panic, might have screamed and thrashed around and maybe eventually have lost consciousness. He needed a focus. That little streak of light was his anchor to reality.

Fixed in reality, he knew his pain. He supposed his nose was broken; how else it could throb and ache as much, he did not know. His arms and legs were twisted and bruised, and of course his shoulders, pulled back unnaturally by the handcuffs, developed a special sharp ache of their own. His shirt was wet in front, probably with blood from his nose. He rolled over gingerly, trying to find a position less painful. That was a futile struggle. Even breathing was painful, and he suspected he had a broken rib.

It would be six or seven hours before Sergeant Murphy returned, and he knew the agony would worsen as those hours passed. Worse, he did not trust Murphy to release him as he had said he would. There were those, Murphy had said, who thought he should not be given another chance. When Murphy returned, it could well be to kill him. He could not lie there and wait for that. Even if it were impossible to escape, he had to try.

He began to work his legs back and forth. The belt would not break, but it might loosen if he could force it down a little. He worked a quarter of an hour, maybe—of course he had no accurate sense of time—before he decided he could not move the belt that way. He rolled across the floor then, even though the awkward, twisting movement brought excruciating pain, until he reached the bottom of the wooden steps. There he tried hooking the belt on the edge of a step, to pull it down toward his ankles. That worked. After a score of useless tries, he caught the belt on a step and tugged it down. When it caught on his shoes, he struggled to kick them off. It was looser anyway, and now as he worked his legs back and forth it slipped and slipped, until finally he was able to free himself from it.

Now he could stand. He forced himself up on his knees, then to his feet. Leaning against the brick wall, he heaved with painful, gasping breaths and felt a cold sweat on his forehead running down into his eyes.

He climbed the steps. Putting his back to the door, he fumbled for the knob, found it, and discovered the door was locked. He turned and clutched the stair rail with both his cuffed hands, to brace himself firmly, and gave the door a hard, angry kick. It broke from the frame and swung around against the wall of the first-floor hallway.

He remained on the steps for a long moment, afraid that Sergeant Murphy had not in fact left the house but would come rushing along the hall now to throw him back down the steps. But the house was silent. He ventured out into the hall, then into the kitchen. Murphy was not in the house.

Bob sat down on a chair in the kitchen. With his right hand he twisted the cuff on his left wrist. It was tight. It was not going to come off. He tried the right one with his left hand. It was even tighter. A moment's notion that he could soap his wrists and hands and slip the handcuffs off was quickly dispelled. He could not get them off. They had to be unlocked or sawed off with a hacksaw.

He turned his back to the kitchen sink and managed to

reach a tap and turn on the water. He put his head in the cold stream and saw gouts of blood wash from his face into the sink. He sucked water into his mouth and spat blood and water. Then he drank a little.

He could get out now. He could open a door and get out of the house. But then what? The first person who saw him would call the police. And how was he to explain why he was handcuffed and why he was beaten and bloody? No, he could not leave the house—at least until it was dark, and even then how would he get home? Besides, Murphy would return at dark, if he kept his promise.

He wondered if he could make a telephone call. He had seen in a movie once a man who dialed a number with a pencil in his teeth. It was fantastic maybe but maybe not impossible. Then . . . who would he call? Moira maybe. Moira had a sense of adventure and of the ridiculous, and though she would ask why he was here in this state, she would not press for the truth when she understood he did not want to reveal it.

He found pencils in a kitchen drawer. There was a telephone in the living room. He knelt on the floor by the telephone stand and tried spinning the dial without removing the receiver from the hook. It wouldn't work. What he had seen in the movie had been only fantasy. On his knees, staring numbly at the phone and at the pencil, he saw how to do it. He broke the pencil. With only a stub in his mouth, he could twist the dial. He could dial Moira—if only Moira were home.

With his back to the telephone, he lifted the receiver and put it down on the stand. He knelt and put his ear to it to listen for the dial tone. Clenching the stub of pencil tight in his teeth, he began to dial—MUrray Hill . . .

When he heard the knob turn in the front door, he hung his head, and his eyes filled with tears. He had failed, and when he sensed that a man—Murphy, he supposed—was standing over him, he shook with sobs.

"Ah. Well. It looks like you've met my colleague Joe Murphy."

It was not Murphy's voice. It was not Murphy. Bob raised his eyes and looked up into the pink, shining face of a very different man.

"Worked you over, did he?" the man asked. He frowned and shook his head. "That's his way. You may consider yourself lucky if nothing's permanently damaged."

Bob did not speak. On his knees, he stared up open-mouthed and heaved with labored breaths.

"My name is O'Shaughnessy," said the man. "Police Sergeant Pat O'Shaughnessy of the mayor's special investigation unit. You need not introduce yourself. You are Robert Hannah. Stand up and turn around, and I'll take off the handcuffs."

Bob scrambled to his feet, and Sergeant O'Shaughnessy stepped around him and unlocked the handcuffs. As Bob flexed his shoulders and rubbed his wrists, he studied the florid face of this new police sergeant. O'Shaughnessy was a smaller man than Murphy: shorter, more compact, trim. His hair was white under his gray fedora. He spoke with a pronounced Irish accent, and his fatherly blue eyes communicated sympathy leavened with humor.

"He knocked me down the cellar stairs," Bob mumbled.

"I shouldn't wonder," said Sergeant O'Shaughnessy. "So you need a visit to a hospital."

Bob nodded.

"But someone downtown wants to see you," said Sergeant O'Shaughnessy. "If you can handle it, we'll have a doctor meet us."

Bob nodded.

Sergeant O'Shaughnessy picked up the telephone, put his finger on the cradle to get a new dial tone, and dialed a number. As he watched the sergeant dial, Bob felt in his pocket. The key to the safe upstairs was still there.

"How'd you know I was here?" Bob asked.

"I didn't m' boy. I was looking for Murphy. Wasn't that lucky?"

"Who do you think you are? *What* do you think you are?" shrilled Mayor La Guardia. "You know who asked me to look into the matter of your father's death. How can I do that if you stick your nib in and get yourself beaten up? Frankly, I don't care if you got your nose busted. What I do care about is that you've fouled up my investigation of something I've started to care about. There's something in this business. But how can anyone find out what, if some stupid Ivy League kid butts in and gets his nose busted?"

The doctor working over Bob in the mayor's office had pronounced him bruised but sound, except that his nose was broken.

"It's out of the woodwork, anyway," remarked Sergeant O'Shaughnessy.

"Ye-ess," agreed Mayor La Guardia. "If Joe Murphy's in on it, that tells the tale. You smoked *him* out anyway, Hannah."

"Like to be there," Bob muttered, "when he looks in that cellar and doesn't find me."

"*Like to be there!*" shrilled the Mayor. "You're more kinds of damn fool than anybody could believe."

"I'd like to kick *him* down those stairs," said Bob.

He sat in a wooden armchair, rueful in his torn and stained suit, his ripped shirt brown with blood from his nose. Sergeant O'Shaughnessy had retrieved his shoes from the cellar and his briefcase from the third-floor office before they left the house, and, even in his pain, on the way downtown in the sergeant's car he had joined O'Shaughnessy's laughing jokes about how surprised—and how distressed—Sergeant Murphy would be when he returned and found Bob had somehow escaped. ("He'll not know how you got away, much less who helped you. Ha-hah! I wish I could see his face when he comes back.") The doctor swabbed cuts and abrasions with stinging alcohol, as Bob winced and grunted. He had straightened the nose between thumb and finger, and it had snapped loudly when he jerked it. His white gauze and tape now covered half of Bob's face.

"He knew who he was, that's the point," said O'Shaughnessy. "Knew who he was and that he was likely to come to the house. He was waiting for him."

"I have something to tell you, Hannah," said Mayor La Guardia. "It's not good news."

"Something—"

"It's about the night watchman who let you go, the one who met you in Chinatown and told you about the walking stick," said the Mayor. "His name was Greschner. He's dead. His body was found in a trash bin in Chinatown last night."

"That was no accident," said Bob.

"I never supposed it was," said Mayor La Guardia. "But does it teach you anything?"

"What's it supposed to teach me?"

"Well . . ." said the Mayor, a little subdued for once. "I guess you were supposed to find out about it before you went to Lindemann's house this afternoon. If you had known, it was supposed to be a warning."

"I can't believe they'd kill the old fellow just to warn Bob," said O'Shaughnessy. "He must have known something pretty important to them."

"Or they thought he did," said the Mayor.

"Murphy knew I broke into the Deutsch, Lindemann offices," said Bob. "He mentioned it. How'd he know?"

"How indeed?" said the Mayor.

"Except for the old watchman and the people in Washington whose names we haven't mentioned yet, nobody knew."

"So you figured," said O'Shaughnessy.

"What?"

"Somebody else knew."

*   *   *

They offered to send him home in a police car. He thanked them and took a cab. He did not go home but to an office on Thirty-fifth Street, and he was glad he was able to reach that office before Harry left for the day. He sat down across Harry's desk and grinned weakly as Harry laughed at his bandages and his torn and bloody clothes.

"You've done something stupid. Wha'd you do stupid, Robert?" asked Harry as he poured a generous splash of rye into each of two glasses.

"If you're interested, I'll tell you the whole story," said Bob. "If we don't have a deal, you're not interested."

"Offer me a deal."

"Some guys want to kill me," said Bob. "I need somebody to stick with me, to prevent it. Twenty-four hours a day, seven days a week, for a while."

"Man's got to make a living," said Harry. "The story around town is that you're broke."

"I'm not broke. Cash in advance."

"By the week?"

"By the week."

"Two hundred plus expenses."

"Two fifty flat, pay your own expenses."

"Deal." Harry tossed off his rye. "For a week, Robert, you're not going to be able to potty without me."

Adriana dropped to the couch and wept. "Oh, darling!" she cried. "I knew it! I had a premonition."

Mrs. Roosevelt agreed. "She did. She told me she believed you were in danger."

They sat together in the living room of the Hannah apartment in New York. Mrs. Roosevelt had brought Adriana to New York on the first train after they received an evening call from Mayor La Guardia. Bob, at this point, the day after his beating, looked worse than he had looked when Sergeant O'Shaughnessy helped him into City Hall and to the Mayor's office. His face had swollen, and his nose had bled again, staining the bandage that covered it. The bruises on his limbs and body had swollen, too, and he was stiff. Every movement, even so simple a thing as rising from his chair and extending his hand to Mrs. Roosevelt, had been painful.

"I'd like you to meet Harry Bledsoe," said Bob. "Harry's an old friend, and he's a private detective. He's going to live with me for a while."

Mrs. Roosevelt cast a skeptical eye on the beefy, jowly man in shirtsleeves, with cigars in his shirt pocket, a glass of rye in his hand, and a stubby revolver hanging conspicuously in a holster under his left armpit. Bledsoe's eyes shifted without subtlety between her, the First Lady, who of course precipitated intense curiosity, and Adriana, who inspired less-than-innocent admiration.

"We are told," said Mrs. Roosevelt, "that the night watchman has been killed."

Bob nodded.

"Why, do you suppose?" she asked.

"I'm worried about that," said Bob. "It seems as if somebody knows a lot of things we supposed were confidential among us."

"What are you saying?" asked Adriana.

"Who knew," he asked, "that I broke into the Deutsch, Lindemann offices? Sergeant Murphy knew. Who knew the night watchman met me and talked to me, told me about the walking stick? Murphy knew. Who knew I might visit Uncle Arthur's house, maybe even when? Murphy knew. How'd he find out so much?"

"You are suggesting. . . ?" said Mrs. Roosevelt.

"I know *you* haven't talked out of turn," said Bob. "I know Adriana hasn't. But who have we all talked to, confided in, who might be passing along everything we say?"

"You have someone in mind," said Mrs. Roosevelt, tight-lipped.

"I do."

"Whom?"

"Pickering," said Bob. "Lionel Pickering. We've taken him entirely into our confidence. He knows everything. I understand he has met with you once or twice when I wasn't in Washington. Think of what you told him. Can you think of anything you might have said to him that he could have passed along to someone in New York?"

"Ohh . . ." whispered Adriana, covering her mouth with her hand. "Oh, I . . . I had dinner with him night before last. . . . I—"

"What did you say to him?" Bob demanded.

"Only that I was terribly concerned that you might be thinking of doing something dangerous again," she sobbed.

"Surely," protested Mrs. Roosevelt, "you don't believe Mr. Pickering is, uh . . . is involved in murder!"

"Who else could be sending messages?"

"Someone in the Mayor's office," suggested Adriana immediately. "We've told Mayor La Guardia a great deal."

"Not that I might pay a visit to Arthur Lindemann's house," said Bob.

"That could have been deduced," said Mrs. Roosevelt. "If it were known—and apparently it was—that you broke into the Deutsch, Lindemann offices, it could be expected that you might try the same at the partners' homes. And, of course, it seems to be general knowledge that Mr. Lindemann spends his weekends out of town. That meant that yesterday was a very likely time for you to commit another burglary. It was not good judgment, you know."

"How did they know I broke into the offices?" Bob asked.

"We knew—I mean, our group. Greschner, the watchman, knew. Mr. Kennedy, Pickering, the Mayor—"

"The President," added Mrs. Roosevelt.

Bob closed his eyes and nodded. "Yes. So who talked to the wrong people? Who got poor old Greschner killed?"

Mrs. Roosevelt glanced distastefully at Bledsoe, who was

pouring himself another shot of rye. "I suggest your body-guard stay sober until we find out," she said primly.

"What they say of you is true, I guess," piped Mayor La Guardia.

"Considering the kinds of things that are said of me, I am not certain that is a compliment," responded Mrs. Roosevelt, leaning forward to bob her head and concede only a very measured smile.

The Mayor laughed. "It's a compliment," he said. "Believe me, it's a compliment."

"Precisely what did you have in mind?" asked Mrs. Roosevelt.

"They say of you," said Mayor La Guardia, "that when you commit yourself to something, you never spare yourself until you have your way."

"That is still not a compliment, Mr. Mayor," she said. "I know you mean it to be one, but it isn't."

"All right," said the Mayor, nodding, raising a finger. "I give up. It is not easy to compliment you. It is too difficult for a man of my limited wit."

Mrs. Roosevelt laughed, and when she finished laughing a broad, warm grin remained on her face. Mayor La Guardia turned down the corners of his mouth and gesticulated with both hands, miming helplessness and surrender. Sergeant Pat O'Shaughnessy shifted his glance jerkily back and forth between them, like a spectator at a

Ping-Pong match, astounded by the dialogue and uncertain of its meaning.

They were in the Mayor's office at City Hall. Mayor La Guardia, in his shirtsleeves, with his necktie hanging loose, turned and propped his feet on the windowsill behind his desk. Mrs. Roosevelt winked at O'Shaughnessy.

"It's a very odd commitment you've made," said the Mayor. "Hannah . . . His old man was a stock jobber. The boy seems to be a professional burglar. We still don't know how he got in and out of the Deutsch, Lindemann offices, but the entry of Arthur Lindemann's home was a neat professional job. I'm beginning to wonder if he missed his calling when he enrolled in law school."

"He may have made a neat and professional entry of the Lindemann house," said Mrs. Roosevelt, "but I judge his exit was rather less."

"Hah!" said the Mayor, nodding. "If not for Pat here, he might have wound up in the East River."

"And why didn't he?" asked Mrs. Roosevelt.

"That's a very good question," said Sergeant O'Shaughnessy, obviously glad of the opportunity to join the conversation. "If Murphy didn't kill him, he didn't want to—or had orders not to. Otherwise, it would have been easy. To catch a burglar in the act and shoot him . . ." O'Shaughnessy shook his head. "No. If he didn't put the young Mr. Hannah entirely out of the picture, it was for some reason."

"Who *is* this Sergeant Murphy, anyway?" asked Mrs. Roosevelt.

"He's what too many of our Irish cops are," said Mayor La Guardia. "He's on somebody else's payroll. I mean, he's on somebody's besides the city's."

"Spare the Oi-rish, please, if you don't mind, Mr. Mayor," said O'Shaughnessy, intentionally exaggerating his Irish accent.

Mayor La Guardia laughed. "We'll argue the point some other time, Pat. Anyway, Murphy is a dishonest cop."

"Do you think he works for Judge Cote?" asked Mrs. Roosevelt.

The Mayor shrugged. "Possibly. And for others. Cote is not the only crook in this city's politics."

"I see," said she. "And did he in fact return to the Lindemann house last evening? Did he come back to find Bob had escaped from the cellar?"

O'Shaughnessy grinned. "That he did. We'd hurried to tap the Lindemann telephone, so we'd know who he called with his unhappy report—but he was too cautious for us and left the house and made his call from a telephone booth."

"Will he try to kill Bob now?"

"I doubt *he* will," said O'Shaughnessy. "I'm afraid *someone* will."

"And this man Bledsoe, hired by Bob Hannah to be his bodyguard. Who is he?"

"An ex-cop, put off the force for drinking too much," said O'Shaughnessy.

"Ah. Is he to be trusted?"

"He's a shamus now," said O'Shaughnessy distastefully. "Spies on erring husbands. Collects bills. Traces skips. Not very popular among his one-time friends on the force. But he's tough. I suppose the boy could do worse."

"He doesn't work for nothing, I suppose," said Mrs. Roosevelt.

"He's paid for what he does," agreed O'Shaughnessy.

She frowned thoughtfully. "Yes. In cash, I should imagine."

"In advance, too," said Mayor La Guardia.

Mrs. Roosevelt put that fact aside in her mind and changed the subject. "Well . . . what has your investigation achieved?" she asked.

The Mayor thrust an arm toward O'Shaughnessy, who began to rub his chin and frown while speaking in the argot of a policeman giving a report. "We questioned people in the building downtown," he said. "That was not productive. They didn't have much to say, and when they found out that Greschner, the night watchman, had been killed, then they refused to talk anymore at all. Murphy is not a suspect in the death of Alfred Hannah. He was on duty at the time, and his whereabouts can be accounted for during all the hours from four until midnight. We can't account for him similarly on the night when Greschner was killed—"

"Have you any suspect at all in the death of Alfred Hannah?" Mrs. Roosevelt interrupted.

"No, none," said O'Shaughnessy.

"But we do have something interesting to tell you," said Mayor La Guardia. "You know the name Martin Fiske?"

"The president of Northeastern United Utilities, I believe," she said.

"And a director of Northern United," said the Mayor. "He had an unhappy experience last night. His home burned to the ground. Westport, Long Island. No one was at home, fortunately, and no one was hurt; but the house was totally destroyed. Arson."

"Oh, dear!" gasped Mrs. Roosevelt. "Oh, there was something in a note . . . something about having 'a little bonfire.' I mean, there was some such reference in a note from someone at Deutsch, Lindemann to Mr. Fiske."

"Where is this note?" asked O'Shaughnessy. "It's evidence."

"Is it something Hannah took the night he broke into their offices?" asked the Mayor.

"No. He . . . It's a piece of carbon paper he took from a wastebasket in the office, some time ago."

"That will be evidence," said the Mayor. "It will have to be produced."

She had intended to catch an evening train back to Washington, taking Adriana with her once more; but when she returned to the hotel, Mrs. Roosevelt found a message waiting—Al Smith wanted to see her and would call at the hotel at seven.

"Where's the girl?" he asked when he had tossed his derby hat on a table and sat down facing her in the small parlor of her suite.

"Resting," said Mrs. Roosevelt. In fact, Adriana was soaking in a hot bath.

Al Smith, no more the Happy Warrior of 1928 but instead a confused and troubled old man, shifted his cold cigar to one corner of his mouth, and his jaw trembled as he clenched his teeth on the butt. "You're smarter than Frank," he said. "Always were. That's why I came to talk to you."

"I'm afraid our conversation will not achieve much purpose, Al, if we begin with an observation like that," she responded.

"Uhmm. Sorry, Eleanor. Sorry. Put it different. I think you're smart enough to listen to somethin'."

"I hope I shall always be smart enough to listen," she said, lifting her chin. "Especially to you."

He gnawed his cigar, twisting his lips around it. "Next year is almost here, Eleanor," he said. "Election year. The way things are buildin' up, it's gonna be a tough year."

"They're all tough, Al. Aren't they?"

"But 1936 may be worse. You and Frank . . ." He shook his head. "You listen to some funny guys. There's a lot of people think Frank is Red."

"You know better than that, Al," she said bluntly.

He shifted his cigar with his lips, from one corner of his mouth to the other. "Not what I came to talk about, exactly," he grunted.

"What *did* you come to talk about?" she asked coolly.

"Well . . . the point of what I said is that Frank's gonna need the N' Yawk people in his corner. No point in goin' out of your way to offend some of them."

"Who is being offended by what?" she asked.

"Eleanor," he said, shaking his head. "Eleanor . . . the Northern United business. Do you and Frank know whose toes you're steppin' on?"

"Judge Cote's?" she asked innocently.

"Cote?" He frowned, shook his head, and waved his hand in a gesture of contempt. "Pip-squeak. Nobody cares what you do to a small-timer like Jim Cote. I'm talkin' about *people*—people that count for somethin'."

"I think you're trying to tell me something important, Al," she said. "I'll be silent and listen. I—"

They were interrupted by a rap on the door. A room-service waiter entered with a tray and put a bottle of rye and a pair of glasses on the table by Al Smith's derby. Smith poured himself a shot and lifted it in salute.

"Eleanor," he said. "This fella Hannah that jumped out the winda. He was on his way to Sing Sing, which was where he belonged. He's where it starts and ends. I mean the Northern United bankruptcy. He put that mess together, and he let it fall apart. He jumped out the winda so he wouldn't have to see the inside of Sing Sing. That's all there is to it. People tryin' to make more of it are makin' a mistake."

"Someone asked you to come and tell me this, I suppose," said Mrs. Roosevelt. "I am sure you yourself are not personally interested in any way."

"No, I'm not interested. All I'm concerned about is to see that some good people don't get embarrassed."

"What good people are those, Al?"

"Well, they'd rather keep their names out of it," said Smith.

"Keep what names out?" she asked. "All the names I know about are deeply *in* and can't get out. The Deutsch, Lindemann partners. The officers and directors of the affected utility companies. What names are to be kept out, Al?"

"You don't know," he said. "That's the point. It would be

better for your husband, politically, if you let the law take its course in this business. I mean, leave it to the district attorney and to the people down in Washington . . . I mean, the whatchacallit, the SEC. Leave it to them. Let them do their job."

"Who asked you to come to talk to me?" Mrs. Roosevelt asked.

He tossed off his rye. "Some respectable men," he said.

"Who? If they're respectable, what are their names?"

He jammed his cigar back into his mouth. "Aww . . ." he growled. "Dammit, Eleanor."

Mrs. Roosevelt shrugged. "Since you've said you're not personally interested, I can't do anything or refrain from anything as a favor to you." She shook her head. "You see, you put me in an awkward position. What was it Mark Twain said, Al? That naked people have little or no influence in society? Yes, I believe that is what he said. The same is true of mysteriously anonymous people."

Al Smith chewed busily on his cigar and shook his head. "I'm only doing a favor for somebody, Eleanor," he said. "*Tryin'* to do one for you." He sighed loudly. "Look . . . in confidence. Did you ever hear of a man called Konstantin von Schwartzberg?"

"No."

Smith nodded. "A very big man. A Kraut, of course. Head of a big company in Germany and head of a group of German businessmen with investments in this country. Very honorable men. Very honest. The kind of money they've got . . ." He stopped and shook his head. "Eleanor, you can't imagine. And titles . . . Anyway, they lost a lot of money because of what Alfred Hannah did, but they don't want it known. I guess they don't want Herr Hitler to know how much money they have invested in the United States. There are some of us, some highly respectable men on Wall Street, tryin' to keep the names of these Germans out of the Hannah investigation. I tell you this in confidence. They've done nothin' wrong, you understand. That's for sure. But it's important to keep their names clear. That fella Hitler could get tough with them if he knew how much they lost in the Hannah business. He doesn't like their takin' their money outa Germany."

"Konstantin von Schwartzberg . . ." she repeated thoughtfully.

"*You never heard it*," said Al Smith, raising the palms of both hands. "Not from me. Tell Frank. Don't tell anybody else. He'll understand why it's absolutely essential to keep this man's name clear. I mean, there's diplomatic implications and all like that, you understand."

Mrs. Roosevelt and Louis Howe sat with the President in the Oval Office, talking while he ate from his lunch tray.

"Poor old Al," said the President. "Poor old fellow."

Louis shook with a deep, painful cough, and his face turned first red and then pale. Mrs. Roosevelt frowned apprehensively as she watched him press his cigarette to his mouth and pull in smoke. She glanced at the President, whose eyes met hers. Both of them were troubled. Louis was losing ground rapidly.

"Konstantin von Schwartzberg," coughed Louis. "I'd guess 'poor old Al' has breached somebody's confidence and accidentally told us more than he realized. Von Schwartzberg is one of the Thyssen group. You know who Fritz Thyssen is?"

"One of the German industrialists who provided the financial support that made it possible for Hitler and his Nazis to come to power," said Mrs. Roosevelt.

"That's right," Louis wheezed. He took a moment to recover himself, then continued. "I've done a little checking. Von Schwartzberg has been in the United States five times in the past three years. He comes over in first-class suites on the *Bremen* and lives in the Waldorf while he's here.

He's well known on Wall Street, but no one seems to know exactly what he does—whether he invests, or if so, in what."

"Is Deutsch, Lindemann his brokerage house?" asked the President.

"I haven't had time to find out much," said Louis. "I think there may be something important involved, though. After all, it's not just anybody who can use Al Smith for a messenger. And maybe, from the way things look, they also use Judge James Cote for an errand boy."

"Curious . . ." said the President. He tipped his head back and settled his gaze on Mrs. Roosevelt. "Babs," he said, "have you stumbled onto something big?"

"Two men are dead," she replied. "Alfred Hannah and the night watchman, Greschner. I'd say that's something pretty big. I'd say that's big enough to justify whatever has to be done to get to the bottom of this thing."

"The ripples are spreading from the Northern United bankruptcy, too," said the President.

"Where is the money?" asked Mrs. Roosevelt.

"Hmmm?"

"Where's the money?" she repeated. "Tens of millions of dollars. It was not spent to build electric generating facilities. Where did the investors' money go? To Germany? Did American investors' money go to Germany to finance Herr Hitler's political campaigns?"

"God forbid," said the President.

"It's no small question," said Louis. "I suggest we poke a crowbar into that little hole Al Smith may have unintentionally opened and see what we can pry loose."

14

"The Securities and Exchange Commission is a young agency, Mrs. Roosevelt," said Joseph Kennedy. "We do not have an entirely unlimited staff or budget, and we are finding our way."

"What's more," said the President, "every step you take, somebody thinks you are stepping on somebody's toes." He chuckled. "Even my mother thinks you are a gang of officious intermeddlers, sticking your socialist noses into the business of honest American stockbrokers who were doing perfectly well without you."

"Your mother thinks I'm a socialist?" asked Kennedy with a broad grin.

"By Mrs. Roosevelt's definition," said the First Lady, "Alexander Hamilton was a socialist."

The President lifted his glass. "I am indebted to you, Joe, for bringing us this wine. I don't very often have the privilege of drinking a Château Lafite Rothschild."

"I'm glad you enjoy it, Mr. President," said Kennedy. "I had a case sent 'round."

The President turned and spoke to the butler who, taking cue, had begun to refill his glass. "Get that out of the pantry," he said. "Have it put in my bedroom. Mrs. Nesbitt will be pouring it into sauces."

"Our cook Mrs. Nesbitt is one of my husband's favorite jokes," said Mrs. Roosevelt primly to Joseph Kennedy.

"Mrs. Nesbitt is a joke, all right," said the President, "but she's not one of my favorites."

They were at dinner in the private dining room, just the three of them, on a warm Wednesday evening—the President comfortable in a wrinkled cream-white tropical-weight suit, Mrs. Roosevelt less so in a pink silk crepe dress, and Kennedy conspicuously less so in a dark blue wool suit. An electric fan whirred and oscillated on a windowsill, but the air it blew in from the White House lawn was hot and damp.

"Your agency is small," said Mrs. Roosevelt, returning to the subject they had been discussing before the President commented on the wine. "Surely, however, this is becoming one of the biggest matters it has confronted. It is no longer just a question of whether the late Alfred Hannah was in violation of the law."

"The agency is small and new," said Kennedy. "I am the *first* Chairman of the Securities and Exchange Commission. Sometimes I have the feeling that the whole world is under our jurisdiction."

"We didn't mean to give you quite that much responsibility, Joe," laughed the President. "Certainly not that much authority."

"I have given new priority to the Hannah and Northern United investigation," said Kennedy. "I've put new men on the case."

"In addition to Mr. Pickering?" asked Mrs. Roosevelt.

"Yes. Pickering is hard at work. He's in charge, but I have three others assigned to the matter now. I'm afraid Pickering has come up with something rather distressing."

"Indeed?"

Kennedy nodded. "I now have a list of the people who did suspiciously timely trading in Ferguson Laboratories stock."

"If there were others, then perhaps Bob Hannah did not have inside information after all," suggested Mrs. Roosevelt with a sly smile.

"Three of the people were executives of Ferguson Labs," said Kennedy. "Their trading in the stock clearly involved the misuse of insider information, and there will be prosecutions. Young Mr. Hannah . . . we know about. The fifth one is the one that's distressing."

"And who was that?" asked the President. "Don't keep us in suspense."

"Cornelius van der Meer," said Kennedy grimly. "On the day when Bob Hannah bought twenty thousand dollars' worth of Ferguson stock, van der Meer bought ten times that much. On the day when Hannah sold his and made a profit of eleven thousand dollars, van der Meer sold his and made a profit of one hundred and ten thousand dollars. That's more than the company executives made by their illegal trading."

"Oh, that's *full* of implications!" said the President, chuckling.

"But we can't do a thing about it," said Kennedy darkly.

"Humm," said the President, drawing his lower lip between his teeth. "Because . . . ?"

"Because we're not supposed to know how Bob Hannah got his inside information," said Kennedy. "To call Hannah and van der Meer on the carpet, we would have to admit we have known for some time—and have not reported to the New York authorities—that Bob Hannah committed a burglary in the Deutsch, Lindemann offices."

The President shook his head. "Babs—"

"I frankly don't care," said Mrs. Roosevelt sharply. "That is a small issue as compared to the murders that have been committed and the disappearance of tens of millions of dollars in the Northern United manipulation."

"I'll accept that," said Joseph Kennedy. "But young Mr. Hannah may have done something foolish and dangerous. If Pickering could find out without much trouble that Hannah and van der Meer made nice quick profits in Ferguson stock, by buying and selling at precisely the right time, so could others find out."

"So could—"

"So could Austin Brinker, from whose desk the information was taken," said Kennedy. "In fact, I would imagine Austin Brinker is not the only one who knew, as soon as it happened. From which he and others may well have deduced that one of the Hannahs, *père* or *fils,* went through the office when no one else was there. Whoever deduced that would have understood perfectly well what the Hannahs were looking for in the offices: evidence in the Northern United matter. It may have been *that,*" said Kennedy, nodding for emphasis, "that moved someone to murder Alfred Hannah."

"*Oh!*" cried Mrs. Roosevelt.

"Joe . . ." said the President. "You've built an assumption on an assumption on an assumption."

Kennedy shrugged. "I said young Hannah *may* have done something foolish and dangerous."

"That got his father killed, you mean," Mrs. Roosevelt protested. "I would not want Bob to hear that suggestion."

"Nor would I," said Kennedy.

The President held his glass in his hand and swirled the dark red wine. He shook his head. "I am beginning to wish I'd never heard of this matter at all," he said quietly.

"I am afraid it was inevitable that you should have heard of it sooner or later," said Mrs. Roosevelt.

The President nodded. "I suppose so." He sipped wine.

She inclined her head toward Joseph Kennedy. "What do you know," she asked, "of this German, von Schwartzberg?"

"Baron von Schwartzberg," said Kennedy, "is one of the Thyssen group, as you know. He is the chief stockholder of a German company known as Nordländische Unternehmungsgesellschaft—"

"Northern Enterprises Corporation," Mrs. Roosevelt interrupted.

Kennedy nodded. "It was his grandfather's company, and his father's, and now his. The company manufactures

high-grade instruments and precision machine tools, as
well as the world's most wonderful and most expensive toy
trains. It also manufactured machine guns for the German
army before and during the World War—and may be
doing it again. The Baron is a very wealthy man."

"Did he lose money in the Northern United failure?"
asked the President.

"It is impossible to tell what investments he has in this
country," said Kennedy. "He works through many inter-
mediaries and dummy corporations, wherever he does
business. I will say, though, I would be much surprised if
he lost money on Northern United. He is extremely
shrewd about his investments."

"What happened to the money people lost in Northern
United?" asked Mrs. Roosevelt. "Isn't it true that a great
deal of money remains missing?"

"It is going to take a long and complicated investigation
to find out," said Kennedy. "Even to find out how much
actually is missing."

"Did Alfred Hannah know?" she asked ominously.

"Alfred Hannah," said Kennedy, "is something of an
enigma, to tell you the truth. I've asked some old Wall
Street hands about him. He came of a good family but a
family that had pretty well exhausted its resources by the
time his generation came along. He worked as a waiter
while he was at Harvard. When he came to New York
about 1908, he was lucky to get a job as a clerk at Deutsch,
Lindemann and Company. But he was sincere and dutiful,
and they took note of him and promoted him. Suddenly,
though, in 1913, the firm made him a partner. I mean,
they just reached down through the ranks and grabbed
this struggling, impecunious young man by the collar and
pulled him up to the top of the firm. Two partners left and
formed a competing firm because of it. Others in the office
never ceased to resent it. It was almost a scandal."

"Have you any doubt," asked Mrs. Roosevelt, "that he
was murdered, that he did not commit suicide?"

"The Street thinks he jumped out that window," said Kennedy. "He had plenty of reason."

"Who is Al Smith working for?" she asked.

Kennedy shook his head. "Everybody," he said. "Anybody. Al is the friend of anyone he thinks has a lot of money. What I'd like to know is, who is Matt Dugan working for?"

"Senator Matthew Dugan?" asked Mrs. Roosevelt.

"He called me this morning," said Kennedy. "His message was essentially the same as Al Smith's—lay off the Northern United matter, let the suicide of Alfred Hannah be the end of it. When I said we couldn't do that but would have to continue the SEC investigation, he made me a speech about what an evil genius Hannah was, about how many people he deceived, and so on. Like Al Smith, he didn't seem to know much about the case, but he was dutifully delivering somebody's message."

"The ripples spread," said the President.

"Waves," said Mrs. Roosevelt. "Not just ripples."

"Matt Dugan claims," said Kennedy, "that Alfred Hannah kept a secret account in a Zurich bank and that as he skimmed off funds from the utility companies he deposited them there. He says Bob Hannah has access to that account—has access, that is, to millions."

"That," said the President, "seems inconsistent with his using insider information to make an eleven-thousand-dollar profit in the Ferguson stock deal."

"It seems to me," said Mrs. Roosevelt, "this mythical Swiss bank account is someone's facile means of explaining away the disappearance of many millions of dollars of investors' money. What could be better? They know you can't check it out."

"Precisely," said Kennedy.

"Well, where is all this getting us, old chap?" asked the President. "It seems to me that every fact you and my missus come up with only leads us deeper into the mystery. When do we begin to come out?"

"I wish I knew, Mr. President," said Joseph Kennedy. "Unhappily, the matter has become too big to ignore, however much we might wish we could."

"I can't seem to discourage him. He insists," protested Adriana.

She had left a note asking Mrs. Roosevelt to call her after the dinner with Joseph Kennedy, but instead Mrs. Roosevelt had gone up to see her. She had found Adriana in bed, reading—wearing peach-colored silk pajamas.

"He insists," Adriana repeated. "I told him I am in love with Bob and intend to marry him, but he says he loves me anyway. He says Bob is not the sort of man I should marry. He . . . Well, you can imagine the kinds of things he says about Bob."

"Not much different from the kinds of things Bob says about him," suggested Mrs. Roosevelt.

"Yes. Well, I don't join Bob in his suspicions of Lionel. He's jealous. He has reason to be."

"How do you mean?" asked Mrs. Roosevelt.

"Oh, only that Bob knows how Lionel feels. I've told him. He had figured it out for himself, but I told him anyway. He doesn't like it."

"You are sure of your own feelings, Adriana? After all, Lionel Pickering is a fine young man, with much promise. Are you sure you are not changing your mind about Bob?"

"No, I'm not. I'm very sure, Aunt Eleanor."

"How would you feel if it turns out that Bob's father was not entirely innocent in the Northern United matter? What if it turns out that Bob has known all along that his father was . . . let us say, *culpable?*"

"Is that what you think?" asked Adriana.

Mrs. Roosevelt shook her head. "No. I've reached no conclusions."

Adriana put aside her book and drew herself up more erect on the bed. "Aunt Eleanor . . . you know about the Ferguson stock, don't you?" she asked.

Mrs. Roosevelt nodded.

"Lionel told me about that, over dinner. I don't know what to think? What do *you* think?"

"How much did he tell you, Adriana?"

"That Bob used information he found in the Deutsch, Lindemann offices to make a small killing in the stock market. It's called misuse of insider information, and it's a crime under the new securities laws that the SEC enforces."

"Did he tell you who else made a great deal of money the same way?"

Adriana shook her head, but her eyes widened, and she seemed to stop her breath.

"Your father, Adriana," said Mrs. Roosevelt gently.

"The same stock?" Adriana whispered.

"Yes. The same trading. Only for ten times as much money."

Adriana's face reddened, but after a moment a small smile came to her face. "I'm not much surprised," she said quietly. "My father has always done things like that. It's one reason I was so annoyed with the pious way he condemned Mr. Hannah. And Bob . . . He needed money so badly. I was afraid to think of what he might do to get some." Her little smile widened. "So he went to Daddy with a proposition to make a quick profit in the market. I suppose Daddy made him a loan."

"That would be my supposition, too," said Mrs. Roosevelt.

"Lionel didn't mention my father."

"He knows."

"I suppose he didn't want to embarrass me," said Adriana. She frowned. "He told me why the SEC can't prosecute Bob for misuse of insider information. That means they can't prosecute Daddy either, doesn't it?"

"Yes."

Adriana's smile reappeared. "Partners in crime," she

said. "Daddy can hardly object to our marriage now. Maybe that's what Bob had in mind."

"Bob needed the money," said Mrs. Roosevelt.

"That's something else Lionel tried to tell me," said Adriana. "That Bob doesn't need money at all. He tried to make me believe that Bob has access to a secret account his father kept in Switzerland, with millions of dollars in it."

"He said that?" asked Mrs. Roosevelt, surprised.

"I told him it's crazy," said Adriana.

"What else did he tell you?"

"Only that, only about Bob's trading in the Ferguson stock and the idea that he can get millions out of that Swiss account any time he wants to." The girl bit her lip. "He's trying to discredit Bob in my eyes. The conversation grew a little unfriendly toward the end, and then he apologized and said he hoped I understood it was only for my own good and because he loves me that he talked that way."

"Have you spoken with Bob?"

"He telephoned."

"Today?"

"Tonight."

"Did you tell him what Mr. Pickering said to you?"

"No. I was afraid it might make him do something foolish. He's capable of it, you know. He can be quite irrational about some things."

15

"It would be better if he didn't see you here," said Bob Hannah to Mrs. Roosevelt. "It would be better if he didn't see either one of you."

"I'm afraid," breathed Adriana.

Bob shook his head. "There's nothing to be afraid of."

"What shall we do?" asked Mrs. Roosevelt.

"If you don't mind," said Bob, "I'd rather you waited in my father's study. Leave the door open. You'll be able to hear anything he says."

Mrs. Roosevelt took Adriana by the hand and led her into the adjoining room, pulling the door three-quarters shut. She sat down in a leather-covered armchair facing the door, and put her big purse before her on the floor. Adriana stationed herself at the window and peered down at the street.

"What if he . . . ?" Adriana whispered, shaking her head.

"Never mind," said Mrs. Roosevelt. "We will interrupt if necessary."

They heard a sharp, impatient rap on the door in the living room.

Bob had of course known who was coming up since he heard the voice from the communicator box, but he let them into the apartment with a sardonic greeting, as if it were an unpleasant surprise to see them—"Sergeant Murphy. What a pleasure. And this, I suppose, is Officer Pup?"

"Very funny, Hannah," growled Murphy. "Officer English. Sixteenth Precinct."

Sergeant Joe Murphy swaggered into the living room as if the apartment were his own, followed by the rather less confident uniformed officer, a blond young man with a flushed face. Murphy stood in the center of the room, looking around, the corners of his mouth turned down, making a show of his skeptical appraisal.

"Ho, Murphy," said Bledsoe. He came in with a glass in his hand. "What are you doing in town?"

"Bledsoe. I heard you'd gone to work for the kid. You taught him to be careful how he goes down steep stairs?"

"Yeah, he won't make that mistake again," said Bledsoe, draining the last sip of rye from his glass.

"Good. Looks like the nose is gonna straighten out, boy," said Murphy to Bob. "Keep it out of the way of fists and stuff, it may be okay."

Bob nodded. He sat down on the couch and crossed his legs. Murphy, without invitation, sat down, too. Officer English, under Bledsoe's unfriendly glare, remained standing, conspicuously uncomfortable.

"You're under arrest, Hannah," said Murphy casually. "Officer English will take you in."

"Forget it, Murph," grunted Bledsoe. He turned a threatening eye on the young uniformed officer. "You too, English. Just relax. There isn't going to be any arrest."

"What you mean there isn't?" piped English nervously. His face turned a shinier pink. "Who are you to say—"

"Murph's a bad cop, young fella," said Bledsoe. "That's why he brought you along. He's not here to make an honest pinch. What he wants is to take Bob out and break his nose again, or maybe worse, and if thunder rolls out of the commissioner's office or higher—which I promise you it will—he'll lay the whole thing on you. Don't be a sucker."

"You'll take orders, English," growled Murphy.

"Well, wait a minute—"

"You want to tell us the charge?" Bob interrupted. "What am I supposed to be under arrest *for?*"

"I could say for bein' stupid and let it go at that," said Murphy scornfully. "You went too far this time, Hannah. Or maybe *you* did it, Bledsoe. Or maybe both of you."

"*Did what?*" Bob demanded.

Murphy looked for a moment at the face of Officer English, as if appraising his determination. "Broke into the old man's house again. Slugged him, put him in the hospital. Ransacked the place. Looked like you took up where you left off, Hannah. Did you find what you wanted this time?"

"You're saying Arthur Lindemann is in the hospital?" Bob asked.

"He'll be okay, lucky for you," said Murphy.

"When is all this supposed to have happened?" Bob asked.

"This morning. Three hours ago."

Bob stood suddenly and walked to the window. "Is Arthur Lindemann *saying* I did this to him?"

Murphy shook his head. "He says he was hit from behind."

"Then what evidence you got that it was Bob?" asked Bledsoe. "Or me?"

"When we search this joint we're gonna find the papers that are missing from Mr. Lindemann's house," said Murphy. "Unless you wanta hand 'em over. It'll go easier on you if you do."

"After you search this joint . . ." mused Bledsoe, nodding. "You got a warrant, Murph?"

"I got a warrant," Murphy nodded, patting the revolver hanging in the holster under his left arm. "English has got one, too."

Bledsoe spoke to English. "Remember what I told you, young fella," he said. "He'll let you pull your service revolver; he'll never pull his. That's the way he works. If anything bad happens, it's on you."

The uniformed officer's face burned an even deeper red. "I'll have to do my duty," he said hoarsely. "A serious crime has been committed, and you two are suspects."

"We were right here all morning," said Bob.

"Sure you were," sneered Murphy. "And each of you is the other's alibi. Take him, English."

Officer English reached for his service revolver.

"Wait a minute!" shrilled Mrs. Roosevelt, emerging suddenly from the adjacent study, leading Adriana by the hand. "Don't . . . don't pull a gun, Officer. *I* can testify that Mr. Hannah and Mr. Bledsoe were in this apartment all morning. We—"

"Mrs. . . . *Roosevelt?*" croaked Officer English.

Murphy gaped. "Mrs. Franklin D. Roosevelt, fer Pete's sake?"

"Let's not allow this confrontation to develop into a tragedy, gentlemen," said Mrs. Roosevelt firmly. She inclined her head toward Murphy. "I will, if necessary—and I trust it will not *be* necessary—testify to the presence of both Mr. Hannah and Mr. Bledsoe right here, in conversation with me and Miss van der Meer for the past several hours. I believe you said the crime against Mr. Lindemann was committed three hours ago? Well, we have been here more than three hours, discussing the plans for the wedding of Mr. Hannah and Miss van der Meer."

"Well . . . it may have been four hours," said Murphy.

"We've been here more than *four* hours," said Mrs. Roosevelt with a precisely measured little smile.

Bob stared at her, unable to hide his astonishment. She and Adriana had arrived no more than thirty minutes ago.

"Uh, well then," stuttered Officer English. "I guess we haven't got a case. Right, Sergeant?"

Murphy filled with breath, indignant but cautious. He glanced from Mrs. Roosevelt to Bob and back again, skeptical but of course unready to call the First Lady a liar. She met his angry gaze with a look of perfect innocence.

"English," said Bledsoe. "How 'bout you waiting outside a minute or two? We might have something to say to Murph that it's just as well you don't hear. I mean, you don't want to get any deeper into something stinkin' than he's already got you. Right?"

The young officer backed hesitantly toward the door, then opened it impulsively and rushed out—glad enough, apparently, to escape the situation.

"Whadda you wanta say to me?" Murphy demanded, glowering.

"Nothin' much," said Bledsoe as his huge fist swung upward and slammed into Murphy's face.

Murphy staggered against the wall, blood spurting from his nose, and dropped hard on his side on the floor. Bledsoe stood poised over him for a moment, ready to kick if he moved a hand toward his holster; but Murphy was stunned and only clutched his broken nose in both hands and caught the blood in his palms and on his sleeves. Bledsoe knelt beside him, reached inside his jacket, and took out his service revolver. He opened it and poured the cartridges on the floor. Then he flipped over Murphy's lapel and ripped the police badge from the fabric. With two powerful hands he bent the badge until it snapped.

Mrs. Roosevelt watched, appalled, as Bledsoe opened the door into the hallway and faced Officer English. He handed the young man the broken badge and the empty revolver. Then he grabbed Murphy by the shoulders of his coat and heaved him onto the floor at English's feet.

"Now, young man," said Bledsoe to the wide-eyed policeman. "On the way back downtown you have Murph explain to you why he's not gonna file any charges or make any fuss about a man bustin' his nose and his shield and taking his service revolver off him. When you understand that, you'll understand why I call him a bad cop and advise you to keep away from him."

Bledsoe slammed the door.

"You may pour me a very small quantity of that," said Mrs. Roosevelt to Bledsoe as he picked up a bottle of rye and splashed a generous shot into his glass.

"I'll be glad to, ma'am," said Bledsoe with a little bow. "I'll get a glass from the kitchen. Miss van der Meer? Bob?"

Both of them nodded.

Mrs. Roosevelt sank onto the couch, her hands trembling slightly. "May I assume you *were* here all morning?" she asked Bob.

"Absolutely. But if Murphy's smart, he'll find out easily enough that you came in from Washington on a train that didn't arrive until—"

"Eleven," she said. "Which he suspected anyway. Or maybe knew. My protection is in what your man Bledsoe said—that Sergeant Murphy was not here to make an honest arrest. What he wanted to do was immobilize you and Mr. Bledsoe while he searched this apartment for papers missing from the Lindemann apartment—or papers someone *thinks* are missing."

"Maybe he wanted something worse," said Adriana in a weak voice. "Maybe he wanted to hurt Bob again."

"That justified my telling a little lie, don't you think?" asked Mrs. Roosevelt ingenuously. She smiled. "It set him off balance. It would have been as well, though, if Mr. Bledsoe had not hit him."

"That's the part of it I enjoyed," muttered Adriana.

"Let's think of what he told us, though," said Mrs. Roosevelt. "I mean that someone broke into Mr. Lindemann's house and attacked him. I assume that is true. Perhaps we should telephone the Mayor's office and find out. Indeed, I'll do that."

When she identified herself to the City Hall operator, she was put straight through to Mayor La Guardia. He confirmed that Arthur Lindemann was in the hospital, though his injury was slight and he would be released shortly. It had already occurred to O'Shaughnessy, he said, that Murphy might have assaulted the old man, but O'Shaughnessy had found that Murphy had been in the squad room at the Sixteenth Precinct during the morning hours when the burglary and assault had taken place. When she told him what had happened, the Mayor laughed. O'Shaughnessy, he said, would have a fatherly talk with Officer English.

Mrs. Roosevelt grimaced over her sip of straight rye, then braced herself and gulped the rest of it, the half shot she had specified. "If Sergeant Murphy didn't break into Mr. Lindemann's house, then who did? And why?" she asked.

"What papers do you suppose he was talking about?" asked Adriana.

Bob blew a noisy breath. "Someone burned down Martin Fiske's house," he said. "Now someone has broken into Arthur Lindemann's house, attacked him, and searched the place. And remember the sheet of carbon paper I rescued from the office trash, the note to Martin Fiske, reminding him to 'clean' his files? Somebody thinks some evidence has not been destroyed."

"You thought so, too," said Mrs. Roosevelt. "You were the first to enter Mr. Lindemann's house."

"Yes. If only I'd had a few more minutes . . ."

"Think of this," said Mrs. Roosevelt. "Sergeant Murphy didn't do it. What's more, Sergeant Murphy doesn't know who did, or he would not have come here supposing *you* did. And if Sergeant Murphy doesn't know who did, then probably whoever he works for doesn't know either."

"Murph's an errand-boy," said Bledsoe. "He didn't come here because it was *his* idea."

"No," said Mrs. Roosevelt. "I feel you are right. So, again, whoever gave him his orders does not know who ransacked Mr. Lindemann's house. Either our conspirators are poorly coordinated or there are two sets of them."

"Murphy didn't kill my father," said Bob. "I've assumed he works for the men who did, but . . . maybe not."

"What about Baron von Schwartzberg?" asked Mrs. Roosevelt. It was the subject they had been discussing when the buzzer sounded and Murphy called from the foyer of the apartment building. "You were saying you have met him."

"He dined in this apartment one night, six months or so ago," said Bob. "He's a very wealthy man, I understand."

"What was the relationship between him and your father?"

"I don't know. But there was one. They talked business alone, in the study there, both before and after dinner."

"Were they friendly?"

"They seemed to be."

"Do you have any reason to think the Baron was an investor in Northern United or any of the other utility companies?"

"I've never seen his name used in that context," said Bob. "In fact, I don't think I saw his name on anything in the Deutsch, Lindemann offices."

"What about Senator Matthew Dugan? Did you see his name on anything?"

"Bingo!" said Bob with a grin. "Griff Bailey's desk calendar. He called the senator and received calls from him, lots of times. On the few pages I had time and film to copy, there are a dozen references to 'Dugan' and 'Matt' and 'MD.' Why?"

"Who has prints from the negatives you took that night?" asked Mrs. Roosevelt.

"I do. You have a set. Lionel Pickering has a set. I have two sets in safekeeping in two different places. I'll tell you where if you really want to know."

"That won't be necessary," she said. "I would like to raise something else, though. Do you want to tell us about the Ferguson stock?"

Bob glanced at Adriana, his face pinched with sudden concern. He drew a breath. "I was dead, flat broke," he said solemnly. "I couldn't afford to carry on the investigation." He shrugged. "I suppose Pickering came up with the story."

"You got the money from my father," said Adriana dully.

"Pickering tells everything," said Bob. "Yes. You can imagine why. He thinks a whole lot better of me now."

Adriana's eyes filled with tears. "You tipped yourself, Bob," she whispered. "When they saw who was dealing in that stock, they knew you'd broken into their offices."

He shook his head. "That's not how they found out," he said grimly.

"Let's don't argue the point," suggested Mrs. Roosevelt. "I have something else to ask. What about the Swiss bank account?"

Bob frowned and shook his head. "What Swiss bank account?"

"You don't want to tell us about that?"

His eyes sharpened. "Oh, I'd love to tell you about that," he said angrily. "If I had the remotest idea what you are talking about."

"A secret bank account in Zurich," said Adriana. "Your father's, that you have access too."

Bob tossed his chin. "Your dear friend Lionel should be a novelist," he said. "He has an overworked imagination."

"I believe you," said Mrs. Roosevelt abruptly. "I believe you don't know anything about a Swiss bank account."

"No. No, I . . ." He hesitated. "But . . . wait. Let me look at something in my father's desk."

Bob rushed suddenly into his father's study, and from the living room they could hear him jerk open, then slam,

a desk drawer. He returned and handed Mrs. Roosevelt a
slip of paper. He shook his head and turned up the palms
of his hands.

She examined the bit of paper, a rough strip rudely torn
from a sheet of fine engraved letterhead. Under the name
and address of Alfred Hannah, in swirling engraved script,
a broadly scrawled note read:

Schw Kr Z—272287248

"I don't know," said Bob soberly. "I honestly don't know.
Since he kept it, it must have meant something. I looked
at it. I couldn't decipher it."

Mrs. Roosevelt frowned over the letters and numbers.
"The letters *S-C-H-W*," she said, "could stand for
Schwartzberg. The numbers *could* be the numbers of a secret bank account. . . . Maybe I'm reading too much into
it."

"If my father had a secret account, what could it mean?"

Mrs. Roosevelt sighed. "A lot of things, Bob. You assume
a certain risk in looking into it."

"The risk that he hid millions in illegal profits in a
Swiss bank, you mean. A risk that he was guilty all
along."

She nodded.

Adriana fixed an apprehensive stare on Bob—her pale
blue eyes wide and brittle. Bledsoe pursed his lips for a
moment and drained the rye left in his glass. Mrs. Roosevelt lowered her eyes and waited.

"We have to know," said Bob quietly. He shrugged. "We
have to know."

"May I have Mr. Kennedy inquire?"

"If it *is* Mr. Kennedy and Mr. Kennedy only. Not Pickering. If you trust Kennedy, I'll trust him. But no one else."

"Agreed," said Mrs. Roosevelt. "And perhaps that's the
most important thing before us right now. When we have

deciphered this note and know the meaning of this number, then the investigation may take an entirely new turn."

"There is an old turn that I'm concerned with," said Bob. "I'd like to know if whoever broke into Uncle Arthur's house managed to open his safe. I'm satisfied there is something important in it."

"How difficult would it be to open it?"

"Not very difficult, I'd guess—if you knew how. If you didn't expect to find a safe, and weren't a safecracker, it might give you a problem. It would take a lot of time, anyway. If whoever was in the house this morning didn't get the safe open, they'll go back. O'Shaughnessy should be told that."

"Promise me *you* won't go back," said Adriana.

"The key to everything may be in that safe," said Bob. "It's got to be protected at least."

"Promise me you won't go back," insisted Adriana.

Moira Lasky crossed her legs and smiled lazily at Bob. She lifted a short amber cigarette holder and pursed her lips to draw in smoke. "I am flattered," she said. "You thought of *me?* Really, seriously, you thought of me? You were calling me?"

He nodded and grinned as he handed her the glass of dry sherry she had asked for. "I was trying to dial you when Sergeant O'Shaughnessy walked in."

"But why me, Bob? What made you think of me?"

"I knew you wouldn't be afraid. I knew I could trust you."

Moira's low laugh rumbled out of her throat. "You are too trusting," she said. "Do you think your face is ever going to look right again?"

"Right enough," he said.

"Good enough for the girl, I suppose," she said archly, raising to her lips the glass of sherry.

"Nothing uncomplimentary to Adriana, please, Moira," he said.

"No. No, she's all right. She'll be good for you."

"I could have called her," said Bob quickly. "But she was in Washington."

Moira smiled. She was twenty-six years old and so a little older than he. The brim of the hat that covered her black hair swept across her forehead and all but obscured one eye. She was wearing a sleek black dress and had put the jacket aside, baring her shoulders. He was stimulated by her. He always had been.

"I'm glad you called," he said to her. "I've had a tough time lately. I've been thinking of you."

She nodded. "Thinking of Moira—who could give you a really good time." She shrugged. "Well, I suppose I'm willing. For old times' sake."

He grinned and shook his head. "Not quite what I had in mind. I was thinking of something more . . . more difficult."

"Oh, damn. Here I am, all ready to give you a good time and you are thinking of something more difficult. What? What, Robert?"

"A scavenger hunt," he said.

Moira turned her head and regarded him skeptically from the corners of her eyes. "I don't think so," she said. "I think you've got in mind something a good deal more serious than a game."

"Moira . . ." he said solemnly. "My father was murdered."

He stood across the street, watching. She had been inside almost an hour, and he could hardly resist the temptation to rush the house, pistol drawn. Every minute he checked his watch. His eyes smarted from staring at the light behind the glass in the doors. She was to blink the hall light twice—a signal he could readily miss if he did not stare. Moira was entirely capable of taking care of herself, he knew; but he was troubled by a sense of having sent her into something beyond her experience. In her way, she was as ingenuous as Adriana.

Back in the apartment, Bledsoe was walking through the rooms, turning lights on and off, talking loudly, playing music on the Victrola, making a show. He had not agreed to this, but he knew how to take orders. He had made a couple of telephone calls before Bob and Moira left the apartment, and he had promised them that Murphy would not recognize Moira.

Bledsoe talked in clichés. That was all right, so long as he did his job. "You two are more kinds of damn fool than anybody I've ever run across," he had complained when he was still trying to talk them out of effecting another entry of the Lindemann house. "If you really have to, I'll come along and put a bash on Murphy. And you take that gun in your pocket, you'll shoot your toe off, that's the best you'll do," he had said.

"I have to know what's in that safe," Bob had insisted.

"They'll double you up, stuff you in it, and dump you in the East River," Bledsoe had grunted.

Besides everything else, Bob needed to go to the toilet. He cursed the Scotch he had drunk before he slipped out the back door with Moira. It lay now as an irritant in his bladder, anxious to get out when he had no way to let it out.

Mrs. Roosevelt had called late yesterday to say that Arthur Lindemann had been released from the hospital and was at home in bed. Mayor La Guardia had told her that the old man was not alone. Someone was in the house with him, taking care of him. Mrs. Roosevelt supposed that was a nurse. Bob supposed it was Murphy—or another one like Officer English, another "Offissa Pup." Moira had been amused at what she thought was a simple assignment: to take care of Sergeant Murphy or Offissa Pup.

He stood on one foot and then another. *He had to go!* What could she be doing? Was she . . . Bob glanced around. Could he . . . here on the street? A doorway? He would have to look away from the light behind the doors. He decided to give Moira another five minutes, then rush the place, pistol in hand. He did not like the prospect of melodrama, but he had become afraid for Moira.

Two minutes passed. Three. Then . . . the light! He could see her shadow behind the glass and curtains. The two blinks! He trotted across the street.

"An hour! Almost an hour, Moira. I was afraid for you."

"Your sleepy friend in there wasn't the dummy you told me he would be," she said wearily.

Bob glanced at the man sprawled asleep in an overstuffed chair in the living room. "He's . . ."

"Out. Chloral hydrate is vicious stuff. When he wakes up, he'll have a bellyache—I mean, a *bellyache.*"

"You're sure he *will* wake up?"

Moira nodded. "He'll wake up. And when he finds out I slipped him a dose of knockout drops, he'll be full of fun. I hope I never see him again."

"Where's the old man?"

"In bed upstairs. So far as I know, he's not aware I've been in the house. I'd guess they have him sedated. The tough boy in there was at no pains to keep quiet."

"The safe's on the third floor," said Bob. "You're absolutely sure that . . . ?"

"The tough boy won't wake up?" She grinned. "He won't wake up. Don't worry about that."

Bob frowned. "Yeah. Well. The safe is upstairs."

"Then let's get to it," said Moira. "My woman's intuition tells me it's not safe to stay in this house one more minute than we have to."

With another quick glance at the man asleep in the armchair in Arthur Lindemann's living room, and with Moira following, Bob mounted the stairs and once more made his way up toward the safe in the third-floor office.

On the second floor he used the bathroom, gratefully and noisily relieving himself. When he came out, he found Moira staring intently at the closed door of Arthur Lindemann's bedroom.

"Are you sure he doesn't have a telephone in there?" she asked.

Bob paused, eyeing the door himself. "I'm sure he *does* have a telephone in there."

"Then you'd better be sure he's asleep."

Bob put his ear to the door and for a moment listened. Hearing nothing, he turned the knob, pushed the door, and found himself meeting an old man's frightened, pop-eyed stare.

"*You! Bob! My God!*" croaked Arthur Lindemann.

The old man was awake. He was sitting up in bed, and had been reading apparently, in the yellow light of a bed lamp. His head was swathed in bandages—but he was alert, and his eyes were fixed on Bob, knowing, understanding, certain.

Bob stood slack in the bedroom doorway. He shook his head.

"Bob!" the old man exclaimed in a hoarse, weak voice. "Come in here."

Bob entered the bedroom and closed the door behind him, leaving Moira unseen in the hall.

"You're in great danger here," said Arthur Lindemann urgently. "Downstairs . . ."

"The man downstairs is asleep."

"He'll waken."

"No, he won't."

"You killed him?" the old man whispered shrilly, his eyes widening.

"Drugged him. He won't be awake for some time."

Arthur Lindemann blinked, and his mouth hung open. "Are you sure?" he whispered. "You have . . . ineffectuated that one? He is very dangerous, I'm sure."

"Who is he, Uncle Arthur?"

"Never mind for now. If we can . . . What time is it?"

"Almost eleven."

"Ah. Time maybe to get away. Others won't come before midnight, I don't think. Help me. Help me get dressed. We can escape! You came for me? No, you didn't come for me. You came for something else. Everyone wants . . ."

The old man rolled over and thrust his legs toward the floor. He was dressed in a white linen nightshirt, and his feet groped for the heelless slippers by his bedside.

"Everyone wants the documents," said Bob grimly. "You have documents that prove my father was innocent."

"I swear I haven't!" shrieked Arthur Lindemann, his eyes widening again.

"Then what's in the safe upstairs?" Bob demanded coldly.

"Never mind that! Never mind it. I swear to you there's nothing there that has anything to do with Northern United. *They* looked. They didn't find anything. If they had, they'd have taken it. We must go! While there is a chance, Bob, we must go!"

"Who killed my father?"

Arthur Lindemann bared his spare, palid shanks, pulling off his nightshirt and jerking at the clothes scattered around the room. He only shook his head in response to Bob's harsh questions, as he dressed in white shirt, gray tie, dark blue pin-striped suit, black socks and shoes, and gray spats. At the end he even settled a black homburg over the bandages on his head and grasped an oaken walking stick in his right hand.

"I want to see what's in the safe upstairs."

"I have no idea what they've done with the key."

"I have a key."

"You have? Oh yes, of course . . ." mused the old man. "You took the key but not the money. I liked that, Bob. It demonstrated a certain quality of character that—"

"I'm going to see what's in that safe."

The old man grabbed his arm. "I beg you not to!" he pleaded. "I swear to you there is nothing in it that has anything to do with your father's guilt or innocence, or anything to do with his death. *I swear that*, Bob. And every minute we remain here is dangerous. They might kill us both if they find you here with me."

"If *who* finds me here with you?"

Grabbing Bob by one arm, Arthur Lindemann tried to push him toward the door. "There will be time to talk," he said. "Now we must go!"

The old man seized the knob and jerked the door open, revealing Moira, who was kneeling and had had her ear pressed to the keyhole.

"Who. . . ? Surely this is not Adriana van der Meer?"

"Uncle Arthur," said Bob, unable to resist a tone of mock formality. "Allow me to present Moira Lasky."

"Who's Moira Lasky?" demanded Arthur Lindemann in a breaking voice.

"She's one of Polly's girls."

"Polly who?"

"Polly Adler."

"Actually," said Moira, rising, "I haven't worked for Polly for two years. I'm an independent."

"Uh . . . a *prostitute?*"

"A call girl, Uncle Arthur. Very classy. Very expensive."

"You trust her?"

Bob nodded. "I've known her for years."

Arthur Lindemann squinted at Moira in the dim light of the hall. He nodded and murmured. "Anyway," he grunted. "The thing that's important is to get out of here. Take an arm, young woman. Help me down the stairs. I'm still a little giddy from being beaten about the head."

Bob and Moira helped the unsteady old man down the stairs.

At the living room door, Bob took a moment to look yet again at the unconscious man. He was well built: slender, muscular, broad-shouldered. He was well dressed in a cream-colored single-breasted suit that fit him properly. His blond hair was cut so close to his scalp that the sun-reddened skin showed through clearly.

"Doesn't look like one of Murphy's boys to me," said Bob.

"He's not," said Moira. "Talks with a thick accent. German."

"Who is he, Uncle Arthur?" Bob asked.

"If we stand here talking," hissed Arthur Lindemann angrily, "you will find out soon enough who he is—from his friends. I tell you, *we must go!*"

"Where do you want to go, Mr. Lindemann?" asked Moira.

The old man glanced back and forth between Bob and Moira, his eyes narrowing. "Why not pick up the package from my desk?" he asked Bob. "It is still there, just as you left it."

"That would be dangerous. To go into that building—"

"What's he talking about?" asked Moira.

"A million dollars," said Bob.

"Oh, no," protested the old man. "Not nearly so much."

Moira's chin rose slowly. "What would be the salvage fee?" she asked.

Their taxicab stopped at the curb, and Moira slipped out of the back seat. Bob extended a hand to her from the front seat, and she took it and squeezed it before the cab rolled away.

Arthur Lindemann had agreed to give her a thousand dollars from the package in his rolltop desk if she could retrieve it and bring it down to the street. He had given her keys: one to the night entrance to the building, one to the Deutsch, Lindemann offices, and one to his desk. If she were caught by a watchman, she was to say she had gotten drunk in the offices and had been left there by Griffin Bailey. Any watchman with experience in the building would know Bailey sometimes brought girls to his office in the middle of the night. The fact that Moira had a record of two arrests for prostitution would give her story additional credibility with the police, if it came to that.

If she were caught with the money, then she was to lead the watchman or the police out to the taxicab. Arthur Lindemann promised to acknowledge that he had sent her to his office, if he had to.

The taxicab cruised the streets of lower Manhattan, allowing Moira twenty minutes to complete her mission before it returned to the curb before the building.

"You know who killed my father," Bob said quietly to Arthur Lindemann.

The old man glanced nervously at the driver. He shook his head. "I swear I don't," he whispered. "I told your mother. I don't even know he *was* killed. It was a shock—"

"All of you are involved in the Northern United thing," Bob went on. "Not just my father."

Arthur Lindemann nodded. "All of us."

"The German that Moira drugged . . . he works for Baron von Schwartzberg?"

"I suppose so, indirectly. I don't know, but who else could he be working for?"

"Why was he in the house?"

"To protect me, they said. Two of them came and brought me home from the hospital. They said my partners had sent them and that they would leave a man with me, twenty-four hours a day for a few days, to protect me from another burglary. I was too confused to question them."

"How long did it take you to figure out they were not there to protect you?"

"When I saw they had cut the telephone wire in my bedroom, I knew I was a prisoner in my own house. They searched. They were quite slow and methodical about it."

"What were they looking for?"

"They didn't say."

A tank truck rumbled by, washing down the street with a great flood of water. After it passed, the wet pavement gleamed with reflections from lights still burning at midnight in the buildings that pressed close on both sides. A derelict rummaged hopelessly through a trash can. At the open door of a delicatessen, a delivery man stood and smoked a cigarette, taking a break from carrying in cartons of bread.

"How did you know someone was in the house with me?" Arthur Lindemann asked suddenly. "You must have planned to knock him out. You didn't bring a girl supplied with knockout drops just by chance."

"A policeman told me," said Bob.

"Not Murphy, surely?"

"No. Another policeman is keeping an eye on things. An honest policeman."

"Most of them are honest," said the old man gravely.

The driver had been watching the time, apparently, for when the twenty minutes was up, he slid the cab to the curb in front of the building, exactly on time. Moira appeared immediately, grabbed the door, and entered the car in a breathless hurry.

"Grand Central Station," she said firmly to the driver.

Arthur Lindemann frowned and gaped. "Did you get it?" he asked anxiously.

"No. I'll tell you why later," she said, casting a suggestive eye in the direction of the driver.

"Why Grand Central?" Bob asked, leaning over the back of the front seat to ask the question and hear the answer.

"Tell you later," she grunted between clenched teeth.

Moira took her cigarette holder and a package of cigarettes from her purse, and with trembling hands she lit herself a smoke. All the way from Wall Street to Grand Central Station, her face remained grimly uncommunicative behind the small orange point of fire at the tip of her cigarettes.

They left the cab at the Forty-second Street entrance to the station and walked down the long ramp into the great cavernous building, where, even after midnight, people slept on the benches, ate from brown paper bags, and still hurried to and from the tracks, in and out of the station.

"Why Grand Central?" Bob asked again.

"Get another cab," said Moira. "We don't want that driver to know where we're going."

"Why? What's going on?" demanded Arthur Lindemann. "Why didn't you get the money?"

Moira stiffened, lifted her chin high, and drew a noisy but shallow breath. "You didn't tell me what I might find in that office," she said.

"What? What did you find?"

"A body," she said. "A corpse."

"My God! Who?"

She shrugged and shook her head. "I don't know."

"What did it look like? Describe it."

"You crazy? I didn't stay around for a close look. It was dark in there, and the man was lying on his face on the floor."

"Griffin Bailey," said Arthur Lindemann fearfully. "Or Austin Brinker."

"I think we'd better call O'Shaughnessy," said Bob.

"I think we'd better get out of town," said Moira. "I was

in that building at midnight. By morning that cab driver is going to know someone was killed there tonight—"

"But he doesn't know who we are," Arthur Lindemann interrupted.

"You think not?" asked Moira impatiently. "How many old men with black homburgs sitting on top of heads wrapped in bandages does a driver haul around in the middle of the night? If that driver goes to the police and describes the passengers who dropped off a girl and picked her up later—"

"We'll go to Washington," said Bob decisively.

"Must we run?" the old man asked weakly. "We've done nothing wrong."

"I don't want to find myself in the custody of Sergeant Murphy, even for half an hour," said Bob. "This can be straightened out, but it will be better if it's straightened out with us at a distance."

"Washington," said Moira glumly. "I know the Roosevelts will be overjoyed to see us."

"You are. . . ? You are a *prostitute?*"

"Yes, ma'am," said Moira.

"But . . . but *why?*" asked Mrs. Roosevelt. "I mean, why would you choose such a life?"

"Before you and Mr. Roosevelt came to the White House," said Moira calmly, "there was, you may recall, a depression. Five years ago, it was more than a little difficult to make your way in this country."

"Oh, my dear!" exclaimed Mrs. Roosevelt. "How perfectly awful for you!"

Moira shrugged. She sat with Mrs. Roosevelt and Bob in the President's study on the second floor in the White House. It was late morning, and Mrs. Roosevelt had interrupted her schedule to receive them and had arranged for coffee and Danish to be served. Moira still had on the black dress and jacket she had worn yesterday afternoon, when she had come to the Hannahs' apartment in Manhattan and had heard Bob's proposition that she join him in his second entry of the Lindemann house. She had had no sleep, except for a few uneasy minutes of drifting off on the drive down from New York to Washington. Her eyes were heavy and dark-rimmed, and she munched gratefully on a cheese Danish.

Bob was unshaven, and his suit rumpled. He had managed to sleep a little in the car, which had been driven by Bledsoe. Arthur Lindemann had collapsed entirely during the trip, to the point where they thought he might need to be hospitalized. On the outskirts of the capital city he had revived and said he would be perfectly all right if only they could find him a hotel room and let him bathe and sleep. He was asleep in the Willard Hotel now, watched over by Bledsoe.

"I have listened with sympathy," said Mrs. Roosevelt to Moira, "to the proposals of groups who want to establish schools for girls who feel compelled to enter your . . . occupation. With education, they—"

"Uh, Mrs. Roosevelt," said Bob. "Moira is a graduate of Wellesley."

"Oh. Well . . ."

"It is a kind thought, ma'am," said Moira. "Let me encourage you. Most of the girls need that kind of help."

"Ah," said Mrs. Roosevelt, regaining her composure, smiling again. "Perhaps we can talk about it another time. For now—"

"I would be grateful if you would telephone Mayor La Guardia," said Bob.

"Yes, of course. As you mentioned when you called. And I will tell him. . . ?"

"First, ask him who was found dead in the Deutsch, Lindemann offices this morning," said Bob.

"Oh! Not another murder?"

"Another one of the partners in the firm, likely," Bob said. "Moira went to the firm offices last night, entirely properly, on an errand for Arthur Lindemann—carrying keys he provided—and she found a body lying on the floor in the outer office."

Mrs. Roosevelt drew a deep breath. "I see. I will place the call."

The Mayor, although not in his office, was located to take a call from the White House. Mrs. Roosevelt told him of the body—though not who found it—and asked him who it was.

"Nobody told me anything about any corpse in the Deutsch, Lindemann offices!" squawked Mayor La Guardia through the telephone line from New York. "And they *would* tell me. You can believe, they would tell me."

Mrs. Roosevelt heard him shouting in his office, ordering someone to check with the police department.

"I can tell you something else, though," said the Mayor. "Arthur Lindemann is missing. He disappeared from his home last night. No one knows where he is."

"I know where he is, Mr. Mayor," said Mrs. Roosevelt. "You need not trouble your police force to look for him. He is quite safe and quite well, and he is where he is because that is where he wants to be."

"And that is *where?*"

"Well, let us not be too specific about it," she said calmly. "He is here in Washington."

"O'Shaughnessy will be relieved."

"Thank Sergeant O'Shaughnessy for his concern and tell him Mr. Lindemann is quite safe."

"This body, this body!" yelled the Mayor into the long-distance line. "No one here knows anything about any body."

Mrs. Roosevelt turned to Bob and Moira and said quietly—"They haven't found any body in the Deutsch, Lindemann offices."

Bob looked at Moira. "You are sure you saw a body?"

She nodded. "Lying on the floor in the reception room. It wasn't somebody taking a nap."

"There was a corpse on the floor of the reception room at Deutsch, Lindemann, about midnight last night, Mr. Mayor," said Mrs. Roosevelt. "I have it on reliable authority."

"Did that little bastard break into those offices again?" the Mayor demanded.

"No. I have it from another witness, who was in the office quite legitimately. It would be well to check as to the whereabouts of the other Deutsch, Lindemann partners."

"I'm doing that right now."

Bob whispered to Mrs. Roosevelt—"Ask him if O'Shaughnessy could identify the man he found unconscious in the living room at Uncle Arthur's house."

"Did Sergeant O'Shaughnessy go to Mr. Lindemann's house last night?" asked Mrs. Roosevelt.

"Yes. As soon as he discovered that young Hannah wasn't at home at two in the morning. He figured maybe Hannah had gone to the Lindemann house again—and got himself in trouble again."

"Who was the man he found unconscious in the living room?"

"Who. . . ? *What man?* Mrs. Roosevelt, for God's sake! What man is *this* supposed to be? How many corpses and unconscious guys you got?"

"Sergeant O'Shaughnessy found no man?"

"No. No. The place was deserted."

Mrs. Roosevelt glanced with a skeptical eye at Bob and

Moira. "No one was found unconscious in the Lindemann living room. No corpse was found in the Deutsch, Lindemann offices. We seem to be dealing with very tidy criminals, Mr. Mayor."

"Not so tidy," said Mayor La Guardia. "In confidence, Mrs. Roosevelt, in complete confidence—including especially from the Hannah kid—I can tell you that Sergeant Murphy has not been very tidy. Two Chinese hookers . . . Excuse me. Two Chinese *prostitutes* have identified Sergeant Murphy as the man who asked a lot of questions in Chinatown about the old night watchman, Greschner—especially about him meeting a young fellow in a joint called Gum Loo. Seems Greschner was a friend of these girls, spent something from his pay on them every week, and they don't like what happened to him. Murphy may have put his neck in a noose. We're not moving in on him yet, which is why this is in confidence. With a little luck we may be able to stick him with the murder of Greschner, but what's really important is to be able to stick that on Jim Cote and his gang. Teach 'em to cheat the city of New York out of thousands . . ."

"Well, thank you, Mr. Mayor," she said. "We must keep in touch."

"You're telling me you have Lindemann there," said the Mayor. "You've *seen* him?"

Mrs. Roosevelt frowned. "Uh, yes indeed. He is altogether well. You need not be concerned."

Bob waited until she had returned the telephone to its cradle, then said, "Thank you, Mrs. Roosevelt."

She settled a severe stare on him. "I have put my neck out very far for you, Bob," she said. "If you have told me anything but the complete truth, you have created an extremely difficult and embarrassing situation for me. I, uh, am a little sorry I shall not be present to hear you explain Moira to Adriana."

Moira smiled, at first tenuously, then her smile spread into a grin, and finally she laughed.

* * *

Peering from beneath his brows and over his eyeglasses, Joseph Kennedy favored Mrs. Roosevelt with a faint, restrained smile. "More than I thought," he said. "More than I had expected."

"The cryptic writing means something, then," said she.

"Yes."

They had met in her office, late in the afternoon. She sat at her breakfront desk, with the chair turned to face him. He returned to her the slip of paper from Alfred Hannah's home desk, and once more she frowned over the cryptic note:

Schw Kr Z—272287248

"It is not so difficult," said Kennedy. "The letters *S-C-H-W K-R* mean Schweizerische Kreditanstalt, otherwise known as Crédit Suisse. It is an important bank, in Switzerland. *Z* stands for Zurich—the Zurich office. The number is of course an account number, the number of a confidential account."

"It is true, then, that Alfred Hannah had a secret account in a Swiss bank," said Mrs. Roosevelt quietly.

"Yes and no," said Kennedy.

"Yes and no?"

He nodded. "Let me explain. Anyone with the number can have full access to the account and will be given any information about it he may request. I telephoned a former associate of mine in Zurich and asked him to go to the office of Schweizerische Kreditanstalt, to inquire as to the status of the account. Because he had the number, the bank answered all his questions. It seems that Alfred Hannah was not the only one who had access to account number 272287248. So did a Zurich lawyer named Friedrich Grossenstadt. Either of them could withdraw funds. The week before Alfred Hannah's death, still another man, not Hannah obviously but not Grossenstadt either, appeared at the bank, had the number, withdrew all the funds, and closed the account."

"How much money?" asked Mrs. Roosevelt.

"One million dollars," said Kennedy. "Actually, the equivalent in Swiss francs."

"So Alfred Hannah *was* secreting his profits in—"

"Uh, a premature conclusion, if you will forgive me," Kennedy interrupted.

"How so?"

"The total number of transactions with respect to this account was two: a single deposit of one million dollars, made in December of last year by Grossenstadt, then the single withdrawal the week before Alfred Hannah's death. It seems like an odd way to stash illegal profits—I mean, all at once, and in an account to which someone else had access."

"Who is this man Friedrich Grossenstadt?" asked Mrs. Roosevelt.

"A Zurich lawyer. Rather prominent. His clientele seems to include a great many businesses that are engaged in international transfers of funds."

"Baron von Schwartzberg?" she asked.

"We don't know."

"It would, I suppose, be futile to attempt to learn anything from Herr Grossenstadt."

"I am afraid so."

Mrs. Roosevelt clasped her hands and put her two index fingers to her lips. "Well . . ." she mused. "What significance do you attach to the attack on Arthur Lindemann?"

"A warning," said Kennedy bluntly. "They burned down Fiske's house, they slugged poor old Arthur Lindemann—"

"And put a bully in his house to hold him prisoner," she added. "It makes no sense."

"To prevent someone from talking to him maybe," said Kennedy.

"Who?"

"I suppose one could guess Bob Hannah," said Kennedy. "In any event, it didn't work. Do you want to talk with Mr. Lindemann?"

"Yes. Where is he?"

Mrs. Roosevelt licked her lips. "This is highly confidential, Joe," she said. "You must not breath a word to anyone. I mean, *anyone*."

Kennedy nodded gravely. "You have my word."

"The President and I are leaving for Hyde Park tomorrow. For a Fourth of July holiday, you understand. Mr. Lindemann is in fear of his life, so we are taking him with us, on the presidential train. We will let him live at Val-Kill Cottage for a while. Why don't you take the train with us? Surely you are going to New York or Boston for the Fourth? You can go that far with us and have plenty of time to interview Mr. Lindemann on the train."

"I shall be honored," said Kennedy.

At eight, Mrs. Roosevelt, gowned in white silk, sat at dinner at an elegantly appointed table in the gracious Georgetown home of Ambassador Jennings Brooke. Home from The Hague for consultations, the Ambassador had reopened the house and was mending his political fences with a series of dinners and balls. Conversation came at her from both sides and from across the table, simultaneously, and Mrs. Roosevelt smiled bravely and tried to sort it out.

The President was in his glory. Grinning and chuckling, he was exchanging quips with Bernard Baruch. Ambassador Brooke and Secretary Hull nodded and laughed—though Mrs. Roosevelt had to wonder if either of them understood half of what they were laughing about, since the President and Baruch had a store of little private jokes that were entirely mysterious to anyone but the two of them. As the waiters cleared the appetizers from the tables, the President stuck a Camel in his holder and lighted up a quick smoke between courses.

Sitting to Mrs. Roosevelt's right was the bullet-headed Texan Sam Rayburn, Chairman of the House Interstate Commerce Committee. She wondered at his presence, for it was known in Washington that Sam Rayburn never went to parties. His great, hard face grim and unmoving, he responded when she spoke to him but otherwise had said almost nothing from the time they sat down together. He was an important congressman, one of the President's most effective supporters on Capitol Hill, and she wanted to make pleasant talk with him. It was not easy.

"Mr. Rayburn," she said, "I don't believe I've met the man sitting over there near the door, the one with gold-rimmed spectacles."

Rayburn glanced at the man she indicated. "That's the new senator from Missouri," he said. "The Pendergast man. Harold Truman."

"Oh," she said. "Yes. He seems to be all alone."

"He will be, till he proves himself," said Rayburn laconically.

"Because of the Pendergast connection?"

Rayburn nodded. "He's got a row to hoe."

To her left sat thin, white-haired Justice Louis Brandeis, a little feeble at seventy-nine but—as she had heard repeatedly—still as sharp of mind as ever, still a formidable judge. It was easier to talk with him, and they discussed the Schechter case briefly, then the changing philosophy of the New Deal, and finally the growth of ugly anti-Semitism in Europe.

"Do you think, Mr. Justice," she asked, "that the industrialists of the Thyssen group are themselves anti-Semites?"

Justice Brandeis shrugged. "If you lend your support to an anti-Semitic political party, perhaps to the extent of making its electoral victory possible when it would otherwise have been impossible, then I would define you as yourself anti-Semitic," he said. "It ain't no very subtle distinction," he added with a wry smile.

"I ask," she said, "because I've heard the name of Baron von Schwartzberg very frequently of late."

"In conjunction with the matter of Alfred Hannah," said the Justice.

"Yes. You know about that?"

"About Alfred Hannah? No. I know almost nothing about him. I do know something, however, about von Schwartzberg. Certain of my friends keep an eye on Thyssen and his group. If there are connections between German Nazis and American fascists, we want to know about it."

"Do you think it possible," she asked, "that some of the money von Schwartzberg invested in the Nazi Party was profit from American business ventures?"

"It would be difficult to find out," said Justice Brandeis. "These people are very skilled and experienced at covering their tracks."

"So far as I know," she said, "the SEC has been unable to connect von Schwartzberg with anything specific."

"Except, of course, for BAE in New York."

"BAE? I'm sorry, I don't think I've heard of it. What does it stand for?"

"Bremener Ausfuhr-Einfuhr," said the Justice. "Bremen Export-Import. That's von Schwartzberg's New York front."

"Joseph Kennedy doesn't seem to know that."

Justice Brandeis smiled tolerantly. "Well . . . Joe doesn't know everything. Maybe he has never had the occasion some of my friends have had to want to know."

Mrs. Roosevelt picked up her glass and took a small sip of cool white wine. "What more can you tell me about this export-import company, Mr. Justice?"

"Very little, I'm afraid," said Justice Brandeis. "It was

very carefully organized some years ago to facilitate the anonymous movement in and out of this country of some of von Schwartzberg's men and Reichsmarks. It is a Delaware corporation. It has all the correct licenses. It is operated very circumspectly. I suspect, however, that it is involved in matters a great deal more important than importing German cameras and toys into the United States."

"I will see that it is looked into," said Mrs. Roosevelt.

The Justice nodded somberly.

"I, uh, am sorry if I have seemed to cross-examine you on the subject, Mr. Justice," said Mrs. Roosevelt. "I'm afraid my interest is rather personal."

"So is mine," said the Justice dryly.

"Because of the anti-Semitism—"

"For that and for a more personal reason," said Justice Brandeis. He sighed. "You see, Holmes brought a young man from Yale to the Court a few years ago, as a law clerk. We all befriended him. I did, especially, even though he was not my clerk. It was personally distressing to me, later, to learn that this young man, as a practicing lawyer in New York, did all the law work to set up this export-import company, which frankly I regard as a front for the Nazis. That's how Holmes saw it, too, and he felt betrayed. He never mentioned that young lawyer's name again after he found out."

"Ah," said Mrs. Roosevelt. "What *is* the name?"

Justice Brandeis tossed his head, and his white hair flew. "The lawyer? His name is Fontaine Pickering. Fontaine Pickering . . ."

"Pickering?" asked Mrs. Roosevelt in a half voice. "Have you ever heard of a young lawyer working for the SEC called *Lionel* Pickering?"

"Brothers," grunted Justice Brandeis.

18

At nine the next evening, the President and Mrs. Roosevelt traveled in a small, slow motorcade from the White House down Fifteenth Street to the Bureau of Printing and Engraving. The presidential Pullman car was waiting at the loading dock at the Bureau, and it was there that they boarded the train—Arthur Prettyman, the President's valet, wheeling him aboard as usual. Ordinarily, the President retired shortly after he boarded. He slept well in the slow-moving train as it rolled through the night toward New York, and he looked forward to quiet nights on the swaying car. Tonight would be different. The rear compartment was crowded with people who had boarded earlier. Mrs. Roosevelt had arranged what the President had already named "a confrontation" aboard the train.

Joseph Kennedy was there. The President greeted him with a warm smile. Kennedy introduced Arthur Lindemann, who impressed the President as a tired old man looking pale and uncertain and shaky. Bob Hannah pressed forward a shy, dark-haired girl and introduced her. Her name was Moira Lasky, and to the President she looked like anything but what his wife had warned him she was. Someone had told Missy, too, and she was unable to conceal her curiosity and stared at the dark-haired girl more than good manners would have allowed. Adriana was seated on a couch, beautiful as ever but tonight bristling with annoyance. Standing behind Lindemann's chair when he sat down again was a burly man no one bothered to introduce. The President quietly asked who he was and was told he was Harry Bledsoe, Bob Hannah's bodyguard.

It was not easy for the President to pretend that all these people were welcome, but he tried, and probably none of them suspected how much he would have preferred to be alone. He gave orders for drinks to be served as soon as the train was underway, and he leaned back, lighted a cigarette, and tried to be comfortable.

Bob Hannah came to the President's side. "I am forever in your debt, Mr. President," he said.

"May I count on that making a Democrat of you?" asked the President with a grin.

Bob smiled. "Yes, sir."

The engine began to chuff, and its drive wheels spun and screeched on the tracks as it strained to pull the heavy presidential car away from the dock. It chuffed in angry bursts as the engineer advanced the throttle, then retarded it, then advanced it again, coaxing into motion the twelve cars of the train the railroads called POTUS. Moving smoothly at last, the train threaded its way through the Washington yards. The engineer whistled for a grade crossing.

Mrs. Roosevelt made a point of sitting down beside Moira. She sensed the young woman's embarrassment. Since yesterday, Moira had bought a new dress, and she looked modest and pretty in pale green.

"Are no reporters allowed in this car?" Moira asked quietly.

"No," said Mrs. Roosevelt. "The President is almost conspiratorial about his privacy aboard this train."

"It would make a lot of bad publicity," said Moira, "if it were known who I am and that I am on the presidential train."

"*We* are not worried," said Mrs. Roosevelt.

Adriana and Missy talked together, a little apart. "He

could have sent her back to New York some other way," said Adriana.

"I wouldn't worry about her, Adriana," said Missy. "What she is imposes inescapable limits on her."

Adriana drew a deep breath. "Oh, I'm not worried, really. It's just that I can't *imagine* . . ."

"Neither can I," said Missy. "But who are we to judge?"

Adriana glanced at Moira. "She seems to have courage, anyway," she conceded.

Arthur Prettyman wheeled in a cart with bottles, ice, and glasses; and the President invited the guests to pour their own drinks. For himself, he said, he would be grateful if someone would put a measure of gin in the glass of lemonade Arthur had brought for him.

Bob talked with Kennedy. "No," he told him. "The old boy has turned silent as a stone. Beyond what he told me the first night, I haven't been able to pry a word loose."

"Well, I hope this night turns out to be something better than a free ride to New York," said Kennedy. He reached for a bottle of Scotch on the bar cart and poured himself a generous splash.

Mrs. Roosevelt handed the President his gin and lemonade. "How long do you want me to stay up?" he asked her. "All right if I excuse myself and go to bed?"

"If you get bored," she said.

Switched onto the B & O tracks, the train rolled out into the Maryland countryside—College Park, Beltsville, heading for the Patuxent River bridge at Laurel, settling into the speed it would maintain steadily throughout the night: twenty-five or thirty miles an hour, no more.

Joseph Kennedy sat down facing Arthur Lindemann. Mrs. Roosevelt sat near enough to take part easily in the conversation. Bob Hannah stood behind Arthur Lindemann, leaning on the back of his chair.

"Are you ready to talk to us, Mr. Lindemann?" asked Kennedy.

Arthur Lindemann had accepted a glass of sherry, and his hand trembled and threatened to spill it. "About what, Mr. Kennedy?" he asked in a guarded, almost hostile tone. He glanced around him, noticing that the car had fallen silent, that everyone was listening to him. "What do you want to talk about?"

"I believe Northern United would be an appropriate topic," said Kennedy dryly.

"What do you want to do? Put me in jail?"

"That would much depend, wouldn't it?" said Kennedy. "It depends on how much you have to confess."

"I have nothing to confess," said the old man firmly. "I have made errors perhaps, but I—"

"Why were you virtually kidnapped from the hospital?" Bob interrupted. "Why are you afraid right now? Why are you afraid to go home? Or to your office? Who are you afraid of?"

"Those Germans . . ." the old man whispered.

Bob raised a finger and opened his mouth, but he was stopped by a severe frown from Joseph Kennedy, supported by Mrs. Roosevelt's reproving stare.

"We know some things about your business, Mr. Lindemann," said Kennedy. "We know that your firm has participated in the transfer of funds and stocks from public contractors to public officials in the city of New York. You have maintained accounts in fictitious names to facilitate such transfers. For example, a great deal of money passed from A. G. DeLoach and Company to Judge James Cote, through fictitious accounts in your office. Is it crude of me to call that graft?"

"I've done nothing illegal," protested Arthur Lindemann. "If the names on those accounts were fictitious, no one told me so."

"Still, you knew," said Kennedy.

The old man shrugged. "A broker is under no obligation to inquire into the identity of people who buy and sell securities. The securities were valid. We received them and sold them and put the funds in the accounts that had been established. The funds were withdrawn—"

"By Judge Cote," said Kennedy brusquely. "So in effect a public official received a large amount of money from a public contractor—which is called graft."

"Which may be," said Arthur Lindemann. "But I was not a participant. I only received and sold stock. No one told me the profits were a payoff."

"A nice distinction," said Mrs. Roosevelt.

"One that is constantly and traditionally made on the Street," said Arthur Lindemann.

"By my father?" asked Bob.

Arthur Lindemann looked up over his shoulder at Bob, who remained standing behind him. "Your father was never involved with DeLoach and Cote."

"With anyone else? With anything like that?" Bob demanded.

The old man drew a deep breath and let it out in a long, noisy sigh. "Is it your idea," he asked, "that Al Hannah was some kind of saint? If so, I am sorry for you. He was a shrewd businessman. Aggressive . . . tough. No, he was not involved with DeLoach and Cote, but in his files you will find transactions not dissimilar."

"And that," said Joseph Kennedy, "brings us to his role in the Northern United collapse."

Arthur Lindemann sighed again. "The indictment charged him with larcenous fraud. That was a gross exaggeration. I for one was confident he would be acquitted."

"Why was he killed?" Bob asked.

"I don't know."

"The Germans," said Kennedy. "The von Schwartzberg group. What was their part in the Northern United business?"

"They were investors," said Arthur Lindemann.

"Big investors?"

The old man nodded.

"In secret?"

"Yes."

Joseph Kennedy glanced at Mrs. Roosevelt, then at the President. "May we assume, then, that these German investors lost their investment in the collapse, like everyone else?"

A bitter smile, fleeting and imperceptible to all but those who were staring hard at him, came across Arthur Lindemann's face. "You may assume the contrary," he said quietly.

The President spoke. "Mr. Lindemann," he said. "Why must we continue to pry this story out of you in bits and pieces? Why don't you just tell us what happened?"

Arthur Lindemann's eyes shifted from the President to Joseph Kennedy. "If you work long enough and hard enough, you will untangle it all," he said. He looked again at the President. "The story is neither short nor simple. It began not very long after the War ended, before the treaty was signed at Versailles, in fact. At first, these Germans simply wanted to secret some funds in the States, to put them beyond the reach of the communist regime they expected to come to power in Berlin. Later they wanted to protect themselves from the big German inflation. Still later, they wanted to hedge their bet on the Nazis. Anyway, at first they were just investors. But they placed a lot of money here, and they were in a position to demand special consideration."

"From Deutsch, Lindemann, you mean," said Kennedy.

"From Deutsch, Lindemann and other brokerage houses," said the old man. "Their demands became so great that some houses refused to deal with them further."

"But you didn't."

"No. About 1924 they became interested in utility holding companies as a means of making large profits." The old man paused and glanced up at Bob. "They could not have done better than to work with Alfred Hannah on that. It was his specialty. They were Griffin Bailey's clients, really, but Griff asked Al to work with him. They began to build the tangle. There were two tangles, actually—the holding-company structure itself and the complex of trading corporations with which the Germans concealed their interest. It is very complicated."

"What was *your* role?" asked Mrs. Roosevelt.

"I am the senior partner," said Arthur Lindemann. "I knew what they were doing."

"Making immense profits from a huge fraud," said Kennedy bitterly.

"No," said Arthur Lindemann. "Any holding-company structure is organized to concentrate the profits at the points where the chief investors can reap them; but in the Northern United case there was no fraud until very late in the game, and when the fraud occurred neither Griffin Bailey or Alfred Hannah was involved in it."

"How can you say that?" asked the President.

"If there was fraud," said Arthur Lindemann, "it consisted of taking dividends out of corporations in the structure when there were no profits from which to pay dividends. That is what the Germans did; they controlled the boards of directors of half a dozen companies and voted dividends that drained those companies—and ultimately the whole structure—of essential funds. That is what caused the collapse, and neither Griffin Bailey nor Alfred Hannah could have prevented it."

"They had lost control, in other words," said Bob.

The old man shrugged. "They never had control. They were the architects of the holding-company structure, not the owners."

"How much money did the Germans skim off?" Kennedy asked.

Arthur Lindemann shook his head. "I don't know. Fifty million, I would guess. Maybe more."

"And transferred all of it out of the country . . ."

"Maybe not."

"Why did my father continue to invest in the stock?" asked Bob.

"I'm afraid he was trying to build himself a plausible defense," said Arthur Lindemann. "If he continued to invest money in the structure, he could perhaps convince investigators or a jury that he had not known the structure was being looted."

"But if he was innocent, why did he need to build a defense?"

The old man turned down the corners of his mouth. He shook his head. "I don't know," he muttered. "Any more than I know how he died. If you'll excuse me for a moment, I must visit the bathroom."

Moira had sat listening, her lips apart, absorbed; and at this point, by chance, involuntarily, her eyes happened to meet Adriana's. Adriana closed her eyes for a moment, then opened them and met Moira's gaze. She let herself smile faintly. Moira moved to sit beside her.

Mrs. Roosevelt turned to the President. "Are you bored?" she asked quietly.

The President chuckled and tossed his chin. "Not yet," he said.

"Joe," said Mrs. Roosevelt. "I'd like to speak with you."

She indicated the corner of the car behind the President, and Kennedy rose and joined her there. The President turned and listened, but no one else could hear as she told Joseph Kennedy what she had learned about Lionel Pickering: that his brother was the lawyer who had formed Bremener Ausfuhr-Einfuhr. Kennedy flushed and stiffened but said nothing.

Moira spoke softly to Adriana. "He used to take me to concerts. He was never afraid someone would see us together."

"I don't know what to say," Adriana whispered.

Moira touched her hand. "You don't have to say anything. There's nothing that has to be said."

Adriana glanced up at Bob. "He's going through an awful ordeal."

Joseph Kennedy poured himself another small portion of Scotch. "Does Bob Hannah know about Pickering?" he quietly asked Mrs. Roosevelt, as if it were an afterthought that had just occurred to him. "Does Adriana know?"

"I haven't told either of them."

"Let's don't for the moment," said Kennedy.

The train rumbled over some switches, and the lights of a town flashed in the windows. The President shook another Camel from his package and glanced at his watch. Harry Bledsoe perhaps shared his thought, since he glanced at his own watch, then turned and opened the door of the compartment. If in fact their thought had been that Arthur Lindemann was overdue to return, their concern was misplaced, for the old man walked through the door that Bledsoe had just opened and again took his seat.

"Why don't you tell us about the million dollars, Mr. Lindemann?" said Kennedy.

"What million dollars?" asked Arthur Lindemann.

"The million dollars in the Swiss account," said Kennedy. "The million dollars on deposit with Schweizerische Kreditanstalt in Zurich."

To this moment, Lindemann had shown only annoyed concern in response to their cross-examination. Now his face reddened and his jaw trembled. "How do you know about that?" he demanded.

"He left the account number in his desk," said Kennedy. "Bob found it after his death."

"Bob . . . Have you used the number?" Arthur Lindemann asked breathlessly. "Have you gotten out the money?"

"No, I . . . How could I? I—"

"Bob didn't know until this moment that the numbers

he gave me were in fact the numbers for a secret bank account," said Mrs. Roosevelt to Arthur Lindemann. "We suspected it, but not until Mr. Kennedy was able to confirm it—"

"*A million?*" Bob choked.

Mrs. Roosevelt shook her head at him and gestured to him to calm himself.

"Mr. Lindemann," said Kennedy firmly. "Why was one million dollars deposited in a Zurich bank account, accessible by Alfred Hannah?"

For a moment the old man covered his face with his hands. "*You* brought this up. You should have left well enough alone." He lifted his face, turned his head from side to side, and glanced up at Bob. "It was a fund for Al . . . to take care of him."

"Where did the money come from?" asked Kennedy.

"I don't know. It was not mine. The Germans, I guess. Von Schwartzberg."

"That's not a guess, is it?" said Kennedy.

"No," the old man admitted wearily. "Von Schwartzberg's group deposited most of the money. Griff Bailey put in some, too. Or so I was told. Personally, I had nothing to do with it."

"Now," said Kennedy. "You say it was to 'take care of' Alfred Hannah. What does that mean?"

Arthur Lindemann glanced around him, as if to find someone who would come to his defense and tell him he did not have to answer the question. He nodded dejectedly. "They knew," he said quietly, "that an SEC investigation was in progress. Someone in Washington told them. They knew the whole scheme was going to fall apart. Von Schwartzberg did not want his name brought into the investigation. He wanted the whole German connection kept secret. Griff Bailey went to work cleaning the files, to eliminate any documentation that could show the connection. He actually went through *my* papers. He went through Al's, through Austin's, too. The whole point was to limit the damage."

"But they knew there would be damage, and they wanted a fall guy," said Kennedy.

"Yes. They put pressure on Al. They talked him into it. The idea was to focus the investigation on him. He would take the blame, ostensibly be thrown out of the firm, seem to be disgraced, even go to prison for a short time if necessary. And, whatever happened, he would never mention the Germans; he would keep their name out of it. They deposited one million dollars in a secret bank account in Zurich and gave him the number. The idea was that he and his wife could retire to Switzerland when it was all over and live comfortably for the rest of their lives."

"Where is that money now, Mr. Lindemann?" asked Kennedy.

Arthur Lindemann shook his head. "It's there," he said. "In the bank in Zurich."

"It is not there," said Kennedy.

"It *has to be there!*" the old man protested angrily. "That was the arrangement."

"Who besides Alfred Hannah had the secret number?" Kennedy asked.

"No one. It was *his* money, his payment for . . . Oh . . ." The old man began to shake his head. "If they thought he took it prematurely, before he had carried out his side of the deal . . ."

"He was not the only one who had the number," said Kennedy. "A Zurich lawyer named Grossenstadt also had it."

"I never heard of him."

"And someone else besides, who went to the bank and withdrew the entire amount a few days before Alfred Hannah's death."

"They betrayed him!" whispered the old man. "Al was betrayed."

"And murdered," said Bob.

"That I don't *know*," insisted Arthur Lindemann, chopping weakly at the air with his right hand. "But I am afraid it is so."

"Why did they try to hold you prisoner?" asked Mrs. Roosevelt. "What were they looking for in your house?"

"Papers!" coughed Arthur Lindemann. "Documents that might reveal the German connection. I am not sure what they most fear, that our government will find out how much money they took out of the holding companies—or that Herr Hitler will find out."

Before the President retired, Mrs. Roosevelt told him she would leave the train in New York and spend a day in the city, then come on to Hyde Park the following day, to be there with him for the Fourth of July and the weekend. The President offered no objection. In the blinding white light of a hot sun on morning haze, she left the train in the yards, and, accompanied by Joseph Kennedy, was driven to the Waldorf, where a suite had been arranged for her.

Bob Hannah and Moira left the train, too—accompanied by the hung-over Harry Bledsoe. Adriana and Arthur Lindemann remained asleep aboard the train.

Mrs. Roosevelt invited Joseph Kennedy to breakfast in her Waldorf suite, and shortly after eight they sat down over coffee and Danish.

"It was a worthwhile night," said Kennedy. He stood at

the window, looking south on Park Avenue. "With what I know now, the SEC investigation will be far more effective."

"Actually," said Mrs. Roosevelt, "I thought we were only confirmed in our suspicions. I cannot say I am much surprised."

"I am," said Kennedy. "Forgive me, but I am surprised that so many of your suspicions have been confirmed."

Mrs. Roosevelt poured coffee from a silver pot. "You realize, of course," she said, "that we remain in the dark on what are to me the most essential points."

"Who killed Alfred Hannah, you mean," said Kennedy. "We can feel certain it was the Germans, the henchmen of Baron von Schwartzberg."

"But *why*, Joe?" she asked. "Why did they kill him? What we know of their conspiracy does not seem to require them to murder Alfred Hannah. Indeed, it would seem to be contrary to their best interests. I suspect we have not yet plumbed the depths of this mystery."

"We don't know who took the million dollars from the Swiss bank account," he said, turning away from the window and returning to his chair, where he picked up a cup of hot black coffee.

"We don't know whose body Moira Lasky saw in the Deutsch, Lindemann offices," added Mrs. Roosevelt.

"Or why, really, they knocked poor old Arthur Lindemann on the head. We don't in fact know that the people who did that are the same ones who came to the hospital and got him and held him prisoner."

"I will mention something else that arouses my curiosity," said Mrs. Roosevelt. She put down her cup and sighed. "What is in that safe in Arthur Lindemann's house? And why is Bob so obsessed with finding out?"

Joseph Kennedy chuckled quietly. "I am afraid we have much to learn," he said. "But can we take our Fourth of July holiday and turn our thoughts to it next week?"

"I hope so," said Mrs. Roosevelt. "I look forward to a quiet few days at Hyde Park, as soon as I soothe Mayor La Guardia and put a rope around Bob Hannah."

"A rope . . . ?"

She smiled broadly. "He has promised to come to Hyde Park tomorrow. If he does not, Adriana will hold me responsible; and I should prefer listening to a harangue by Huey Long to facing the long-faced silence Adriana can affect."

She had time to bathe and refresh herself with talcum and cologne before the telephone rang and Sergeant Patrick O'Shaughnessy told her he was in the lobby and ready to come up to her suite.

"Ah," she said when he was in the doorway. "The Mayor—"

"The Mayor is on a boat circling Manhattan," said O'Shaughnessy. "After which he goes to Ebbets Field for a Dodgers game. Van Lingle Mungo is pitching, and the Mayor is taking the afternoon off to see him. He sends his apologies, but he did not expect you in town today."

"*I* did not expect to be in town today," she said.

"I have something a little embarrassing to tell you," said the big florid Irishman.

"I am not easily embarrassed," said Mrs. Roosevelt with a measured smile.

"I hope not," said O'Shaughnessy. "It has to do with a young woman I understand came to Washington with Bob Hannah."

"Moira Lasky?"

O'Shaughnessy nodded. "Yes. I am afraid she—"

"She is a call girl," said Mrs. Roosevelt. "Is that what you wanted to tell me?"

"Uh, yes . . . it is. She has an arrest record. Uh, she spent a few days in jail last year. I—"

"I know," said Mrs. Roosevelt.

"I, uh, have never met her," said O'Shaughnessy. "I . . . we, uh, pulled the file. She has, uh, nothing else on her record. She has no FBI sheet."

"It was Moira Lasky," said Mrs. Roosevelt, "who found the body in the Deutsch, Lindemann reception room. She entered quite legally, with a key afforded her by Arthur Lindemann. He sent her on an errand, which she did not complete when she found a corpse lying on the floor."

"Oh, yes. The body," said O'Shaughnessy. He shook his head. "We have no idea who it could have been. Frankly, we are inclined to discount the story. The young woman, after all—"

"—is a prostitute." Mrs. Roosevelt completed his sentence.

"Well . . . yes."

"I am inclined to trust her."

"We will continue to inquire," said O'Shaughnessy soberly.

"Have you arrested Sergeant Murphy?"

"No. But we have some more information about him."

"An ugly man, Sergeant Murphy," observed Mrs. Roosevelt. "There is a streak of violence in him."

"Violence, yes," said O'Shaughnessy. "We reviewed the autopsy report on the dead night watchman, Greschner. He was severely beaten before he was killed. It seems very likely that Murphy tortured him to find out everything he knew—and then murdered him."

"Which," said Mrs. Roosevelt, "would explain how he knew Bob Hannah entered the Deutsch, Lindemann offices."

O'Shaughnessy nodded. "And some of the other things he knew, he may have found out from the Jim Cote crowd. We've been looking into that. The Mayor says Murphy worked for somebody besides the city. Well, that's who he worked for: Judge Jim Cote and his crowd. Confidentially speaking, the Mayor is about to lower the boom on Judge Cote."

"Sergeant O'Shaughnessy," said Mrs. Roosevelt. "I am going to ask Mayor La Guardia not to . . . lower, uh, not to lower the boom on Judge Cote just yet. We don't want to frighten off the bigger fish, if I may mix my metaphors so awkwardly."

"Well, uh, don't worry about mixing up anything," said Sergeant O'Shaughnessy. "Mayor La Guardia wants to give you his whole cooperation."

She smiled brightly. "I entirely understand," she said.

Sergeant O'Shaughnessy nodded. "There is one thing more," he said. "The *Europa* docked yesterday afternoon. From Hamburg. One of the passengers was Baron Konstantin von Schwartzberg."

Bledsoe's head was aching, and he was feeling nauseous when he and Bob arrived at the Hannah apartment. Moira was still with them, though she had said she could stay only long enough to drink a cup of coffee.

The two men stepped back and allowed Moira to walk first through the door.

"My God!"

Bob pushed past her. The apartment had been ransacked and was in shambles. Furniture had been overturned, upholstery had been cut or ripped. Drawers and cabinets were open and their contents strewn across the floor. Bob wandered, stunned, from room to room. Every room was the same, except perhaps for his father's office, which was worse—more thoroughly torn apart. There, even the carpet had been pulled up, the draperies torn down, pictures ripped from their frames. Sometime during the two days they had been gone, someone had spent hours here, tearing everything to pieces.

"Who could hate you this much?" Moira whispered.

Harry Bledsoe shook his head. "Not hate," he mumbled. "A search. Systematic . . . They didn't miss much."

"What were they looking for?" Bob asked—asked himself, since neither of the others could know as much as he about what had been the object of the search. "What was left to look for? His files—"

"Not files," interrupted Bledsoe. "Something smaller."

"A bank book," said Bob. "A deposit slip. The number for another Swiss account. Anything that would tell where a million dollars went."

"I would have supposed they took it themselves, to cheat your father out of it," said Moira. "If they didn't . . . If they didn't, maybe that explains what they were doing in Arthur Lindemann's house: looking for evidence of where the money went."

Bob paced through the rooms of the apartment that had been his home for the past ten years, shocked by the violation and the senseless damage—glad at least that his mother had not been here to see it. Little things, personal things that could not possibly have held any significance for the men who had broken in and committed this outrage, were scornfully tossed about, broken, for no reason. His father's desk pen set, mounted on a base of black marble—given to him five years ago by Bob's mother—had been thrown against the wall and was shattered. Someone had stepped on one of the pens, crushing it and staining the carpet with ink. His mother's photograph had sat for years on his father's desk, in a silver frame. Now the glass was broken and the picture scarred. Harry could call it a systematic search. It was that perhaps, but it was also a desecration.

Bob picked up the telephone and dialed the special number he had been given by Sergeant O'Shaughnessy.

The doorbell rang before O'Shaughnessy could answer, and Bob put down the telephone and went to the door. Griffin Bailey was there, alone.

"Bob, I—" The sharp, angry voice stopped as Bailey's face stiffened and his eyes widened at the sight of the living room. "I . . . My Lord, what's happened?"

"It's obvious enough, isn't it?" Bob said curtly. "Some friends of yours paid me a visit while I was out of town."

"Friends of mine?" asked Bailey indignantly. "Why friends of mine?"

"Your Kraut chums," said Bob. "But I don't think they found what they were looking for."

"My . . . my what? 'Kraut chums?' Do you refer to your father's and my German business associates?"

"The Huns," sneered Bob.

Griffin Bailey, who was taller than Bob, shook his head and looked down on him with eyes narrowed by concentrated contempt. He was the old Griffin Bailey, the one Bob had known since he was a boy: pallid, spare, haughty, and incapable of concealing his scorn. He was not accustomed to contradiction, and he was unskilled at dealing with it.

"You are an ignorant boy," said Bailey.

"Yes, but I've been chopping away at your shins with my little hatchet," said Bob. "I wondered when you would come to see me."

Bailey looked past him again, surveying the damaged and littered living room. That the sight troubled him, that he had not been ready for it, was apparent.

"I . . . I am looking for Arthur," said Bailey.

Bob shrugged and turned his back on Bailey. "He's not here," he said.

Bailey followed him to the center of the room. "I suppose not. But I am sure you know where he is. You will be very foolish if you don't tell me."

Moira and Bledsoe had returned and stood regarding Bailey with open hostility.

"If I knew," said Bob coldly, "you are the last person I would tell."

"I don't know what motivates you," said Bailey coldly but quietly, trying to talk so Moira and Bledsoe would not hear. "You should listen to me. You have no idea of the extent of your ignorance."

Bob glanced at Moira and Bledsoe, and they took the cue and backed out of the room.

"How much did you make on the Ferguson Laboratories stock?" asked Bailey. "A hundred thousand dollars? Two hundred?"

"Nothing like that," said Bob. "I had to borrow—"

"You're a fool, then," said Bailey. "You could have made a lifetime's fortune. And it would have been in your family tradition. How do you suppose Alfred Hannah became wealthy? Do you have any idea?"

"There is a point to this, I suppose," said Bob.

"Indeed there is. Quit being a fool. You can still be a secure and wealthy man."

"How?"

A cold smile crossed Bailey's face. "Remember where your interests are. Don't forget that the Roosevelt crowd, whom you seem to have befriended, are traitors to their class. Your interests, and your father's, and mine . . . are identical."

"Then why was my father murdered?"

Bailey drew back his shoulders, lifted his chin, and looked down his long, thin nose. "Stupidity," he said. "In the pursuit of identical interests, men often use faulty judgment. I much doubt that you have inherited the predilection. You will be offered an opportunity to demonstrate that you haven't."

"Am I to understand my father's murderers want to make a deal?" asked Bob.

"It is within the realm of possibility," said Griffin Bailey thinly.

"It is within it from this side," said Bob.

"You begin by telling me where Arthur Lindemann is."

Bob shook his head. "You begin by going back to whoever sent you to carry their message and tell them they'll have to do better than send a demand for information. What do they offer? Tell them I want to know what they offer and what safeguards I have against their betraying me like they did my father."

"God help you if you're being stupid," said Griffin Bailey, and he turned on his heel and retreated through the still-open door.

"I am afraid," said Moira.

Mrs. Roosevelt nodded. "So am I," she said.

"I feel powerless. I feel there is nothing we can do."

Mrs. Roosevelt frowned deeply and nodded again. "That is a feeling I do not like," she said.

"He will get himself killed," said Moira.

"Well, I do not intend to stand by and let it happen," said Mrs. Roosevelt decisively.

"We don't dare go to that house. If I encountered that German I gave the knockout drops . . ."

"We dare if Sergeant O'Shaugnessy will go with us," said Mrs. Roosevelt. She reached for the telephone.

Once more Bob stood at the door and peered through the glass into the long center hallway. The house was lighted, in the living room at least, and he thought he saw a light from the bedroom shining yellow on the wall at the top of the stairs. Though Uncle Arthur was not at home, it was obvious that his house was occupied.

Bob glanced nervously around, half expecting someone to bound up the steps from the sidewalk. Again he peered into the house.

As he stared, suddenly a man burst from the living room, pulling a small automatic pistol from inside his jacket. Bob drew a breath, fixed his determination, and threw his weight into a powerful kick against the door. The latch broke from the wood, the door swung back, and the glass shattered and fell.

The man spun toward the door, lowering himself to a crouch and leveling his pistol on Bob. "Ach!" he grunted. "Ach! Halt!"

Bob slowly raised his hands. "Okay . . ." he breathed. "Take it easy."

The man stood. "*Hereinkommen*," he said, gesturing to Bob to come inside. "So. Hannah, *nicht wahr?* Ve expected you." He stepped closer to Bob and felt him for a weapon. "Sooner or later, ve knew you vould come."

"We just bet you did," said Harry Bledsoe as he crashed the butt of his heavy snub-nosed revolver down on the German's skull. The German sank to his knees and fell headlong.

This had been their plan: for Harry to break in at the back door, alerting the German and bringing him into the hall, then for Bob to smash his way in at the front door, monopolizing the man's attention as Harry rushed up to slug him.

"Careful!" snapped Bob quickly. "I think there's another one. Probably upstairs."

Harry glanced up. He nodded. "Some way, I think you're right." He pushed Bob ahead of him, back along the hallway, out of sight and out of the range of fire from anyone upstairs.

They stood in the back part of the hall, silent, listening for a sound from above. They heard a sound, the creak of a loose floorboard.

Harry pointed to the kitchen, to the back door he had opened. "That's our retreat if we need it. It's dark out back."

"I don't want to retreat," said Bob. "We came here to get into that safe."

Harry slipped along the wall and risked a glance up the stairway to the second floor. "What we got here is a Mexican standoff," he said. "If he's armed up there—"

"He's got a phone anyway," said Bob. "He'll call for reinforcements."

"Damn! Damn . . ."

The German on the floor rose to his knees and began to

clutch his head between his hands. His hands came away red with his blood. "*Gott verdammt . . .*" he muttered.

"C'mere, Fritz," said Harry.

The German stared at him, blinking.

Harry aimed his revolver at the German. "I said c'mere. Never mind that automatic. Just kick it back here. How many are upstairs?"

The German raised his eyes. "Nobody upstairs," he mumbled.

"We—*Hold it!*"

A uniformed police officer appeared in the front door, with another behind him.

"God gimme it ain't Murphy," growled Harry.

Others came in through the kitchen. There were four of them. When all four were in the house, Sergeant O'Shaughnessy walked in, followed immediately by Mrs. Roosevelt and Moira.

The safe was intact. If it had been opened, it had been opened with a key and closed again. Bob pushed the long thin key into the lock, as Mrs. Roosevelt stood behind and watched.

O'Shaughnessy had agreed: Bob could open the safe, provided Mrs. Roosevelt was with him as a witness, to see to it that he did not take anything valuable. Downstairs, the two Germans were in custody. They had not been able to offer any satisfactory explanation as to why they were in the Lindemann house—whereas Mrs. Roosevelt had assured Sergeant O'Shaughnessy that Bob had permission from Arthur Lindemann. Moira waited downstairs, too, with Harry Bledsoe, who had helped himself to the rye he found in the kitchen.

"I hope you are right about there being something important here," said Mrs. Roosevelt. "You have risked a great deal to gain entry to this safe."

"There has to be something," said Bob quietly as he

pulled on the handle and the big, heavy door slid out on its smooth bearings.

The oversized file drawer contained no more than half a dozen files, each tidily bound in a bulging red expanding pocket. One by one, Bob pulled pockets from the drawers, untied the ribbon that held them shut, and riffled through the papers inside.

"Canceled checks . . ." he muttered as he looked through one. "Stock certificates," he said as he looked through another. "Looks like stock in old companies that aren't in business anymore." He shook his head. "I wouldn't be surprised to find a stale sandwich in here." He untied the ribbon and opened a third file. "I . . . *Oh, my God!*"

For a long moment he stared silently into the open file pocket; then in a frenzy he began pulling papers from the pocket, scanning them, and tossing them one after another on the rolltop desk. His face turned deep red, and he pulled a succession of noisy breaths, all the while shaking his head.

"What is it, Bob?" Mrs. Roosevelt asked quietly and sympathetically. "What have you found?"

He pulled a big, slightly faded photograph from the file pocket and silently handed it to her. The room was only dimly lighted by the single bulb in Arthur Lindemann's desk lamp, and Mrs. Roosevelt put her hand to her mouth as she stared at the surprising picture. It was of a nude woman: a photograph of a young woman, wearing the broad-brimmed hat that had been stylish twenty years ago, and her shoes and stockings, and nothing else.

"That is my mother," said Bob quietly. "The picture was taken, I suppose, in the next room. He has a studio there."

"Oh, I'm sorry, Bob," said Mrs. Roosevelt. "It is embarrassing."

"Actually, she looks quite happy," he said. "There are others here, several others. And this"—he reached for one of the papers he had tossed on the desk—"is a love letter from my mother to Arthur Lindemann."

"I am sorry we've intruded," said Mrs. Roosevelt. "May I suggest we replace everything in the pocket, put it back in the safe, lock everything up, and go?"

Bob shook his head. "Read this," he said somberly. He handed her another letter. She read a part, only a part:

> *The baby is healthy. We have named him Robert Theodore Hannah. You would be proud of him. You will be proud of him, darling, as you see him grow up. Al is abiding by every word of his agreement and by its spirit also. He speaks of him as his son, as he should—with a great deal of pride, which I cannot believe he could entirely dissemble. In all, Arthur, I think we have made the best of an exceedingly bad situation. If you were free, and if I were, it could have been different. As it is, we must live with what we have done, and I want you to love our son even if you can't acknowledge him.*

Bob picked up, then dropped on the desk, a typewritten document. "This," he said, "is a copy of his will. He leaves me his entire estate."

"You are his son," whispered Mrs. Roosevelt.

Bob was contained and silent on the morning train up the Hudson. He and the First Lady sat alone in one end of the coach. Mrs. Roosevelt knitted and required no conversation from him, and most of the time he stared out the window, although he seemed hardly to notice what was outside: the bleak, littered railroad yards at first, or later the river and the lush green valley.

Harry Bledsoe sat two seats away, with the two Secret Service agents who kept professionally wary eyes on Mrs. Roosevelt. Last night, while Mrs. Roosevelt and Bob were upstairs opening the safe, Bledsoe had stayed downstairs, listening to the interrogation of the two Germans. The first, the one he had slugged, was named Heinrich Gottsmann and was an employee of Bremen Export-Import Company. The one upstairs had turned out to be the man Moira had knocked out with chloral hydrate last week—another employee of the German export-import company, named Hans Braeder. They had insisted they were in Arthur Lindemann's house at his request, to guard against burglary; but Sergeant O'Shaughnessy had refused to accept that and had taken them both into custody.

Mrs. Roosevelt had suggested, without really hoping it would be accepted, that Moira come along on the train and spend the Fourth at Hyde Park. She could stay at Val-Kill. Moira had responded with thanks but had said she had been away too long, that two dozen telephone messages had accumulated with her answering service, and that she had two engagements for this afternoon and evening. Mrs. Roosevelt had also suggested, knowing it would not be accepted, that Joseph Kennedy come to Hyde Park. As she had expected, he had gone along to spend the holiday with his family on Cape Cod.

This train would not pull into the siding at Hyde Park. They would leave it at the station at Poughkeepsie, and Secret Service agents would drive them on to Hyde Park. It was only when the train was slowing for the station stop that Bob finally heaved a sigh and spoke:

"What in the world am I going to say to him?"

"Mr. Lindemann, you mean?"

"Yes. He bears some part of the responsibility for the death of . . . of my mother's husband. He—"

"Bob," she interrupted. "I think you can still call Alfred Hannah your father. After all, he earned your respect and love, did he not, over many years? Isn't that enough to justify the name? You can call both of them your fathers."

"Well . . . Even so, what can I say to Arthur Lindemann?"

"Perhaps," Mrs. Roosevelt suggested, "you should simply tell him what you know and let him speak. Remember, he has been long denied the opportunity to say to you a great many things he has probably been very anxious to say."

Bob nodded and again looked out the window.

Harman Knox, the agent in charge of the detail that had accompanied the President to Hyde Park, was at the wheel of the President's car, which he had brought to the Poughkeepsie station to pick up Mrs. Roosevelt. A second car, a Secret Service sedan equipped with radio communication, waited behind. The agents on the platform and those on the train were experienced in the somewhat delicate technique of letting people approach Mrs. Roosevelt, to greet her, sometimes to shake her hand, without allowing a crowd to press too close around her or to impede her slow progress toward the car. As she made her way, smiling broadly, calling to familiar faces in the small crowd in the station, she glanced back at Bob Hannah and kept gesturing to him to keep near, not to be separated from her.

Harman Knox was a small man but a hard, wiry former athlete whose affability could change in an instant to threatening hostility if he judged someone was pressing too purposefully toward the President or Mrs. Roosevelt. When they were in the car and he had started the engine, he relaxed a little but remained grim and apparently troubled. He drove out of the station, followed by the other car, and only then did he begin to speak.

"We've developed a problem this morning," he said, glancing at Mrs. Roosevelt and also at Bob. "Miss van der

Meer is missing. She left the house before the President and his mother came down for breakfast. The President is deeply troubled, I must tell you."

"Why?" asked Mrs. Roosevelt. "She may have gone for a walk. She—"

"No. The President's concern is about the man who called for her. She went with him. He—"

"Who?" Bob demanded impatiently.

"A Mr. Pickering. Mr. Lionel Pickering."

"I'll kill him," muttered Bob.

"You may have reason," said Mrs. Roosevelt ominously. "There is something you and Adriana don't know about Mr. Pickering."

"I know all I want to know about him."

"I think not. I assume you *don't* know that his brother, Fontaine Pickering, is the attorney for Bremener Ausfuhr-Einfuhr."

"Pickering! Then he . . . All along!"

"Probably," agreed Mrs. Roosevelt.

"And he's got Adriana!" Bob cried in a breaking voice. "*They've* got Adriana!"

"We mustn't assume anything. Maybe he only wanted to talk to her. He was smitten with her, you know. I suspect that was genuine."

"No . . ." sighed Bob, shaking his head. "He was trying to pump her for information—and everything he learned, he was feeding it back to the Krauts in New York. Think of the things he must have reported back to them! Maybe he caused the murder of . . . of my father." He paused, frowned. "How long have you known?"

"I learned it only last week," said Mrs. Roosevelt. "I didn't tell you because you are precipitous, Bob. At times, you've given us cause to doubt your discretion." She touched her hand to her mouth. "I wish, though, I'd told Adriana."

"What can we do? Where do we start?"

Knox spoke. "The President alerted the state police," he said. "We have notified Mr. van der Meer, who has employees checking places where she might have gone if in fact she just went for a walk. Technically speaking, it is not a matter for the Secret Service, but we will assign two agents to it as soon as we reach Hyde Park."

Bob lapsed into a tense, miserable silence as the two cars sped up the highway between Poughkeepsie and the village of Hyde Park. When they turned into the lane leading to the Roosevelt mansion, he stiffened and seemed ready to open the door and jump out of the car before it stopped.

Two New York State Police cars were drawn up before the broad front porch. Bob ran up the steps and entered the house without knocking on the door—Mrs. Roosevelt hurrying behind, clutching her white straw hat to her head.

"We've got this note," said the President. He was in his little Hyde Park office, to the right of the entryway, and he put down the telephone when he saw Bob and Mrs. Roosevelt. "It was handed to the gardener by a man who ran away as soon as he'd delivered it."

Bob took the note, which read:

> *When Lindemann is with us, the girl will be sent home. Let him out on the railroad track just this side of Staatsburg, on the straight stretch. We'll be watching, and if there's anybody in sight, no deal. The girl will walk up to him and tell him where to go. If there is any attempt to interfere, we'll be in a position to shoot. You have till noon.*

"It could be worse," said the President.

"I fail to see how," said Bob despondently.

"She couldn't be far from here," said the President. He pointed at the note, which Mrs. Roosevelt was now reading. "If they're talking about an exchange in the next two and a half hours, she has to be somewhere nearby. In fact, since they don't say *at* noon but *until* noon, that would seem to mean they are prepared to make the trade on a few minutes' notice any time this morning. I can't believe Adriana is more than five miles from this house."

"And what good does that do us?" asked Bob.

"The state police have blocked every road and highway out of the area," said the President. "I've sent for big, detailed maps. Putting it all together, I'd guess there are no more than a very few places where they could be holding her."

Bob shook his head. "They'll kill her if—"

"If it comes to it," said the President, "Arthur Lindemann has said he will go out on the railroad track and exchange himself for Adriana—that is, if we haven't recovered her by the deadline. I'm sure he means it. He's not a bad old fellow, really."

"Franklin," said Mrs. Roosevelt. "We learned last night that Arthur Lindemann is Bob's father."

"Really!" said the President. "Well, he's back in the living room, with Mother. And two police guards. He's given us an option."

"Where's Cornelius?" asked Mrs. Roosevelt.

"Rampaging," said the President. "Stalking up and down the roads with a shotgun. I wouldn't want him to know our plans."

"We *have* plans?" Bob asked.

"Of course we have plans," said the President, almost idignantly. "First, I want to see those maps."

The maps he referred to—topographical and political maps of the region, prepared by the United States Coast and Geodetic Survey—had in fact already arrived and were in the hands of a police sergeant who waited outside the office, unwilling to interrupt the conversation taking place inside the Hyde Park office of the President of the

United States. Hearing them referred to, he brought them
in. The two sheets that covered the Hudson River Valley
from Poughkeepsie to Kingston showed the lay of the land,
its use (woodland, farmland, village, etc.), the roads and
railroads, and, in the rural areas at least, every house and
barn of any consequence.

The President squinted through a large magnifying
glass. "I've lived in this neighborhood all my life," he said.
"Ridden horses over all these roads, in past years. Look
here—" He pointed to a tiny black square on a road running from Route 9 back into the hills east of the river.
"That's the old Overmeyer farmstead. That old stone house
has been abandoned for forty years. Old stone structures
like that don't fall down, though. Suppose you decided to
make a hideout of a house like that . . ."

"You couldn't see the track south of Staatsburg," Bob
objected. "Wouldn't they want a place from which they
could observe the rendezvous point, even through a strong
telescope?"

"Exactly," said the President. "Assuredly they would.
That's why I sent into town for these maps. What we have
to do is identify the places from which they could watch
the track."

"Fifty places," Bob objected, leaning over the President's
shoulder and squinting at the map.

"Yes, fifty houses," said the President. "Fifty if you assume they are holding some family hostage. Four or five if
you assume they are in an uninhabited house or a remote
barn."

Mrs. Roosevelt leaned over the map. "This . . ." She
pointed tentatively at a tiny black square on the map. "The
old Mayfair place?"

"Precisely," said the President. "And the Morgenstern
barn. Van Rensselaer, here." He paused, drew a breath.
"My childhood," he said. "I hunted over these lands. Col-
lected birds and butterflies. Flowers . . . Some of the stuff

in the frames out there. After we went iceboating on the river, I remember coming in and having hot cider with cinnamon . . . in the old Vanderstaat house, here."

Mrs. Roosevelt nodded emphatically. "We ate apples one winter day, marveling they had not frozen in the root cellar."

The President glanced up at Bob. "You see?" he asked. "They are very likely hiding Adriana in a house or barn we know well. And that," he added with confident emphasis, "gives us an advantage."

"We'll set to work on the houses you suggest, Mr. President," said the state police sergeant. "I have enough men to cover them."

"Very carefully," said the President. "Wait for them to come out. These men are capable of killing. Unfortunately, we've seen evidence of that."

Mrs. Roosevelt touched Bob's arm as they left the office where the President was operating his command post with grim enthusiasm. The two of them were supposed to be on their way to speak with Arthur Lindemann, but she tipped her head toward the dining room, and they passed through that room and through the kitchen and out of the house at the rear.

"Are you carrying your pistol?" she asked Bob.

"Yes. And Harry has his."

"Never mind Harry," she said. "You and I. We'll take horses. We can be where the troopers cannot, in the woods and fields; and I have ridden the trails around here for many years and can find ways to look at some of these houses without being seen. Only . . . I require circumspection on your part, no bold, impulsive excursions. We work carefully together or not at all."

Bob nodded. He followed her to the stables, where she ordered the stableboy to saddle two horses. She closeted herself in the tack room for a few minutes and emerged wearing stained and tattered breeches and a workman's blue cotton shirt. Having found no boots, she still wore her low-heeled white summer shoes, and on her head a farmer's high-crowned straw hat.

"Anyway, I'll hardly be recognized if anyone spots us," she said shyly as she raised a foot and thrust it through a stirrup.

The boy had saddled for her the sleek black mare he knew she favored, and for Bob he had chosen the only other really serviceable horse in the stable, a slightly swaybacked bay that had seen better days. Bob had put aside his double-breasted jacket and stuck his pistol in the waistband of his trousers. He pointed to a battered old cap hanging on a peg, and the stableboy handed it to him. Possibly it would disguise him a little.

"The Vanderstaat house first," she said. "It's on the river. They could row across and make their escape on the other side."

She knew the land, as she had said she did. They abandoned the trail very soon after they left the house and rode headlong into what seemed to Bob like an impenetrable thicket. After only a moment of forcing the horses through underbrush, they emerged on the riverbank, in tall grass and stunted brush, and they rode north, passing across the back of two estates without being seen from the houses. If they could do that, he supposed they could approach the Vanderstaat house, which she said was a likely place for the kidnappers to be holding Adriana.

It was better to be moving, to be doing something, even something foolish, if that was what this was, than to sit helplessly in the mansion and wait. He wondered if Mrs. Roosevelt felt that way, too, or if she were only taking him on a wild ride to placate him. He was conscious of the unreality of the whole situation: of riding an aging, swaybacked horse along the banks of the Hudson River, following the ludicrously dressed wife of the President of the United States, in an unlikely search for the girl he loved, who had been kidnapped by men he did not know, for motives he did not understand. The chase had an impetus of its own. Doubtful though he was, he urged the horse forward, following Mrs. Roosevelt, fixing his mind on keeping up with her and wondering which turn she would take next.

She drew her horse to a halt. Bob caught up with her.

"The house," she said, "is there." She pointed ahead and to their right. "All this is grown up now, but in the old days, when we came in from the iceboats, we went up to the house on a walk that followed this ravine. The boathouse is gone. The ice on the river took it away years ago. But you can approach the house from here and come within a few yards without being seen."

He dismounted and tied the horse's reins to a small tree.

"Bob," she said. She touched his arm firmly. "We are here to find out if Adriana is in the Vanderstaat house. If we learn she is, we go back for help. You must promise me you won't try some wild assault."

He nodded.

"I am most serious," she said.

He nodded again.

He set out ahead, and she followed. It was as she had said. In the tangled grass, under the cover of nettles and briars, he could feel from time to time the abandoned paving stones of what had once been a walk laid through this ravine. A freshet of water trickled down the low center of the ravine, and the stones had been laid just to the right, set into the gentle slope of the bank. The house was at first entirely out of sight, but as they came closer Mrs. Roosevelt cautioned him to crouch. Shortly the roof and chimneys, then the upper windows, of the house were in sight when he raised his head.

Near the end of the ravine, he lowered himself to his belly and crawled. When he looked around, he saw to his amazement that Mrs. Roosevelt was crawling behind him, pressed down to the earth and wetting her clothes in the mud, just as he was.

He turned and whispered, "You don't have to do this."

"Adriana has been like a daughter to us," she said reproachfully. "You may be assured that the President would be here, too, if he could."

He parted the weeds that blocked their view of the house and peered at the grounds. "No cars," he whispered.

"I notice," she said quietly, thoughtfully. "It's unlikely they . . . On the other hand, the railroad track is only a quarter of a mile from here. They could—"

"A quick way to find out," he said. From the mud under him he pried loose a rock the size of a goose egg, and lifting himself to his knees, he threw it with an accuracy that surprised him—noisily shattering a window on the side of the house.

"Bob!"

"We don't have time to lie here in the mud wondering."

"But—"

He raised himself and stared at the house. The shattering of the window had produced no reaction from inside. He turned to Mrs. Roosevelt, shrugged, then stood. "I owe the Vanderstaats five dollars," he said.

They scrambled hurriedly back down the ravine to their horses and mounted.

"The van Renssaeler place," said Mrs. Roosevelt. "It is a ruin, and I thought it less likely than this house, but someone in an upstairs window there, looking through binoculars or a telescope, would have a view of the straight stretch of railroad track. I think we should check it next."

"I wish *we* had binoculars," said Bob as he reined his horse around to follow Mrs. Roosevelt.

"It is on the opposite side of the track," she said. "I think we can ride across, even if it does let them see us. They won't recognize me in these clothes, and you look like a farm hand."

They rode away from the river, up the slope of the land toward the embanked railroad tracks, the New York Central line for Hudson and Troy. As they crossed the tracks, Mrs. Roosevelt pointed out the ruin of an old stone farmhouse, standing in a weeded grove atop a knoll on the east side of Route 9. She led Bob across the highway and into a farm lane that passed through a pasture and ended at the boundary of an apple orchard. She turned her horse into the orchard, he followed, and shortly he realized that the trees hid them from the ruined house that was now above them and only two or three hundred yards away.

She stopped and dismounted. "We have to be careful," she said.

The apple trees grew in neat lines, thick with leaves and heavy with small, hard green fruit. If they moved into the open lanes between the lines of trees, they could be seen. So long as they moved from tree to tree, keeping in one row, they were hidden. They tied their horses to a tree and trotted forward, moving closer to the house.

The orchard ended some fifty yards from the untended land that surrounded the knoll and the grove and the house. They could go no closer without being seen. Bob swung himself up into the lower limbs of the next-to-last tree in the row, to try for a better look at the house. He climbed a little higher, among the leaves and apples, and surveyed the scene.

In a moment he dropped down. "There's a car there," he said.

Mrs. Roosevelt shook her head. "There shouldn't be," she said. "No one has lived in the house for fifteen years."

"There's no sign of work, no sign that anyone has begun to clean the place up," said Bob. "There's just a car. A Packard, I think."

"A Packard?" She frowned and licked her lips. "Someone hired to clean up the premises wouldn't come in a Packard. Nor would squatters. No. I think we've found the house

where they are holding Adriana. Of course, we can't be
sure."

"We don't have much time," said Bob, looking at his
watch.

Mrs. Roosevelt took his arm in a firm grip. "You must
not do anything foolish," she said. "We must ride to a telephone and call for help." She pointed toward the far end of
the grove. "The farmer who owns this orchard has a telephone, I am certain. We can have police here in five minutes."

"I'll stay and watch," said Bob decisively.

"You must not try to go in alone," she said, squeezing
his arm tightly. "You *must* not."

"I have to stay and watch, anyway," he said. "What if
they leave?"

"I assume I cannot persuade you to come with me," said
Mrs. Roosevelt. "Nor would there be any point in trying to
extract a promise from you. But I beg you to use your
head, Bob. Please don't do anything foolish."

She turned and trotted away, back toward her tethered
horse.

He heard her horse's hooves, thumping on the soft earth,
the clattering of gravel, as she urged her horse into a gal-
lop and rode for help.

For himself, he knew as well as she did that he would
not simply lie here on the ground in the border of this ap-

ple orchard and wait for someone—likely as not clumsy state troopers—to arrive and establish a standoff. He climbed into the tree and again surveyed the space between himself and the house.

The place was a ruin, as Mrs. Roosevelt had said. It had never burned, but for some reason—perhaps because it was too small—it had been abandoned and allowed to fall into disrepair and decay. Someone had, over fifteen years, broken all the glass out of the windows. The slates had slid down from parts of the sagging roof, leaving great holes where rain could fall into the house. Rose vines that had undoubtedly once been tended and kept as a pride of the house grew now in an untended tangle, spreading over the ground and climbing where they could, onto the front porch, up the chimney, dragging down the old, rotted trellises. Fences were down. What had been a lawn was now a field of weeds.

The weeds and brush, though, had not grown high in the shade of the big trees that surrounded and overhung the house. It would be impossible to crawl through any kind of cover and reach the house unseen by anyone keeping guard.

At least it was not possible on this side. Bob dropped from the tree, retreated some distance back into the orchard, and then worked his way eastward. His thought was that anyone keeping watch from the windows would be more likely to be watching the railroad track, not the lane approaching the house from the east. It was easy enough to circle to the east, out of sight on the lower slope of the orchard, and to approach along a line of trees for a different perspective.

It did not look much different, except that from here he could see a fence row: a line of weeds and brush that grew along the two sides of a ruined fence. To attempt to crawl along that line and approach the house that way would be hazardous; yet he felt compelled. Very likely, Adriana was inside.

Keeping his belly pressed to the earth, he worked his way through the brambles on the fence row, constantly entangled, ripping his clothes, taking painful scratches from the thorns. Much of the brush was blackberry bushes, hung now with red, unripe blackberries. He remembered being told as a boy that snakes often lay in these thickets, hiding from the sun and living off the small rodents that sought shelter in the tangle. He remembered someone saying that copperheads smelled like cucumbers, and twice he was certain he smelled cucumbers. He paused and listened for the movement of a snake. He peered through the tangle at the house. Foot by painful foot, he slipped forward.

The fence row brought him to within ten feet of the big, dark blue Packard. He lay looking at it for a long moment, then, seized by an impulse, he rose to his feet and ran in a crouch to the rear of the car. He knelt behind it then and, clutching his pistol in his hand, waited to see if he had produced any reaction from the house. He had produced none. He thought—maybe imagined—he could hear voices from inside, but he could not be sure.

It was an exposed place, there behind the car—exposed to anyone who came up the rutted lane. He knelt there for a couple of minutes, just the same: the couple of minutes it took him to press one of his keys down into the valve stem on the left rear tire and let out air until it collapsed. Only when he was satisfied that the car was disabled did he slip along its side, now only partially hidden from the house, toward the front bumper.

Pressed to the hot steel of the front fender, he watched the house for what seemed a long time. From the car to the front porch was a matter of some ten yards. If he could trot across those ten yards without being seen, he could crawl along the foundation, in the partial cover of the untrimmed shrubs and roses that grew all around the house. He took off his shoes, tied the laces together, and hung the shoes around his neck. Pistol in hand, he trotted across the open space and dropped into the cover of a ragged old shrub.

Now he did hear a voice. He was sure of it. It was Adriana's voice, making not words but sounds, half groans, muffled expressions of pain and protest. Her voice came to him from the window just above him. Driven, almost unconscious of the risk, he rose and looked in through the open, glassless window.

It was Adriana. She lay on the dusty floor, in the midst of a litter of broken plaster, in what had once apparently been the living room of the little stone house. She lay on her side. Her hands were tied behind her back, her ankles were bound together, and she was gagged with a white rag that was knotted behind her neck and pulled so tightly that it forced her jaws apart. She was in pain, and gagging, and she grunted and groaned and seemed to be pleading with someone out of sight to come and relieve her.

He could not do it. Obviously somewhere in the house there was one man, maybe two, maybe more. He had to hope that the help that Mrs. Roosevelt had gone for would not come. Adriana was a hostage. If whoever was in the house were threatened, Adriana would become a shield, and they would take her away. He looked at her for a moment, but she did not see him. He dropped to his knees.

He began to crawl around the house, finding all the entryways, all the windows. Twice he dared to rise again and look in a window. He saw what he was afraid of: two men in the back of the house, in what had probably been the kitchen, one scanning the railroad track a quarter of a mile away, through binoculars, the other drinking beer from a bottle. He wondered if there were not a third man in the front somewhere—wondered, that is, until he saw the one with the beer abruptly leave the rear window and stride out of the kitchen.

He heard the man's footsteps echoing through the empty house, heard him mutter something to Adriana, heard her try to force a plea through her gag.

If he climbed in, through the window where Adriana was . . . If he shot one of the kidnappers . . . If . . . He would risk her life as well as his own. He raised himself to the window of her room once again and chanced another look.

Adriana had rolled over and now lay facing him. Her white summer dress was soiled with black grime and brown plaster dust, and the skirt was twisted up around her, exposing her silk stockings and her bare legs above them. The man with the beer bottle stood at the front window, shifting his glance from the Packard and the lane in front to Adriana and back—a glance that would certainly have caught Bob when he crouched beside the Packard and then ran from the car to the house, if the man had not gone to the back of the house to have a beer with his companion. Adriana's eyes were on him, and she still tried to beg him for some relief from her bonds. He told her to shut up.

A diversion . . . Bob wondered if he could make a diversion. What if he threw a rock at the Packard? If he hit the Packard with a rock, would the man in front run outside? If he did, what would the man in the rear of the house do? If both of them ran outside for a moment, he could swing himself through the window and be ready to defend Adriana when they came back. He knew he could shoot one. Then . . .

"Willi!"

The one in the rear was yelling.

"Willi! *Kommen Sie hier! Schnell! Sehen Sie mal an!*"

The man at the front window ran for the back of the house. Bob dropped away from the window and fell to his knees outside. The sound of the voices changed. The two men had stepped outside the house at the back.

"Der Alte, nicht wahr?"

"Ich glaube ja."

Bob rose and looked, knowing their attention was fixed for the moment. At first he could not imagine what had aroused them; then he saw—far away, on the long straight stretch of railroad track, a solitary figure trudging northward. He was far away, and it was difficult to see; but Bob recognized him after a moment. It was Arthur Lindemann—still dressed in black homburg, dark blue suit, white shirt, spats on his black shoes, carrying a walking stick—slowly making his way along the railroad track, turning his head, looking all around him, now and then stumbling. He stopped, raised his cane as if to summon someone, looked around, and then trudged forward.

"Schön!" said one of the Germans.

Bob fell to hide himself as one of the Germans set out down the slope toward the tracks, trotting and jumping. The other one returned to the house.

The one who had remained would stay at the back of the house and watch. That was certain. Bob rose, slipped around the house, checked the lane, and, once again carrying his shoes around his neck, walked in the front door.

He was conscious of the click as he pulled back the hammer of his pistol. He slipped into the room where Adriana lay and silenced her with an urgent sign of warning. Her eyes widened, but she ceased even to groan. He slid along the wall, trying to remain out of the line of sight through the door into the kitchen.

Reaching that door, he braced himself and stepped into it. The German did not notice him: his eye was pressed to the telescopic sight of a big, sleek rifle. He had steadied it on the windowsill and knelt, watching his companion approach Arthur Lindemann on the railroad track.

"Put the rifle down," Bob said.

The German's head jerked around; and quickly, in a surprisingly fluid, fast movement, he swung the rifle barrel around and up. Bob squeezed the trigger of his pistol. The shot struck the German in the middle of the chest, and he dropped the rifle and doubled over on the floor.

Bob stepped past him and looked out the window. The other one, Willi, had heard the shot, and from halfway to the track he was now running back to the house as fast as he could come. He had a small automatic in his hand. Bob picked up the rifle, found Willi through the telescope, centered the cross hairs on him, and dropped him as he ran.

Then Bob raced back to the first room, to Adriana.

"Baron von Schwartzberg is here," she told him breathlessly. "I heard them talking."

They had kissed ardently; but now, feeling helpless to offer her any adequate comfort as she stood squeezing and rubbing her chafed wrists, Bob tried awkwardly to knock some of the dirt off her dress. The corners of her mouth were bruised from the tight gag. Her stockings were shredded around her ankles from the rubbing of the coarse hempen rope.

"Where is he?"

Adriana shook her head. "I only heard them say he is here. They are all afraid of him. Oh, Bob, Lionel Pickering is one of them."

"I know."

He took her to the back window with him as he went to look down on the track. Arthur Lindemann was still there, but now he was surrounded by men, state troopers in uniform and others. Two men had run to Willi and knelt over him.

"That's what they wanted," Bob explained to her. "Him for you. He was walking up here alone to make the trade."

"Foolish old man," she whispered.

"He's my father, Adriana," Bob said quietly. "That was what was in the safe: all the evidence that my mother and that old man are my parents."

"*Oh, Bob . . .*"

"Did you hear anything as to why they want him so much?"

She shook her head.

He put his arm around her. "We'll get you back to the house," he said. "With a bath and some rest, you'll be all right."

"Look," said Adriana, pointing. "Look at the funny-looking farmer coming."

She was pointing at an ill-clad figure in a high-crowned straw hat, galloping a horse up the slope from the tracks. Bob had to tell her it was Mrs. Roosevelt.

Willi was not dead, the state troopers said. The other German, the one on the kitchen floor, was. They searched the house and the Packard, then took Adriana in a police car back down to the Roosevelt mansion, where they had already taken Arthur Lindemann, who was puzzled but not hurt. In half an hour everyone was ready to leave the house. Bob remembered that the swaybacked bay from the Roosevelt stable was still tied to an apple tree, and he said he would get it and ride it back. Mrs. Roosevelt said she would wait there at the stone house until he brought the horse, and then they would ride down together.

It took him only five minutes to trot down through the orchard, find the horse, and ride it back. When he rode out of the orchard he pulled the horse to a sudden halt. Another car had arrived and was parked beside the Packard. He was alarmed at first, until he saw Mrs. Roosevelt amiably chatting with whoever had come up in the green Model A Ford. Then he rode on to the house and confronted another suprise. She was standing there talking to Lionel Pickering.

"Look who's here, Bob," she said with a broad smile that seemed for all the world Rooseveltian and genuine. "Mr. Pickering. I've just been telling him about the excitement that's happened this morning."

Bob dismounted and walked up to the two of them.

"Good morning, Hannah," said Pickering smoothly but cautiously. He glanced at his watch. "Or good day, actually."

"I'm surprised to see you here," said Bob.

"He's just been explaining to me that Joe Kennedy sent him—and when he heard at the house about all the excitement here, he drove right up."

Pickering nodded, but his nod was cut short by the hard jolt of Bob's fist, breaking his nose, knocking him sprawling against the side of the Packard. He rolled over in the dust, and when he was on his back his hand came out of his jacket, holding a small automatic. He drew it only halfway. Bob's revolver was leveled at his face.

"I'd really like to kill you, Pickering," Bob said. "Even Mrs. Roosevelt has agreed I have ample reason to. But for the moment, just give the gun a little toss."

Pickering threw the automatic beyond his reach, and Mrs. Roosevelt stepped over and picked it up. Bob stuck his revolver back in his pants.

"You didn't come up here by chance, Pickering," said Bob coldly. "Not for the little story you've told or for any other chance. You are the errand boy, running back and forth between the Baron and his two thugs. You came up to see if they'd got Arthur Lindemann, and you were to take the word back to the Baron. All I want to know is: Where is your boss? Where's Baron von Schwartzberg?"

"You're wrong, Hannah," grunted Pickering through the hands that clutched his bleeding nose. "You've got an overactive imagination."

Bob grabbed Pickering by his shirt and necktie and hauled him to his feet. "You've got a broken nose now, you son of a bitch. What do you want me to break next?"

"Oh, Bob, be—"

Bob tapped the already broken nose with a short jab that sent a fresh gout of blood down over Pickering's mouth. "Where is he, Pickering? Would *he* protect *you?*"

Pickering raised his hands flat toward Bob as he shook his head and retched. "I'll—" He coughed. "I'll tell you. He's at the Beekman Hotel in Rhinebeck."

"Figures. The Baron *would* stay at the best. Room number?"

"Two-oh-four," breathed Pickering painfully.

"You have a room there too, I imagine," said Bob. "Give me the key."

Pickering reached in his pocket and handed over the key to room 206.

"One more thing, Pickering. How many men are with him?"

Pickering weaved and slumped back against the door of the Packard. "One man," he said. "Griffin Bailey is with him."

22

Rhinebeck had always impressed Bob as a beautiful village, with its quiet, tree-lined streets, its air of genteel burgher tranquility. It was quiet today, on this Wednesday afternoon before the Fourth of July. The holiday would be celebrated with a parade, with picnics, and with a grand display of fireworks tomorrow night, which was advertised on a hundred gaudy red-and-white posters tacked to trees and poles all over town. The village seemed to bask in anticipation, with no one moving purposefully on the streets. Few cars sat headed in to the downtown curbs. The stores were open, but few customers went in and out. The village had a Sunday-afternoon, not a Wednesday-afternoon, air.

He pulled the green Model A up to the curb in front of the Beekman Hotel. Leaving the van Rensselaer house, he had driven away in Pickering's car. Looking back as he sped down the rutted lane, he had seen Mrs. Roosevelt trotting off, leading the bay horse. She had abandoned Pickering with the flat-tired Packard, supposing apparently that he would not go far before the state police returned to the house and picked him up. She would ride once more to the nearest telephone, to send help to the Beekman. He had no doubt of that. He hoped he would have a few minutes with Baron von Schwartzberg and Griffin Bailey before the police arrived.

Another Packard, much like the one at the house, was parked before the hotel. It might be the Baron's. Or Bailey's. He did not pause to look at it but hurried into the tiny, dark lobby of the old hotel. The two girls behind the counter knew him, and one of them grinned, pointing at his torn and dirt-stained clothes, "Been wrestling?"

"Two-oh-four," he said sharply. "Who's in two-oh-four?"

The young woman glanced at the book. "A Mr. Black," she said. "Why?"

"The state police will be here any minute," Bob said. "That's who they'll want to see. Is he alone?"

"I think there is another man with him," said the other girl.

"Don't do anything," said Bob firmly. "Don't come up. Don't call the police. The state police are on their way. And don't tell anybody but the police that I am here."

"What's going on, Bob?"

He swung away from the desk and hurried up the stairs. He found Room 204 and Room 206, opened the door to 206 with Pickering's key, and went inside.

The room was small, comfortably furnished, and pleasantly warm and fragrant with the air that blew in through a big old oak tree just outside the window. As he had feared, though, there was no door connecting the two rooms. He put his ear to the wall. The hotel was well built, with double walls, and he could hear nothing.

He was quite familiar with the town and the hotel, and, on his way into Rhinebeck at the wheel of the Model A, he had recalled what he knew and pondered how he could use it. He knew how the stout old oak brushed the walls of the Beekman. He had slept on this floor one windy night, and he remembered how the wind had brushed the outreaching limbs of the tree against the wall and window. It had kept him awake then, but it might be helpful to him now. The question was: Could he reach a strong limb from the window of Room 206 and make his way out into the tree? He knew he could not climb up from street level. The lower limbs had been trimmed to prevent just that.

He stood at the window and looked at the nearest branch. He could reach it. He could throw himself from the window, grab that limb, and hang there. Then, if he didn't lose his grip and fall, he could pull himself up and into the tree, from where he might be able to find a way to the window of Room 204.

It was a good, bold idea. But it was unworkable. As he studied the limbs, he saw that none big enough to support him came near the window to Room 204.

He leaned out and studied more. If he threw himself onto the limb he could reach and climb into the tree; he could climb higher, even to the roof. Or . . . maybe—just maybe—he could reach the windowsill of the room above 204.

All the windows were open. They were protected only by fly screen. If he reached any window, he could easily punch through.

He had few options. Maybe none. Shortly the police would come, and in the civilized procedures that would follow he might never find the chance to learn what he was determined to know. As quietly as possible, he pulled the screen out of the window frame and climbed onto the sill. He crouched and jumped.

It was easier than he had expected, reaching the nearest limb and grabbing it. It bent until he was afraid it would break, and it dipped and swung him inward, toward the trunk; but it held at last, and he hung there, clinging to it with both hands, swinging. Even so, as he had expected, he was now in a position from which he could get a grip on another branch and reach the trunk. He made his way up the tree until he was well above the second-floor windows.

Level with the third-floor windows, he worked his way out a limb and looked into Room 304. It appeared unoccupied. The bed was smooth, and he could see no luggage. Grasping a higher limb, he swung his feet and kicked in the screen. Swinging again, he swung his legs through the window, let go, and fell into the room, scraping his back painfully on the windowsill and landing hard on his bottom.

Quickly he stripped the bed of sheets and a spread. He knotted them together, dragged the bed to the window, and tied the first sheet securely to the bed frame. He tested his knots, then climbed out the window and lowered himself down toward the window to Room 204.

"This is utterly insane. You cannot. You can't do things like that in this country."

Hanging on the brick wall of the Beekman Hotel, two and a half floors above the ground, Bob heard the sharp, angry voice of Griffin Bailey. It was what he wanted to hear. Gingerly turning himself over, he wrapped his ankles around the sheet above and hung head down. With the oak shielding him from at least casual observation from the ground, he hung with his head just above the window.

"Not only can I, but I will," said a harsh voice from inside the room below his head. The voice, which Bob had never heard before, spoke Oxonian English, only slightly

arked by a Teutonic accent. "One of you has the money.
ne of you. At first I supposed it was Hannah. Now I be-
eve it is you or Lindemann. And Lindemann is a dodder-
g old fool. Besides that, my inquiries tell me he does not
eed the money the way you do. No, Bailey. No. I am be-
inning to think it is you. Anyway, when Pickering brings
s Lindemann, we will ask him."

"You will be a fugitive from justice," said Bailey. His
oice was thinned by anxiety. "You will never get out of
e United States. *Use your head, Konstantin.*"

Konstantin. So it was the Baron—Baron Konstantin
n Schwartzberg. Bob strained to hang onto the sheets
d listen. He was sweating, and the sweat ran into his
es. He dared loosen the grip of one hand only for an in-
ant to wipe the stinging sweat away.

"You think I would come here and omit to provide my-
lf an escape? *You* use your head, Bailey."

"They will extradite you."

"You think the Führer would extradite me?" the Baron
ughed. "Me? The man who brought sixty-five millions of
llars home to the Fatherland?" He laughed scornfully.

"So, if you got sixty-five million, then why do you pro-
se to kill for one million?"

"Because it was *stolen* from me," the Baron said simply,
ying a threatening stress on the word *stolen*.

"Lindemann . . ." whispered Bailey hoarsely.

"I don't think so," said the Baron. "I've made careful in-
iries. You are not well off, Bailey. Lindemann is."

"The Northern United debacle ruined our firm. We'd
rely recovered from the Depression," said Bailey.

"And Lindemann?" His German accent betrayed itself in
s pronunciation of Lindemann—"Leen-de-mahn."

"He made his a long time ago," said Bailey, resentment
ingling with the fear in his voice. "Anyway, what makes
u think Brinker didn't get the money?"

"Don't be a fool. He didn't have the number. Only fo[w]
men did: Hannah, Lindemann, Grossenstadt, and you."

"Grossenstadt, then," said Bailey.

"No. He has been loyal to me for many years."

"Then why not Hannah? Why do you exclude him?"

"The night my men killed him, they followed my i[n]
structions to offer him his life in return for the money. [H]
did not give up the money."

"He did not want to impoverish his wife and son."

"His wife has enough to live on, modestly. And his son [is]
not his son. Young Hannah is the son of Arthur Li[n]
demann."

"How do you know that?"

"My men saw the documents that prove it. They are [in]
his safe in his home in New York. We left them ther[e]
That matter is none of our concern."

"But—"

"I think we are running out of alternatives, Bailey.
think you stole my million dollars."

"If you get it back. . . ?"

"Of course. Then all is forgiven."

Bob could hear Bailey's heavy sigh. "It was simp[ly]
transferred to another number account, in the same ban[k]
It was done for me by a Zurich correspondent of mine, hi[m]
self entirely innocent. I gave him the original accou[nt]
number, and he went in and used that number to move t[he]
funds to a different account. I don't have the new numb[er]
with me. It is in my office in New York."

"You lie."

"No!"

"I want the number now."

"You'll kill me!"

"I will kill you in any event, Bailey. It is only a questi[on]
of *how* you die."

"*No!*"

Bob was at the limit of his ability to hang from t[he]

sheets when he heard Bailey's terrified scream and the sound of a struggle. He let down his feet, used them to push himself out from the wall of the hotel, and swung toward the window. He crashed through the screen and fell forward to his knees on the floor of Room 204.

The Baron had just used a knife to slash Bailey across the cheek, and Bailey was slumped against the wall, moaning, clutching his cheek, the blood oozing from between his fingers. The Baron swung around in a fury and thrust the knife toward Bob.

Abruptly the Baron stopped and stood balancing himself warily on the balls of his feet. "So," he said. "It seems you have a pistol. And I have only a knife."

Baron Konstantin von Schwartzberg was a prepossessing man: tall, slender, handsome. The flesh of his face was stretched tightly over prominent, finely drawn cheekbones and jawbone, and the smooth, reddish skin seemed to have been newly scraped with a razor. His thin, bluish lips had a cruel cast, and his pale blue eyes were cold and revealed nothing of his thoughts or emotions. He must have been fifty years old, Bob supposed, but he looked not more than forty. He sat on the one chair in the room, erect and calm.

"I interrupted an interesting conversation," said Bob. "I'd like to hear the end of it."

"It will make little difference what you say you heard," the Baron told Bob. "We will deny it, and we are two."

"Lionel Pickering faces a life sentence, if not in fact the electric chair under the Lindbergh Law, for his part in kidnapping Adriana," said Bob. "He'll try to bargain for a lighter sentence, and he'll talk. Then there's Willi. The same. Also, you left two men in my father's house in New York. They're in police custody. Burglars. No, I think there will be evidence enough against you to put both of you in prison for a long time."

Griffin Bailey staggered to the basin in the bathroom, to press a towel to his bloody cheek.

"Who threw my father Alfred Hannah out the window?" Bob demanded.

"The man you say you shot," said the Baron. "His name was Günther."

"How very tidy," said Bob. "If one of your men is dead, he's the one you say committed the murder."

The Baron shrugged. "The matter will be laid at the door of the one who ordered it."

"Yes. You."

"If you can prove it."

"What was the million dollars?" Bob asked. "Why was there a million dollars in a Swiss account?"

"It was to be Alfred Hannah's compensation for . . . You have an American expression for this."

"For being the fall guy."

"I believe that is the correct expression," said the Baron. "It was to be his compensation for whatever he had to suffer to save my name and to conceal the connection with the Fatherland. When the million dollars disappeared from the Zurich account before Alfred Hannah carried out his part of the bargain—that is, gave his testimony and so forth—we supposed he had taken the money and was preparing to conceal himself both from American law and from us. Of course . . ." He glanced into the bathroom. "Of course, Bailey there encouraged us to think so. Does that surprise you?"

"Not in the least," said Bob.

The Baron continued. "It is not true what I said, that my men tried to force the information out of Hannah before he was killed. I only said that to Bailey to see if he would acknowledge his own guilt—which he did. You heard him, did you? You were hanging out there? You are an astounding young man. If you were as intelligent as you are physically strong, you would join me in my escape to Germany, where the qualities of a young man like you are truly appreciated."

"I'm afraid your Führer will have to do without me."
"As you wish. You decline a wonderful opportunity."
A minute later the police arrived.

"Point by point, if you please," said Cornelius van der
Meer. "For the simpletons like me. Just how did they loot
those companies to the extent of sixty-five million dollars?"

Adriana was upstairs. Her mother had cleaned the
ropeburns on her ankles and wrists, and Adriana was now
in the bath. Mrs. Roosevelt had brought Bob to the house,
insisting it was time he and Cornelius made their peace.

"At first all they had in mind was to put some of their
wealth beyond the reach of a government they didn't
trust," said Bob. "The Baron and his friends thought Germany might go communist, so they decided to invest in
American businesses."

"But they were greedy men," said Mrs. Roosevelt. "In
Europe they were the managers of cartels, and they
thought they could do the same kind of thing here."

"As their investment in American business got bigger,
their motives changed," said Bob. "They built a huge, complex holding-company scheme. Investors thought they
were buying shares in companies that owned real assets.
Actually, it was mostly paper. The von Schwartzberg
group held the key directorships and methodically looted
the structure over the years."

"By taking dividends?"

"Yes. There were no profits, but they took dividends
anyway—out of the money investors were putting into the
companies when they bought the stock. They kept selling
securities and just skimming off the proceeds."

"But the SEC—"

"Two things happened to them," said Bob. "Their new
Nazi government put pressure on them to bring ever more
money home to the Fatherland, and the United States out-

lawed such stock shenanigans and created the SEC to in-
vestigate and prosecute."

"As time went by," said Mrs. Roosevelt, "it all got more
and more complicated for them. The things they did to conceal their crimes were themselves crimes—until ultimately it came to murder."

"Sixty-five million dollars!" said van der Meer. "Sent
home to Germany."

"Maybe more," said Bob.

"And besides all that," said Mrs. Roosevelt, "Deutsch,
Lindemann and Company was acting as a conduit for graft
by New York City politicians."

"Alfred Hannah—"

"Was part of it," said Bob. "Of some of it, anyway. Von
Schwartzberg tapped him for the fall guy. He was to guard
the secret, take the rap, and go to Sing Sing. They put a
million dollars in a Swiss account for him, which he would
withdraw when he was released."

"Then why was he murdered?"

"The money disappeared from the Swiss account. They
supposed he was welshing on them. Actually, it was
Griffin Bailey who had withdrawn the money."

Cornelius van der Meer frowned and shook his head.

"I think it would be appropriate for you to take note,
Cornelius," said Mrs. Roosevelt, "that it was this young
man's determination and courage that confounded their
scheme and set in motion the wheels of justice."

"Umm. Yes. Noted," muttered van der Meer.

"And will he not, then, make a worthy son-in-law?"

"Umm, yes. Suppose so. Granted. It's settled. Nothing
much I can do about it anyway."

"Except welcome him to the family," said Mrs. Roosevelt, smiling delightedly.

Van der Meer sighed. He fixed a still-skeptical eye on
Bob. "Yes. Well . . . I suppose so."

"And give him and Adriana the hundred and ten thousand dollars you made off his insider information as a wedding present," said Mrs. Roosevelt. "Technically, both of you should be prosecuted for that transaction, but if the money is used to set up a fine young couple in a new home—"

"Eleanor! Damn! A hundred and— Oh, damn!"

23

On the Fourth of July, the President took his station on the front porch of the mansion and there received his fellow townsmen of Hyde Park who stopped by to exchange a word of greeting with him. He made a short radio address during the morning, and by noon the reporters and photographers had been gently shooed away, leaving the estate to him and his guests and visitors. At noon, sandwiches and lemonade were served. His mother, Sara Delano Roosevelt, sat to his left; his wife sat to his right—both of them in summer dresses and broad-brimmed white straw hats. Bob and Adriana sat on the steps below the President. The day was bright and warm, and the distant popping of firecrackers contributed to the holiday air.

"I suppose all is well that, uh, that ends halfway well," the President said to Bob and Adriana when for the moment there were no visitors in earshot.

"Halfway well," said Bob solemnly. He put down his glass of lemonade. "I killed a man yesterday."

"You saved my life!" shrilled Adriana.

"Yes, I think you are something of a hero, young man," said the President.

"Thanks to being very cautious and circumspect," said Mrs. Roosevelt, her smile broadening as she spoke.

"I had not supposed he was that," said Sara Delano Roosevelt tartly.

"And so . . . the wedding," said the President. "And you'll go back to law school in the fall?"

"If I'm not compelled to spend the next year as a witness at the various trials," said Bob.

"I think we will see a lot of pleas entered," said the President. "And there will be plenty of other witnesses against the Baron, if he chooses to be tried. I suspect Herr Hitler will order him to plead guilty, to avoid the publicity of a spectacular trial—and, unless I mistake my man, the Baron will obey Herr Hitler. Something in the Teutonic character, you know."

"Let us hope so," said Sara Delano Roosevelt. "It would be *distressing* if Eleanor's part in this unsavory business were to become a matter of public knowledge."

"Indeed, let us do hope so, Mother," said the President. "And here now are the Nelsons. Ho, there, old boy! A happy Fourth to you!"

Half an hour later a square old Cadillac came around the turn in the drive. Betsy Hannah—Bob's mother, Alfred Hannah's widow—was at the wheel, and in the seat beside her was Arthur Lindemann. He got out quickly, came around, offered her his hand, and led her to the porch.

Betsy Hannah was a petite, plumpish, dark-haired woman. She approached the President and his two ladies, not just deferentially, but shyly, with her eyes down, her cheeks pink.

"Betsy," said Mrs. Roosevelt. She stepped down from the porch and extended her hand. "How very nice to see you."

"Thank you," said Betsy Hannah. She looked up at the porch. "Mrs. Roosevelt. Mr. President."

"There are some chairs here," said the President, gesturing. "Have a seat. Join us for lunch. It's good to see you both."

Arthur Lindemann, too, seemed reticent and hesitant as he accepted a chair dragged up for him by Bob. "Bob . . ." he murmured quietly.

"Father," said Bob.

The old man's mouth trembled, and he put a hand to his eye to catch a tear. Bob put an arm around his shoulder and clasped him tight. Adriana took Arthur Lindemann's hand and squeezed it.

"We'll explain," said Betsy Hannah.

"You needn't," said Mrs. Roosevelt.

"But we should. And we want to," said Betsy Hannah firmly. She looked at Bob. "In other circumstances it might have been a more private explanation."

"It still can be," said the President.

Arthur Lindemann shrugged. "Not for long," he said. "It will be made public. We have become public people, I am afraid."

"You'll learn to live with that," said the President dryly.

"Maybe even to enjoy it," said Mrs. Roosevelt.

"Times have changed," said Arthur Lindemann. "Twenty years ago we had no options. Today, I think we might have. I was married then. My marriage was not very old. Divorce was out of the question in those days. Betsy was married. Her marriage was new. It was out of the question for her, too. But we were in love."

"Arthur was in love with his wife. I was in love with Al. And we were in love with each other, just the same," said Betsy Hannah. "Is it possible?"

"Romantic love is a deception," said Sara Roosevelt.

"You understand," said Betsy Hannah simply to the President's mother.

"I arranged," said Arthur Lindemann solemnly, slowly, "for Al to receive one hundred thousand dollars, in a series of payments. I arranged for him to be made a partner in Deutsch, Lindemann and Company. It almost broke up the firm when we promoted him so far, but I insisted on it. It was, after all, *my* firm."

"Al carried out his agreement to the letter," said Betsy Hannah. "It might have happened, Bob, that you would never have found out. He spoke of telling you someday, but he never seemed to reach the point where he really wanted to."

"I do not entirely understand what all this means," said Sara Roosevelt.

"We'll explain it later, Mother," said the President.

"You were willing yesterday to give yourself up to those men, to save me," said Adriana to Arthur Lindemann. "That was very fine of you. I am grateful. I told my father. He is grateful."

"I'm surprised you got away from the state troopers, old fellow," said the President.

"I was not a prisoner," said Alfred Lindemann. "I told them they had no right to restrain me."

The President and his wife and mother remained on the porch all afternoon, greeting a constant stream of Dutchess County neighbors who came by, some for just a word, some for a glass of lemonade and a cookie or two. A delegation from the Odd Fellows, another from the Masonic Lodge, stopped to salute the President, the Odd Fellows to present him a certificate. Arthur Lindemann and Betsy Hannah left, saying they were going to pay a call on Cornelius and Christina van der Meer. It was about four o'clock when a Buick came around the turn and stopped before the house—and Moira Lasky got out.

"Moira!" called the President, casting a highly amused glance at his mother. "Welcome! Come up and have a chair and a glass of lemonade."

Moira, too, was hesitant to mount the four brick steps to join the President on his Hyde Park porch. She nodded at Bob and Adriana, licked her lips, and placed a tentative foot on the first step. The First Lady stepped down and took her hand.

"Mother," said the President. "This is Miss Moira Lasky, a friend of Bob's from New York."

"How do you do?" said Sara Roosevelt coolly.

"How very nice to meet you," said Moira. "I hope you will forgive the intrusion on your holiday." She turned to speak to the younger Mrs. Roosevelt. "Some things have happened in New York."

"Will you have lemonade?" asked Sara Roosevelt.

"How very kind," said Moira. "I will, if it's not any trouble. It has been warm and dry, driving up from the city."

"What's happened?" asked Bob.

Moira glanced back and forth between him and Sara Roosevelt, who was pouring lemonade from a pitcher. "Uh . . Mayor La Guardia has, uh, moved against the Cote gang."

"If you're going to talk politics, *I* shall go inside and refresh myself," said Sara Roosevelt. "I suppose it's important?"

"I'm terribly sorry," said Moira. "I'm afraid it is important."

"Well, if you drove all the way from New York to bring the news . . ."

As Moira stared after her open-mouthed, Sara Roosevelt left the porch.

"She's been looking for an excuse to go in for a nap," said the President. "So, tell us the news."

"I've heard rumors of *your* news," said Moira. "But . . . we know now who it was that I found dead on the floor in the Deutsch, Lindemann offices. It was Sergeant Murphy. They dragged him out of the East River. He still had the key to the offices in his trousers pocket. Lint from the of-

fice carpet had been ground into the fabric of his suit. They
had dragged him across it, obviously."

"Who killed him, and why?" asked Bob.

"Sergeant O'Shaughnessy is not sure who. But Murphy
also had Griffin Bailey's unlisted telephone number, written with pencil on a matchbook cover. As to why . . . well
Sergeant O'Shaughnessy believes it was to keep him quiet
He'd been fingered by the two Chinese girls and was to be
charged with murder. Everybody knew he would talk as
soon as they got him to jail. Whoever killed him did so to
keep him quiet."

"And Bailey knows who that is," said Bob.

"How do you suppose they got him to the Deutsch, Lin
demann offices?" asked Mrs. Roosevelt.

"The fact that the Bailey phone number was written on
a matchbook cover suggests that he'd spoken to Bailey
only a little while before he was killed—otherwise he
would have copied the number onto a notepad or some
thing. O'Shaughnessy thinks Bailey may have been
tricked into calling him and sending him to the firm's of
fices, where somebody was waiting to kill him. When
went up, I interrupted things before they could get the
body out, but they didn't kill me, too, because they didn't
know who I was or why I was there and they already had
one body to get out of the building without being seen."

"Speculative," said the President.

"Mayor La Guardia says they'll put it all together," said
Moira.

"And what about Jim Cote?" asked Mrs. Roosevelt.

"The Mayor called in reporters this morning," said
Moira, "and accused Judge Cote of taking payoffs from city
contractors whose cases are before his court. Yesterday he
got a federal subpoena for the records of the Deutsch, Lin
demann firm, which he says will prove that Cote took pay
offs from DeLoach and Company and from others, through
phony stock transactions."

"Premature," said the President.

"Well, the fat's in the fire," said Moira. "And with what happened here yesterday, it's going to be a little difficult to get it out."

Moira joined the three Roosevelts and Bob and Adriana for dinner. Mrs. Roosevelt insisted she could not set out down Route 9 for New York tonight, but must stay overnight. After dinner, the three younger people drove to Rhineback for the street dance and fireworks. The President and his wife and mother settled themselves in the living room for coffee and brandy.

"You see, Babs," said the President, "what comes of trying to play cupid? If you hadn't interfered in the van der Meers effort to prevent their daughter from marrying Bob Hannah—"

"Franklin," Mrs. Roosevelt interrupted. She shook her head.

"And if you hadn't called in Joe Kennedy and hadn't—"

"Really!"

"Seriously," he said. "It was a good piece of work, Babs. You won't get credit, you know, but—"

"I didn't do it for credit."

He reached for her hand. "I know that," he said quietly. "I can't think of anything you ever did just for the glory of . I wish a lot of other people knew you the way I do."

"I wish a lot more people knew *you* the way *I* do," she said, smiling warmly at him. "Neither one of us is what the world supposes, are we?"

"I thought," said Sara Roosevelt, "that it was *wrong* to support that girl in her defiance of her parents. I cannot say I find very much to admire in either one of those young people. In *my* judgment," she went on, shaking a finger for emphasis, "Adriana would do well to take a cue from Miss Lasky. Now, *there* is a young woman who exemplifies the values we used to cherish."

Sara stared in astonishment as first Franklin then Eleanor began to shake with helpless mirth. "I shall never understand your generation. *Whatever* do you find so risible?"